The Resurrection Protocol

A JAKE ANKYER ADVENTURE

D K Harris

Published By Harris Informatics, Inc. in cooperation with CreateSpace, an Amazon Company.

ISBN-13: 9781493703661
ISBN-10: 1493703668
LCCN: 2013921567
CreateSpace Independent Publishing Platform
North Charleston, South Carolina

Printed in the United States of America

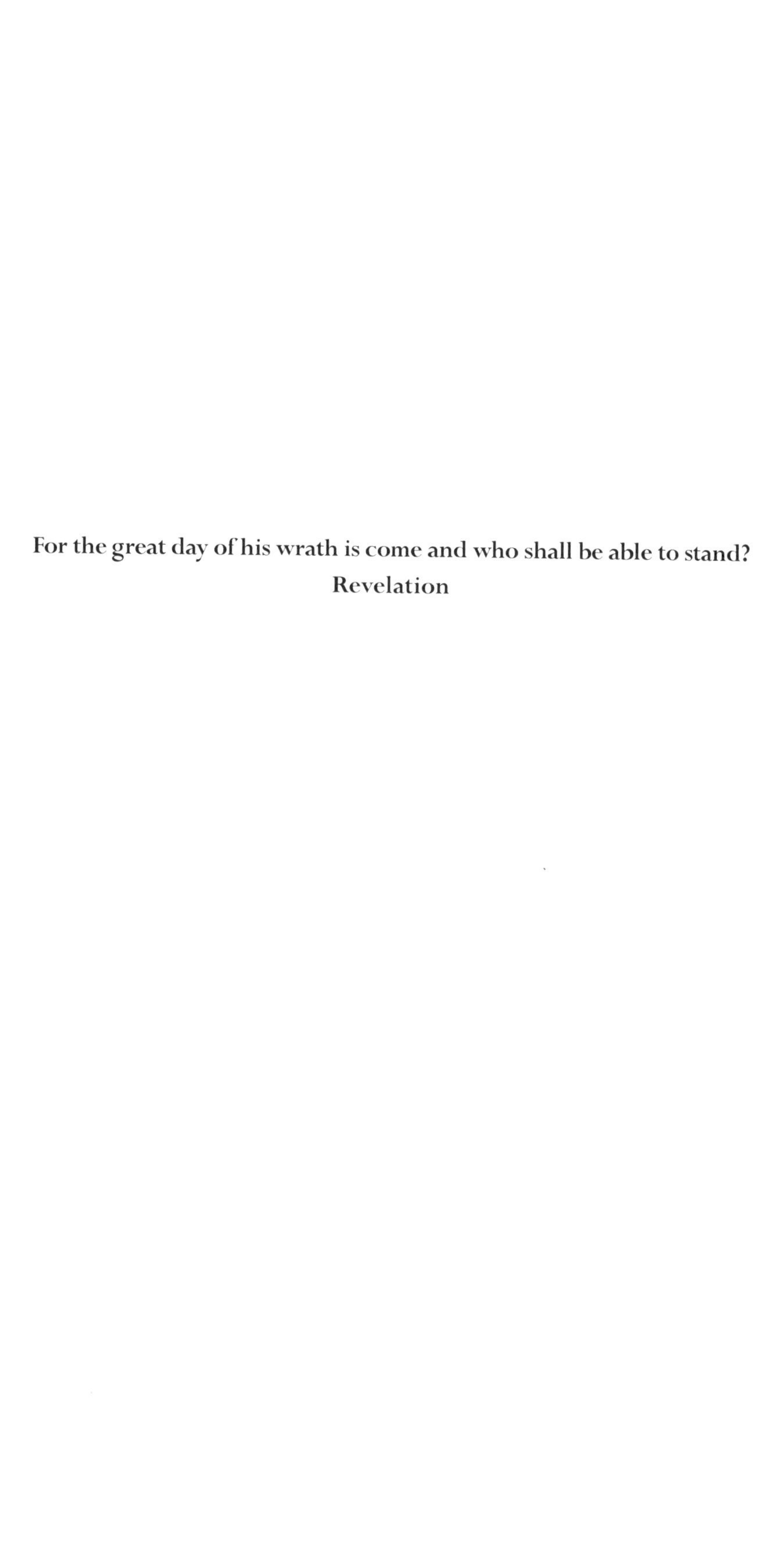

For the great day of his wrath is come and who shall be able to stand?

Revelation

CHICAGO
AUGUST 8, 2011

Doctor Angus McGinty PhD, D.Sc. looked out the window from the back seat of the Jaguar XJL Ultimate Sedan heading toward the Gold Coast in Chicago. Reflected back by the window was an image of a thirty nine year old researcher with a receding hairline, hooked nose, white beard and weepy eyes. While his intellect could make up for some of his perceived appearance limitations and lack of physical stature, a large financial payoff wouldn't hurt either.

During the past 6 months, more or less...he felt like he was in a time warp, testing his grip on reality. Doctor McGinty's main interest, second only to making money, was nanotechnology inhalation therapy. This involved engineering inhaled therapeutic substances into very small particles (nanometer sized and virtually invisible) that could quickly and efficiently deposit the medicine into the deep lung. Toiling away at the Nalco "start up" pharmaceutical lab outside of Dallas Texas, Doctor McGinty was hot on the trail of a cure for asthma when the dawn of discovery shined its light down. He realized that his nanotechnology research technique could be applied to cocaine, allowing him to convert a pound of cocaine to the equivalent of a hundred pounds of highly concentrated material without changing the properties or effects of the new 'nano cocaine' and at the same time generating truck loads of cash. Doctor McGinty confided his discovery to an acquaintance at a "coke" party (one of Doctor

McGinty's leisure activities). Before he could say "ca-ching" Doctor McGinty was invited to the hacienda of Arturo Ramon Rodrigues-Zappa, located 15 miles outside of Taxco, Mexico. Upon Doctor McGinty's arrival at the hacienda, a very nice hacienda indeed, he was introduced to the hacienda's patron, Mr. Rodrigues-Zappa, and promptly deposited in a locked, dirt floor room in a subbasement of the estate.

Doctor McGinty, in his headlong pursuit of extending biopharmaceutical excellence to cocaine, had overlooked the basic principles of business supply and demand. Mr. Rodrigues-Zappa on the other hand, as the founder and current head of Mexico's second largest Zappa drug cartel, knew all about supply and demand. He also knew that given the chance, Doctor McGinty's discovery would flood the market with 'nano cocaine' reducing the cost of 'real' cocaine to almost nothing and requiring Mr. Rodrigues-Zappa to eventually vacate his hacienda. Mr. Rodrigues-Zappa's immediate thought was to remove Doctor McGinty's head from his body and ship it back to Nalco Pharmaceuticals. Prior to doing so, his second thought was to call Ibram el Farsi, his link to the Emir, and seek the Emir's guidance. The Emir was the principal owner of the Swiss bank that laundered Mr. Rodrigues-Zappa's ill-gotten gains.

Mr. Rodrigues-Zappa's second thought proved insightful. The next day Doctor Angus McGinty was a passenger on a private Gulfstream G650 jet seated across from his new best friend, Ibram el Farsi, who was very affably describing to Doctor McGinty his new life as a valued employee and sole researcher at a private Colorado research facility owned by the Emir. As a reward for surprising the Emir with an intelligent decision not related to massacring competing drug cartel members, Mr. Rodrigues-Zappa received an electronic funds transfer of $ 2,000,000 deposited to his account in the small, boutique, Swiss bank owned by the Emir.

Twenty minutes out of O'Hare General Aviation, and five minutes from the Gold Coast, the Jaguar hit one of many Chicago potholes and jarred Doctor McGinty from his reverie. He turned to Ibram el Farsi in the back seat next to him.

"I'm concerned he will not like my report."

Ibram replied, "The most important thing to remember is not to correct anything he says. The Emir does not countenance criticism of any kind or in any form. I don't pretend to understand the underlying science of your findings but the results themselves seem to be what the Emir desires. We will find out soon enough. One thing to keep in mind is that the Emir is very generous with good results and can be less than generous with bad."

"What does 'less than generous with bad' mean?"

"It means Doctor McGinty, that if the Emir does not like your answers, you could very well be a guest of Mr. Rodrigues-Zappa tomorrow or the next day. Also, and this is very important, do not lie or over promise on anything. Give the Emir an accurate recitation of your progress and you should be ok. But do not exaggerate under any circumstances."

At that moment the terminal screens embedded in the backs of the Jaguar's front seats started to glow and an image of two crossed scimitars appeared. Ibram picked up the phone and began speaking in Arabic. He paused, spoke again and hung up. Ibram looked over at McGinty.

"The Emir was going to wait until tomorrow for your presentation but has decided he wants to hear it tonight.

"When?" McGinty asked.

"In about fifteen minutes."

"I need more time to review my notes and to make some adjustments to the DVD material," replied McGinty.

"We will be at our destination in ten minutes," said Ibram.

"You will have five minutes after that. Prepare yourself."

The 510 horsepower Jaguar Ultimate sedan shot forward as if the driver had been in on the phone call. McGinty started to think about the overnight accommodations at Mr. Rodrigues-Zappa's hacienda as the skyscrapers in distant downtown Chicago started to come into McGinty's view. He also thought of the nanotechnology breakthrough with the VX provided to him by Ibram. It would be an interesting conversation with the Emir.

FBI HEADQUARTERS
935 PENNSYLVANIA AVENUE
WASHINGTON DC
FEBRUARY 13, 2012, 11:00 AM

George Makin sat in a winged back chair in FBI Assistant Director Vann's office half listening to Vann explain what was happening, having difficulty processing his voice. At 48 years old he thought the purpose of the meeting was to give him a 'bump up' in responsibilities placing him on a well-deserved runway for retirement. His 5'11", 180-pound frame had held up well over the years. The divorce from Megan two years earlier, and no children, left Makin flexible for moving into a lucrative, post-FBI career anywhere in the world. He had not seen this coming.

Makin had just placed his FBI-issued side arm on the conference table along with his credentials and badge. "George, this situation simply has not occurred in my experience, but it has now," said Vann.

"You are resigning from the Bureau and you will be rehired by the National Security Agency effective immediately. Your compensation and benefits at the N.S.A. will be comparable to what they are in the Bureau. If and when your assignment at the N.S.A. is completed, you will have the option of staying with the N.S.A., rejoining the FBI, or entering retirement status from the Bureau at an Assistant Director level along with normal retirement benefits."

"Sir," said Makin "what is it I am volunteering for?"

Vann looked pensive, unsure how to continue. "George, I simply don't know."

"The Director called me this morning and instructed me to bring you in. He said that there is something called a 'Priority Red Protocol' involving the Bureau and the N.S.A., which provides for an unconditional staff transfer to the N.S.A., at their request, no questions asked. According to the Director this protocol has not been activated, to his knowledge, until now. And N.S.A. specifically asked for you."

"The only comment made was that your experiences as Special Agent in Charge of the Washington Violent Crime Task Force unit, along with certain case experience, which again, they did not elaborate upon, were contributing factors in the request. And here's where it gets particularly strange, George. The Director asked the same question you just did and was told that the situation was such that the FBI was to be insulated from knowledge of the mission and therefore only cleared for information on a 'need to know basis'."

"And he bought into that?" Makin asked.

"He did call the White House and as soon as he mentioned a N.S.A. Priority Red Protocol he was directed to adhere to the N.S.A. request, no that's inaccurate, I should have said N.S.A. demand."

"Oh, there's one more thing" Vann said. "There's another agent who is in the same situation you're in and who will be joining you at the N.S.A."

"Do you know Doctor Margie Tallon from the Chicago office Evidence Recovery Team?"

"I do know her," said Makin. "She is absolutely brilliant. She received her MD from Yale and graduated second in her class. I've worked with Margie on a number of cases. I think she's one of four pathologists assigned to the Evidence Recovery teams across the entire Agency."

"Actually one of three pathologists who are sworn agents," said Vann.

"Doctor Tallon is the total package," said Makin. "I'm amazed the Director would let her go."

"He definitely was not happy about it. But this Priority Red Protocol overrides any other consideration," replied Vann.

"That's it then," said Vann. "You'll have your sidearm and credentials returned should you decide to rejoin the Bureau after this is all over, whatever 'this' is. There is a N.S.A. car waiting out front to take you to a meeting in half an hour."

THE CONSTABLE CLUB
EMBASSY ROW
WASHINGTON DC
FEBRUARY 13, 2012
11:45 AM EASTERN STANDARD TIME

The N.S.A. car pulled up in front of a limestone building. The driver turned to the back seat. “Mr. Makin, this is the Constable Club. Please ring the door bell at the entrance.”

Makin exited the car and walked up a thirty yard, bluestone path with rectangular reflecting pools on either side and stopped at the entrance. Two marble urns, fronting an exceptionally ornate ironwork gate, which could have been the work of the Chicago architect Louis Sullivan, flanked the recessed entrance. The building itself was five stories high and roughly sixty feet wide. Above the entrance was a stone plaque reading: The Constable Club 1967. Makin pressed the doorbell button. The ironwork gate slid across the entrance and a large oak door behind it opened.

“Good morning, Mr. Makin. Welcome to the Constable Club. My name is Neil. I will be escorting you to the meeting room. After your meeting I will brief you on the various functions of the Constable Club which you may find useful from time to time.”

Makin noticed the Navy SEAL insignia on Neil’s pinstriped suit lapel.

“I see you were a Navy SEAL. Thanks for your service,” remarked Makin.

Neil replied "Actually sir, I am still on active duty and will be assigned to you for the duration."

"The duration of what?" asked Makin.

"I believe that will be discussed at your briefing sir," replied Neil.

Makin noticed the entrance hall for the first time. The floor was white marble tile flanked by twin, wrought iron staircases ascending to a second floor. Nearby was a large, marble fireplace with an oil painting of an admiral holding a sword and keeping a watchful eye on Makin. Other oil pictures of naval officers hung from the walls on the second floor landing.

"Neil, I have to tell you that this club is spectacular. What are the membership requirements?"

"Membership is closed sir. Please follow me," said Neil.

Makin followed Neil around a staircase to a door, where a light shone on Neil's eyes. The door opened. They entered a wood paneled elevator, the door closing immediately behind them. "Biocular optical recognition sir, in case you are wondering. I'll get you set up after the meeting," said Neil.

There was no perceptible movement of the elevator, either up or down, just a low whining sound. A moment later the door opened to a medium sized room with a fire in a fireplace at one end [including an oil painting of another admiral], several leather library chairs around a mahogany table, and what appeared to be an antique tea cart. Standing in the middle of the room was a sixtyish man, about five feet eight and dressed in herringbone tweeds and a bow tie.

"Thank you for bringing Mr. Makin up, Neil."

"I'll deliver him back to your capable hands at the conclusion of our meeting."

"Yes sir", replied Neil taking three backward steps into the elevator, the door to which silently closed were the door had been. leaving a seamless walnut wall.

"Mr. Makin, my name is Doctor Asher Finkel. I serve as a senior member of the National Security Agency...your new employer so to speak. I am going to call you George and you may call me Asher. I like to keep things informal as we tend to work closely in this part of the N.S.A."

Finkel walked over to one of the leather chairs and sat down.

"Have a seat George. My job at the N.S.A., among others, is to oversee and coordinate Priority Red Protocol projects, which occur from time to time. Your transfer to us here at the N.S.A., no that's not correct, I should say your retirement from the FBI and re-employment at the N.S.A., is necessary due to a security level which exceeds FBI security access and, its fair to say, just about all other security access levels of virtually all other government agencies and individuals except the President. This necessitates that we bring in certain skill sets and levels of expertise for let me say special projects and, like you, place them under the security and operational umbrella of the N.S.A. We then return everyone to his or her parent agencies under arrangements similar to the one Mr. Vann discussed with you."

"The Constable Club is a club with one organizational member, the N.S.A. You will in effect be an associate member of the Club as long as you are associated with the specific project you are becoming involved in. When you are in Washington you will be working out of this building and staying here as well. Your personal mail has already been redirected to this address. You will find the accommodations here quite comfortable and your living quarters will reflect the ambience I'm sure you have noticed in the parts of the Club you have observed so far. You will also be issued a special, secure smart phone. Keep it with you at all times. This will provide us the ability to physically locate you. All calls you make or receive with the phone are transmitted over a secure network. This building is designed to prevent electronic eavesdropping of any kind, or at least those we know of. You will give your personal smart phone to Neil who will return it after your involvement in the project is completed. Finally, we have a Navy SEAL Team in residence here. Their responsibility is to undertake missions we periodically request as well as to provide security for this building and its residents. Neil, who escorted you here, is a member of the SEAL team and will assist you in navigating your new environment."

"Oh, and one other thing. You need to sign this supplemental security agreement on the table here. It simply reads, "I, George Makin, agree to all N.S.A. security restrictions and understand I am subject to substantial penalties for breach of this Agreement". Everyone involved in a N.S.A. Priority Red Protocol project signs one of these. Don't worry about the "restrictions" or "substantial penalties". Just don't discuss any thing you hear or talk about here with anyone other than your colleagues in the Priority Red Protocol project. Bring any questions you have to me. So there you are. Sign the document and we can proceed. Any questions?"

Makin signed the paper and handed it back to Finkel.

Makin looked at Finkel and replied: "I have one question at the moment. Why me?"

"George, bottom line, you are very effective at what you do; so effective in fact that your superiors at the FBI have kept you in the field limiting your opportunities for organizational advancement. Special-Agent-in-Charge of the Violent Crime Task force is an excellent position, but you will never rise above it. In fact your name has surfaced a number of times for Associate Director positions but your fieldwork has eclipsed consideration for a management position with a larger portfolio. Your tenacity and ability to solve complex cases is superb and a situation has developed in this country that requires your substantial experience and skill set. But that will become evident in the briefing. At the conclusion of this project, assuming a positive outcome, your ascension to FBI Associate Director status, assuming it is something you still desire, will become a reality."

Finkel escorted Makin through open polished cherry double doors into an adjoining room. The room was large and rectangular with cherry paneled walls, bookcases on either side of the entrance, and a long mahogany conference table. Several people were already seated. Makin took a seat designated by a place card with his name. Finkel said: "We have one more guest to arrive, after which I will introduce everyone." Finkel left the room. Each of the people nodded at Makin but did not speak.

Five minutes later every head at the table turned and watched as a woman whose physical attributes could only be described as spectacular, walked over and sat in the seat next to Makin. "Good afternoon Mr. Makin. Nice to see you again," she said.

"Nice to see you as well Doctor Tallon," said Makin.

Doctor Margie Tallon, MD, projected a 5 foot 10 inch, perfectly formed female body, weighing in at 132 pounds, and wrapped in a dark blue, pinstriped, mid length skirt and jacket ensemble. She wore a light, pastel blue blouse and what appeared to be a medium sized emerald pendant, suspended slightly above approximately one half inch of cleavage formed by two Sports Illustrated caliber Swimsuit Edition breasts. Her medium length dark blond hair and bangs accentuated slightly oval, dark brown eyes and a mouth terminating with a hint of a pout, possibly suggesting Egyptian heritage along with the other perfectly assembled components of Doctor Tallon's genome. Makin recalled his "total package" comment to Vann earlier that day.

"The one everyone, including instructors, at the FBI Academy wanted to follow around the "O" course," he thought. "Total package" indeed.

Doctor Finkel entered the room, the doors closing behind him, and seated himself at the head of the table. He paused, looking at each person seated.

"I and the National Security Agency very much appreciate each of you being present today. I will introduce everyone starting with myself. My name is Asher Finkel. I hold an MD degree and PhD in behavioral science. My job at the N.S.A. is to coordinate resources designed to deal with events, which are designated as Priority Red Protocol in nature. A Priority Red Protocol event is an event, which places the United States in a serious and potentially destructive situation, either physically, politically, or both. Such an event is outside the portfolios of specific government agencies. However, the N.S.A. is legally enabled to draw relevant professional and various other assets from other organizations such as each of your parent agencies to address the situation. Each of you has been temporarily transferred to the N.S.A. as an employee. This was done to insulate you from any potential legal or Congressional oversight you might otherwise be exposed to as a consequence of your participation in this project and, with a few exceptions, provide linkages as necessary with your parent agencies. You have also signed a security agreement that limits any discussion of matters you become privy to with just this group. You may be requested to relay operational requests to your parent agencies, but only with my authorization."

"With that I will introduce each of you along with your former respective affiliations. To my immediate right, Colonel Joseph Braun, Defense Intelligence Agency; next, Mary Hendricks, Central Intelligence Agency; next, Martin Semanski, Department of Defense, and Mary Lou Hastings, Federal Bureau of Investigation. On my left, Captain Arthur Moreland, Joint Special Operations Command; George Makin, Federal Bureau of Investigation; and finally, Doctor Margie Tallon, a physician specializing in forensic pathology and also from the FBI. Regarding the FBI affiliations,

George Makin and Doctor Tallon have been transferred permanently to the N.S.A. on special assignment. Mary Lou Hastings will serve to coordinate activities from this group as necessary, and at my direction, with the FBI Washington Office and its branches as I conclude necessary and as consistent with the security requirements now in place."

Finkel paused to collect his thoughts, and then continued speaking.

"In July 2011 an N.S.A. analyst was routinely reviewing archival material collected during Operation Iraqi Freedom. Included in the material was film footage of Saddam Hussein's execution by the Iraqis. The video most people are familiar with shows Saddam Hussein being led into the gallows, speaking for several minutes, and then dropping through the gallows' hatch. This particular video was shot by an Iraqi present using a cell phone secreted into the execution. The image was poor quality and quite jerky."

"There was also a second video shot at the morgue which shows the body of Saddam on a gurney. A sheet is lifted revealing his head. This video shows a red gash under Saddam's jaw. There has been speculation that the gash resulted from a post mortem knife wound inflicted at the hanging, but more likely, it resulted from the rope being the incorrect length for Saddam's weight causing the skin below the noose's knot to separate. Various reality web sites have circulated the video, mainly via YouTube."

"However, there is a third video, which was also provided by the Iraqi morgue to an Army pathologist. This video has not been circulated publicly and shows the same neck wound as the second video, but in this depiction, there is a morgue attendant pulling the wound apart to better visualize the neck. The Army pathologist dutifully included the third video with the other materials received from the Iraqi's and shipped it off to the US. It eventually somehow found its way to the Uniformed Services University of the Health Sciences in Bethesda, Maryland. The material was archived and indexed into an Iraq war files database for future research. The N.S.A. analyst noticed the entry of the third Saddam morgue video, which she was not aware existed. She requested and obtained a digital copy for review."

Finkel took a sip of water and continued. "When the analyst digitally enhanced the neck wound visible in the third video, she observed what appeared to be a metal object in the neighborhood of the third cervical vertebra. Further enhancement revealed a screw. Please open the folder in front of you. The first document is a photo of the enhanced image." "Doctor Tallon, any comments?"

"Without CAT or MRI scans, ideally with contrast media, I would be guessing," said Tallon.

"Guess away doctor," replied Finkel.

"Well", said Tallon, "if there is a complete break at the third or fourth cervical process, it can be lethal, or at least result in paraplegia and the need for continuous respiration assistance. Since this is the body of Saddam Hussein, who appeared not to suffer any mobility problems before or after his apprehension, the actual damage would have had to be relatively minor. The screw is likely holding a plate in place, and the purpose of the plate and screw would be to stabilize the vertebra. Also, with an injury at this level there might be chronic neck stiffness, requiring the person to turn their body slightly to the side instead of turning their neck to speak with someone at their side.

"Exactly" said Finkel. "That's what we thought."

Mary Hendricks spoke. "As far as we know Hussein had no history of neck surgery. In fact, the CIA requested a full body CAT scan after he was captured and there was no indication of any injury to his neck or anywhere else. Period."

"I agree," said Finkel. "As a matter of fact, we obtained a copy of the complete medical file for Saddam, including all CAT scan and MRI files and looked at them as well. No injury."

"This one got by us at the Defense Intelligence Agency, completely" said Braun.

"It got by everyone," said Finkel. "At that point we had an anomaly," continued Finkel.

"It was more than a simple curiosity but not definitive enough to be conclusive."

"Please continue, Colonel."

"JSOC was ordered to send a SEAL team to Tikrit" said Braun.

"Once there the team was to proceed to the cemetery Hussein was buried in, locate the grave, drill down into it, and take a core sample from the corpse."

"Keep in mind" said Finkel, "as far as the world is concerned Saddam Hussein is dead. Digging up the body and removing it for examination was not an option as we did not want to be accused of desecrating a grave and more importantly, we did not want to provide any inferential evidence that we were not certain that Saddam was dead. Pulling up a core sample of the corpse for DNA evaluation was our only option. Please continue Colonel Braun."

"The SEAL team had the geo coordinates of the grave site. A Black Hawk helicopter dropped them about a mile from the objective. Once at the cemetery they encountered a single guard who was neutralized. They drilled three times into the gravesite. The drill extracted core samples containing both bone and flesh. The team then withdrew with the body of the guard and jogged a half-mile to the extraction point. They then buried the guard five miles into the desert and returned to base. The bio sample was handed over to the CIA."

"I will pick up the story from there," said Finkel. "The biological samples were flown to a CIA laboratory in Virginia where multiple DNA analyses were conducted and compared to Saddam's DNA profile taken immediately after his capture. Twenty-four hours later the DNA results were sent to the N.S.A. The results are conclusive. No match. The body in that morgue in Iraq, and the one that was buried in the grave in the cemetery in Tikrit, is not Saddam Hussein."

CHICAGO
GOLD COAST TOWNHOUSE
AUGUST 8, 2011
8:15 PM CENTRAL STANDARD TIME

The Jaguar arrived at a three story, classic, Chicago Gold Coast townhouse. The driver turned left into a driveway with a slight decline, opened a garage door with a remote opener, and pulled into a large, three car space. Ibram el Farsi quickly left the car and motioned McGinty into an elevator, which rose with a low whining sound to the townhome's second floor. The elevator doors opened into an expansive room furnished with white leather and chrome chairs. At the end of the room was a waist high cabinet. El Farsi walked over to the cabinet and pressed a remote control. A 50-inch HD TV screen emerged from the cabinet. Ten feet in front of the cabinet was a flat desk with a 15-inch Mac Book Pro computer. El Farsi walked over to the desk and pressed the 'return' key on the computer. The computer screen came to life with an image of two crossed scimitars similar to the image on the screen in the Jaguar. At the same time the 50-inch monitor was activated and showed a blank screen with a small, blinking green rectangle in the lower left hand corner of the screen.

"Doctor McGinty, please take a seat in front of the computer and insert your CD ROM into the drive," said el Farsi.

McGinty did so and three links appeared on the 50 inch screen: Trial 1 Animal A, Trial 1 Animal B, Trial 2 Subject 1. El Farsi walked over to an alcove and returned with a glass of water and set it on the desk.

"Your nerves are showing, Doctor McGinty," he said.

At that point a female voice emanated from a speaker somewhere in the room. Where exactly, McGinty couldn't be sure.

"Doctor McGinty, my name is Zainab Malibi. I hold a doctorate in molecular biology. I am a colleague of the Emir's and will be listening in and viewing your presentation."

"I thought I would be making my presentation to the Emir" said McGinty.

"The Emir is here with me and will speak if he feels it necessary. Now please proceed and be as concise as possible," said Malibi.

"As you wish", said McGinty wiping his sweaty hands on his pants legs.

"My field of specialization is biomedical nanotechnology. I convert organic substances into very small, highly aerodynamic particles between two and three nanometers in size. A particle is effectively made invisible to the naked eye. Nanotechnology techniques are useful in medical applications for inhalation medicines used to treat asthma and pneumonia. A nanoparticle that is breathed in goes to the deepest part of the lung because of its ability to very efficiently fly into the lung without getting caught in the mucous membranes in the nose or mouth. Once in the lung the particle is rapidly absorbed into the bloodstream. Any questions so far?"

"Continue," said Malibi.

"Converting substances to nanoparticles is difficult to do and requires a variety of chemical reagents as well as advanced laboratory techniques and equipment," said McGinty. "By the way, your laboratory in Colorado is first rate and is even better with the additional equipment I have been able to obtain with the help of Mr. el Farsi. Also, considering the nature of the material you asked me to convert to nanoparticles, having a bio safety level 4 facility is extremely helpful. I think there are only fifteen or so facilities in the entire United States. I could not do the work without it."

"Move on Doctor McGinty," said Malibi.

"As you know," said McGinty, "I managed to apply the technique I've just described to cocaine. The resulting substance, which I call nano cocaine, is more effective than untreated cocaine and produces highs much greater with much smaller amounts of material. Mr. Rodrigues-Zappa did not appreciate this for some reason, and that landed me in his Mexican dungeon. The same technique, however, also applies to the material you had me test, that being the VX nerve agent."

McGinty paused then continued.

"Mr. el Farsi supplied me with three fluid ounces of VX. Given VX toxicity this is enough to sicken 100 adult humans at a minimum. After application of the nanotechnology techniques, the resulting nano VX, if I may call it that, is a quantity large enough to sicken 1000 or more adults."

"What do you mean by sicken?" asked Malibi.

"Sorry," said McGinty. "What I meant to say was kill."

"But surely this is theoretical," said Malibi.

"No," said McGinty. "It can be practically applied and I can demonstrate that with the videos I brought. The videos are the result of experiments conducted at your Colorado facility. They reflect the results of only a few particles of inhaled nano VX."

"Proceed," said Malibi.

McGinty clicked the first link, Trial 1 Animal A, on the computer. A video showing a box with a white rat appeared on the fifty-inch HD screen. A clock was located in the lower right corner.

"A liquid spray of a small amount of the VX you supplied is now introduced into the rat's enclosure. Watch the time-lapse clock."

The rat in the box continued to crawl around the box. When the clock showed one hour the rat had slowed down and vomited. The time-lapse clock continued and showed 1 hour and 30 minutes. The rat had stopped moving and its breathing was shallow. At 2 hours the rat stopped all movement. "In this first video," said McGinty, "it has taken 2 hours for the rat to die from the first contact with the normal VX."

McGinty clicked on the second computer link, Trial 1 Animal B.

"In this video a rat is exposed to a few particles of nano VX."

The rat crawled around the box and vomited, arched its back, hemorrhaged from its eyes, mouth and anus and then stopped moving. The time clock showed 10 seconds.

"Not only did the nano VX cause the rat to exhibit the usual VX symptoms, it caused the rat to bleed out, accelerating its death, and causing it to expire almost instantly," said McGinty. "Also, and very importantly, nano VX kills so quickly, it is unlikely that atropine, the antidote for VX, could counteract the effects of nano VX in time."

"You're saying that there is in effect no antidote for nano VX," said Malibi.

"Correct," said McGinty.

"But what about the effect on humans?" Malibi asked.

McGinty clicked on the second video link, Trial 2 Subject 1. The screen showed a white room with a man seated at a desk. He was about 5 feet 8 inches and appeared to weigh about 150 pounds. "Mr. el Farsi was helpful in obtaining a human subject," said McGinty.

"He was a homeless person who was paid fifty dollars to come in for what he thought was a part time job," said el Farsi.

"When the clock in the lower corner of the screen starts, that will signal that the nano VX has been introduced into the room. "Starting now!" said McGinty.

The clock started. At 5 seconds the man vomited. At 7 seconds he fell to the floor, his back arched and bleeding from the eyes and ears. At 13 seconds the man stopped moving and lay in a widening pool of blood leaking rapidly from the seat of his pants.

"Total elapsed time from introduction of the nano VX to death was 15 seconds. I did an autopsy in the bio safety level 4's clean room. The subject's back was broken from the spasms and his kidneys, liver, spleen and colon had partially jellified and hemorrhaged. The extensive damage to the colon accounts for the substantial loss of blood from the anus. Once he had inhaled the nano VX, which was almost immediate, there would have been no way to save him even if we wanted to. This damage was in addition to the neurological damage normally associated with VX. It appears that conversion of normal VX to the nano version causes it to produce the additional findings you observed in the video, including a tremendous spike in blood pressure which accounts for the massive organ failure," said McGinty. "There is an additional feature of nano VX that is of interest. Once released, the nano VX actually seeks out the organism it infects. This may be a result of body temperature or normal inhalation and expiration. Whatever the mechanism is, once the nano VX is released, it proactively pursues its victims. There is no place to hide!"

A disembodied male voice asked: "Doctor McGinty, can this nano VX be manufactured in large quantities?" The voice had a Middle Eastern accent.

"Yes. Assuming I had access to sufficient quantities of normal VX and the necessary equipment for mass production or 'scale up' as we refer to it," replied McGinty.

"You can be supplied with approximately four tons of VX. The equipment can be in place in at the Colorado facility according to specifications you provide within a month. How long will it take to manufacture the nano VX?" asked the voice.

"Sixty to ninety days at the outside," replied McGinty. "I should tell you that based on the laboratory results you have seen during this demonstration, it would take only two tons of VX converted to nano VX to involve the entire Eastern United States assuming an efficient delivery system."

"We need to discuss that," said Malibi.

"The other thing we need to discuss is my incentive for doing this work," said McGinty. There was silence for a moment then the male voice said, "That is an excellent question Doctor McGinty. Your continued existence would be one incentive. We could always send you back to Mr. Rodrigues-Zappa, or Ibram could break your neck right now."

McGinty flushed and a bead of sweat formed on his temple.

"But your impertinence is not completely without merit. Based on your results demonstrated this evening, I think a financial reward is not inappropriate. An account as been established for you at a Swiss bank. It already has one million dollars in it. If you complete the work we have discussed, four million more dollars will be added and you will be given the bank's name and the account pass code."

"That is very generous," said McGinty.

"You mentioned a delivery system before, Doctor McGinty. How would that work?" asked Malibi.

"It would depend on where you wanted the nano VX dispersed," McGinty replied.

"For the purposes of our discussion let us assume the Eastern seaboard of the United States," said Malibi.

"In that case dispersal of the nano VX would be relatively easy," replied McGinty. "With the dispersal mechanism I have in mind and the quantity of nano VX converted from normal VX, almost every living, air breathing being, including people, from Florida to Maine, and probably Nova Scotia, would be infected and die within two to three days, depending on wind currents."

THE CONSTABLE CLUB
EMBASSY ROW
WASHINGTON DC
FEBRUARY 13, 2012
12:25 PM EASTERN STANDARD TIME

"By the way," said Finkel, "there are sandwiches and drinks at the end of the room in case anyone wants lunch. Please help your self." No one at the table moved.

"I thought not," said Finkel.

"That's the way I reacted when I first received the report. So let me summarize. We have an enhanced photograph of a corpse reputed to be Saddam Hussein, post hanging, which shows a gash in the neck revealing a surgical artifact. It appears that this could be the result of a cervical fusion procedure where a metal plate may be screwed into the vertebrae above and below the graft to hold the bone in place while it heals and fuses. Also, this kind of surgery often results in limited range of motion in the neck making turning of the head limited, which also appears to be the case with the Saddam we see in the video on the scaffold at the hanging. When the hangman talks to him he turns his body to look at him rather than just his head. We are speculating somewhat since after the hanging they sent his body from the morgue directly to Tikrit for burial without a normal autopsy."

"So far this makes sense," said Tallon. "Too bad about the lack of an autopsy."

"I agree," said Finkel. "But this is Iraq we are talking about after all."

"The second issue is the DNA provided courtesy of the Navy SEAL team which indicates that Saddam's body is not in his purported grave," added Finkel.

Makin raised his hand and remarked, "I can see where the evidence supports the conclusion that Hussein is not the person who was hanged. The question I'm wrestling with is how did he manage it?"

"That's not an inappropriate question by any means," said Finkel. "The N.S.A. has concluded that there was a switch between the time Saddam was handed over to the Iraqis and his execution. We have discovered in the meantime that the religion of all the Iraqis involved with Saddam after the transfer, at least as far as we can tell, was Sunni Muslim, the same as Saddam. Not one Shi'a or Christian in the whole bunch. The strong, religious bias could have worked in Saddam's favor. Couple that with the known fact that Saddam used a number of body doubles, some with surgical enhancements, and it's not a stretch that a switch was made after the handover. This would have allowed Saddam to escape, resulting in the body double sacrificing himself, probably in support of the cause and in return for a substantial payment to support his family. We are also in the process of trying to tie the Saddam grave DNA to a name but an identification has not been made as of yet."

"There are two additional elements we need to be aware of. Actually as I think about it there is a fourth," continued Finkel.

"The second element is financial. With the cooperation of our friends at the CIA (Finkel nodded to Mary Hendricks) we have determined that Saddam was looting Iraq over a period of over a dozen years prior to the first Iraq war. Substantial oil revenues were converted to bearer bonds and fine diamonds graded as brilliant, colorless, and flawless. The best grade possible. The bonds and diamonds were shipped out of Iraq in diplomatic pouches and we think disbursed in either Swiss or Cayman Island banks or both. Saddam may, in fact, have control over a bank in Switzerland and we are checking on that. We think this was, or is, Saddam's retirement nest egg."

"How much are we talking about?" asked Semanski.

"It's a rough estimate," said Hendricks, "but we think in the neighborhood of between three and four billion dollars."

"The third element, and the one which is very troubling, centers around the remains of a body found by some hunters about five miles south east of Texas Creek, Colorado in a mountainous area," said Finkel. "At first they thought it was a deer carcass mauled by a bear or a mountain lion. Upon closer inspection, it turned out to be a man, or what was left of a man. Parts of the flesh and some organs were still intact and since Texas Creek has only a population of around 70, the remains were sent to the Denver coroner's office 183 miles away. So far so good. Nothing of interest to us. However, after the forensic evaluation of the organs, the pathologist started to exhibit neurologic symptoms consistent with some kind of nerve agent, which was subsequently found to be in the lung tissue of the cadaver. To make a long story short, the remains were sent to a CDC bio safety level-4 lab and were ultimately found to contain the nerve toxin VX. That did get our attention. They also found the VX had been altered, and under electron microscopy, revealed VX micro particles in the shape of dimpled golf balls for lack of a better description. One particle in particular was different from the others. This particle also had a molecular identifier that indicated its origin. The origin was the United States. The identifier also associated the particle with a batch of VX provided to the Iraq government during the Iran–Iraq war. In effect what was found was George W. Bush's Iraq weapons of mass destruction, or at least some of it."

"Jesus!" exclaimed Braun.

"It gets even more interesting," said Finkel.

"The "dimpled golf ball" VX I mentioned a moment ago, which was revealed under the electron microscope, is in fact, a new kind of VX changed from conventional VX through nanotechnology conversion, to a type of VX which is substantially more efficient and lethal."

"So what we have here is the possibility that Saddam Hussein is still alive with access to several billion dollars; and he has managed to transfer to the US some or all of the VX originally supplied by the United States to Iraq; and has coincidentally figured out a way to make the VX substantially more lethal using some kind of nano…? What did you call it?" asked Makin.

"Nanotechnology" replied Finkel. "I should also add, that the reason Bush and his Administration were so sure that they would find WMD in Iraq was that the US supplied it to Saddam in the first place. They could not find it because Saddam had at some point transferred it out of the country, possibly to some place in the United States."

Makin chimed in again. "As outrageous as this sounds, it may actually be true. You couldn't make this up!"

"I agree George," said Finkel. "Which brings us to today's meeting. I think you can see where the circumstances warrant the N.S.A. calling for a Priority Red Protocol event to be initiated. If Saddam is alive, it could destabilize Iraq and lead to a Sunni uprising, not to mention the consequences if he has access to some kind of radical VX, or even conventional VX, which has been used to kill at least one person we know of in the United States. We know, for a fact, that Saddam used VX to kill the people in the Kurdish village in northern Iraq. We now think that event could very well have been a test of the lethality of VX along with a delivery mechanism. From his perspective it worked quite well. The Kurdish village was completely wiped out."

"So what do we do?" asked Makin.

Finkel paused and surveyed the people at the table.

"What we do," said Finkel, "is find him if he is still alive and, hopefully, stop whatever he has in mind for this nanotechnology VX. And we do it without anyone knowing, Finkel added. At this juncture I would like to excuse everyone except George Makin and Doctor Tallon. I will contact each of you individually utilizing the smart phones you were issued, as circumstances require," said Finkel.

Neil appeared at the doorway. "Please follow me," he said.

When the others had left the room, Finkel moved to a chair opposite Makin and Tallon. "This entire meeting falls within the security requirements everyone has agreed to. However, certain information also falls within a "need to know" policy and what we are about to discuss does not pertain to the participants who just left the room and should not be discussed with them."

At that point, Neil walked through the door carrying two rectangular boxes, which he placed at the opposite end of the table. He sat in a chair next to the boxes.

"So as I understand it, you want Doctor Tallon and I to find someone who may or may not exist and stop some kind of terrorist attack based on an autopsy performed on a partial cadaver. How could that possibly be accomplished?" Makin asked.

"You and Doctor Tallon are going to find Saddam Hussein, and then we are going to kill him...this time permanently...and replace the Saddam Hussein body double in the Tikrit grave with the real Saddam." said Finkel.

"I'm not sure how you would accomplish the swap, but even if you did, there is no way to track him. He could be anywhere!" said Tallon. "Not to mention killing him if we did find him, she said. And assassination is not in my job description," she continued.

"Your respective points are well taken, which brings me to the fourth element in our previous discussion," said Finkel. "When the VX contamination was discovered in the human remains recovered outside of Texas Creek and it was subsequently determined that it was the result of conversion to a nanotechnology form, that information may have given us a lead. It turns out that converting biochemical substances to nanotechnology substances is not all that easy. In fact it is quite difficult. In addition to highly specialized equipment, it requires specialized expertise. We discovered that there are five scientists, all located in the United States, who have this expertise. Four of them have been accounted for, interviewed, and eliminated from consideration. The fifth scientist, a Doctor Angus McGinty, disappeared about eleven months ago from his job at Nalco Pharmaceuticals. He was working on converting asthma drugs into an inhalable nanotechnology form for ingestion into the deep lung, which could be a big breakthrough for asthma inhalation therapy. We wouldn't even have known about the good Doctor McGinty except that Nalco has a small research contract with the Biomedical Advanced Research and Development Authority (also known as BARDA), within the Office of the Assistant Secretary for Preparedness and Response in the U.S. Department of Health and Human Services. The contract involves converting certain drugs into inhaled, nanotechnology therapeutics for use in therapy for anthrax exposure. McGinty's name was included on a list of senior scientists working on parts of the contract. Because of the sensitive nature of the work, BARDA is routinely notified of any changes in status of scientists involved in the project. When McGinty disappeared, the Nalco human resources manager contacted BARDA and informed them. BARDA made a note in their contract vendor database, which is appended to one of the N.S.A. databases. This, in turn, yielded Doctor McGinty's name along with the four others. Since the other investigators were cleared, we had to assume by process of elimination, that McGinty was a possibility for the source of the nanotechnology VX."

Finkel continued. "We sent an investigator to the Nalco Company in Dallas Texas. The investigator's Nalco employee interviews yielded a name of a friend of McGinty's who, as it turns out, shared a recreational cocaine habit with him. Our investigator found the friend, one Bengie Butafucco, and persuaded him that if he ever wanted to see the light of day again, he would assist in helping find Doctor McGinty. The investigator's argument proved persuasive and the investigator was informed by Mr. Butafucco that Doctor McGinty told him that he had an idea for converting cocaine into some "nano thing", which would make it more powerful, resulting in a greater high with much less cocaine per snort. That conversation and a couple more resulted in our investigator coming up with a name - Arturo Ramon Rodrigues-Zappa, a Mexican drug lord in the Zappa drug cartel. It now appears that the enterprising Doctor McGinty decided to pay Mr. Rodrigues-Zappa a visit to explore a business opportunity for converting conventional cocaine to nanotechnology-based cocaine. It's at that point that Doctor Angus McGinty disappeared.

"I gather the next step is to find a major drug lord located in the middle of a drug cartel somewhere in Mexico and talk him into giving up McGinty," said Makin.

"Something like that," said Finkel. "We contacted our law enforcement colleagues in Mexico and carefully inquired where Mr. Rodrigues-Zappa might be located. I say carefully, as some Mexican law enforcement officials are often paid more by the drug cartels than by their own government employers. We were advised that Mr. Rodrigues-Zappa periodically resides somewhere south of Mexico City. Based on this sketchy information, and N.S.A. being the kind of organization it is, the exact location of Mr. Rodrigues-Zappa's residence, or at least one of them was identified. N.S.A. satellite surveillance has targeted a hacienda outside of Taxco, Mexico. Taxco was at one time a major silver mining town, although in more recent times it has been taken over by the cartels. Rodrigues-Zappa's hacienda appears to have a considerable amount of activity in the daytime as well as the evening, probably guards and other associates of Mr. Rodrigues-Zappa. We think this is where we will find Doctor McGinty."

"Can I take a moment to get a sandwich?" asked Makin.

"Absolutely," replied Finkel.

They all got up, went to the 18th century black walnut sideboard, selected sandwiches and drinks and returned to their seats. Makin took a bite from his sandwich, chewed thoughtfully and asked: "Even if Zappa is there, how do we get through all the guards and if we do, how do we convince Zappa to cooperate?"

"That's something you will not need to do," said Finkel.

"We have reached the point in our meeting where I will tell you about a resource at our disposal and, incidentally, the reason I requested earlier that your new associates leave the room. The resource is surgical in nature, and it is only deployed when absolutely necessary."

"And this resource will convince Zappa to cooperate?" asked Makin.

"Unquestionably," replied Finkel.

"Ok," said Tallon. "What is it?"

Finkel took a sip of his Coke and asked, "Are either of you familiar with Trappist monasteries?"

CHICAGO
ASTOR STREET TOWNHOUSE
AUGUST 8, 2011
8:15 PM CENTRAL STANDARD TIME

"Tell us more about this nano VX dispersal mechanism you mentioned," said Malibi.

"It's quite simple," said McGinty. "The normal average human body temperature is 98.6 degrees Fahrenheit or 37 degrees Celsius. It is routine to heat-test biomedical substances designed for introduction into the human body to evaluate the extent to which the human core temperature may cause molecular decay or otherwise interfere with the action of the medicine or substance. When I created nano VX, I conducted the normal heat test over a range of temperatures from 20 degrees Fahrenheit below zero to 500 degrees Fahrenheit above zero. Under the electron microscope the nano VX particle showed no change over the range of temperature tests. This brings me to the nano VX delivery system. Steam is an excellent medium for releasing material into the atmosphere. Materials mixed with steam are released into the atmosphere and can be carried substantial distances by wind currents. With the quantity of nano VX converted from your normal VX, the nano VX would saturate the steam and droplets and would be widely dispersed into the atmosphere at various levels depending on wind currents. It would then condense into moisture and convert into rain. Because of the tendency of nano VX to be rapidly inhaled during respiration, and due to its aerodynamic properties, the nano VX particles in the rain droplets would be widely dispersed. The nano VX detaches from the droplets and seeks out and is absorbed into the lungs of any air-breathing animal it comes in contact with. Again, depending on wind currents, the nano VX could be quickly dispersed over a period of several days. The entire operation could be accomplished using steam generators forcing the steam into the atmosphere. Since steam is virtually invisible. It would be almost impossible to tell where the steam is coming from, making the source of the nano VX completely undetectable. It would be an invisible, efficient weapon of mass destruction if ever there was one."

"Brilliant!" said Malibi.

The Emir's voice filled the room. "I have one question for you Doctor McGinty. What you propose is likely to kill hundreds of thousands of Americans, if not millions. Does that not bother you?"

McGinty replied: "It doesn't bother me at all. What did they ever do for me? Besides, the five million dollars is, as you put it, a financial reward of considerable interest and certainly better than the alternative of another visit to Mr. Rodrigues-Zappa."

"Ibram," said the voice, "please fly Doctor McGinty back to the Colorado facility immediately. Doctor McGinty, you will convey your equipment requirements to Mr. el Farsi and you will be provided the necessary materials for the scale up process as you call it, along with the VX we have at our disposal. You will have until November to complete your work, after which time you will receive your reward."

"I have one request," said McGinty.

"What might that be?" replied Malibi.

"I want to be absent from the location the nano VX is released from," said McGinty.

"You definitely do not want to be anywhere nearby when the steam infused nano VX is ejected into the atmosphere."

"Doctor McGinty," said the male voice, "I can assure you that you will be nowhere near the place where the steam carrying the nano VX will be released."

The crossed scimitars image on the computer screen disappeared.

Ibram said: "Doctor McGinty, we must return to the airport immediately. Your presentation was quite impressive. I think if your work produces the results you expect, you will become a very rich man."

LIBRARY
EMIR'S RESIDENCE
GOLD COAST, LONG ISLAND NEW YORK
AUGUST 8, 2011
10:30 PM EASTERN STANDARD TIME

The soft light reflected on the oblong, polished quartz table in the two-story library. Several hours earlier, the setting sun shown through the 16th century stained glass windows and illuminated the Persian carpets which surrounded the table and led out to the central book stacks. An older man sat at the head of the table. He was wearing a pair of dark beige slacks and a lightweight, black, silk shirt. To his right sat Doctor Zainab Malibi. Across the table from Doctor Malibi sat Sheik Abu Mactar Kahn, a vibrant, massive, physical presence, dressed in white cotton robes, and who never left the side of the older man. A HD television screen and a computer monitor had gone blank earlier, after having displayed the people and presentation during the earlier Chicago Astor Street townhouse briefing with Doctor McGinty.

"Your opinion?" asked the older man in a soft voice directed toward Doctor Malibi.

"The scientific assertions of the infidel appear correct," she said. "Converting the VX to nano VX certainly extends the effectiveness of our material. It also increases the material's aerodynamics allowing it to travel great distances carried by the steam. In my opinion, the steam is as important as the nano VX. It is the perfect medium and is invisible. The Americans will see the effects of the nano VX on the population but will have no idea where it is coming from or how to stop it. We will, of course, install the steam devices at strategic locations across the country, not just the East coast, to achieve the maximum death rate will we not?" asked Malibi.

"Of course" said the older man. "I am only sorry some Americans might inadvertently be spared in this country of devils."

"It will be a small matter to purchase older buildings with tall chimneys and install the steam generators and nano VX steam receptacles," continued Malibi. "Another thought has occurred to me," she said. "If the wind currents from the East Coast deposit the nano VX steam into the jet stream, there is a possibility that the nano VX will travel to England and other European countries that conspired with the American devils at the United Nations to take our country from us. The damage would not be as great but the American infidels would be viewed as infecting the World. Their power, if they had any left, would be reduced to ashes."

The older man looked down for a moment and then again toward Malibi. "The World will quake and Saddam will arise from his tomb in Tikrit, surround himself with his Sunni brothers, and assume his rightful place again in the country that was ripped from his grasp," he said.

"What about McGinty?" Malibi asked.

"Ah, our friend Doctor McGinty, who would kill millions of his fellow Americans for money because they did nothing for him as he said. We will place funds into the bank account established for him and leave an anonymous note thanking him for making the death of his fellow Americans possible. A fitting memorial to the white bearded, fish eyed infidel McGinty who would trade the lives of his countrymen for a few dollars. When the time comes, and the nano VX steam sites have been prepared, Abu Mactar, my friend, you will leave Angus McGinty at a site and expose him to the nano VX. As the nano VX descends down upon him and invades his body he can contemplate his creation."

"Allahu Akbar," said Abu Mactar, his massive muscles rippling under his robe in the soft light of the library.

THE CONSTABLE CLUB
EMBASSY ROW
WASHINGTON DC
FEBRUARY 13, 2012
2:00 PM EASTERN STANDARD TIME

"The Trappists are a Catholic religious order," said Tallon.

"They take a vow of silence and are self supporting."

"Last I heard," said Makin, "they sell fruit cakes and operate farms to support themselves."

"You are both partially correct," replied Finkel. "Trappists are comprised of Catholic monks and priests and do in fact take a vow of silence, but they will speak as a situation calls for communication. The Carthusian Catholic religious order, on the other hand, is much stricter than the Trappists and do not converse with anyone outside the order, and seldom with each other," said Finkel. "You are also correct, Doctor Tallon, that Trappists are self supporting," said Finkel. "They farm, and yes, make fruitcakes. They also manufacture and sell caskets and funeral urns at a Trappist monastery in Iowa. For our purposes one of the Trappist monasteries in particular, Holy Innocents, is financed through an agreement with a N.S.A. cover company called Jam Pot Limited and the monks actually ship jam supplied by Jam Pot to their Web site customers. But what they also do is house and support the N.S.A. resource. We were thinking about funding a Carthusian monastery but their rigorous code of silence made working with them impractical."

"To give you additional context," continued Finkel, "during the second Gulf War, there was a rumor of a secret weapon, which was used to hunt down and kill most of the leaders of the Iraqi resistance and Al-Qaeda operatives. Many of the individuals targeted were included in the famous deck of cards distributed to American and allied forces. One General, in particular, was asked by a reporter how it was that so many key fighters were being killed, and the General replied that the US had a secret weapon. The General was subsequently removed from Iraq, brought back to the Pentagon, retired, and informed that if he mentioned anything related to a secret weapon to anyone, he would lose his pension and be subject to treason proceedings. However, even at that, the press picked up the scent and stories regarding a top-secret technology started to circulate. Even Bob Woodward got into the act on a segment of the CNN Larry King Live broadcast. Woodward suggested that the weapon was on the order of the Manhattan Project atomic bomb. Another theory was that the US had deployed a ray gun-like device that could melt vehicles and people. And there were even wilder speculations. As it turns out, the speculations were, in fact, partially true. There is a secret weapon, which we prefer to call the N.S.A. resource and it was, in fact, used to destroy most of the senior Iraq and Al-Qaeda insurgents. But it is deployed by the N.S.A., and not by the military, and it is not a ray gun or other similar device. It is a man."

"What are we talking about here, some kind of Shaolin commando?" asked Makin.

"Not quite," said Finkel. "No. What we are talking about is a human being whose physical and mental processes are very highly tuned. Most people use only forty five to sixty percent of their abilities. Some a little more, and some a little less. A Navy SEAL like Neil is trained to operate physically at around sixty percent that produces the physical and intellectual competence Navy SEALs require, and which, I might add, is significantly higher than that of the average soldier. The resource located at Holy Innocents monastery functions at a level of ninety five percent of physical capacity and at eighty nine percent of mental capacity, both far above normal. This has been achieved through research and advances in highly elastic stem cell biomedicine. The resulting augmented muscles and neuro receptor enhancements effectively close the synaptic gaps between neurons. Brain cell activity is much more efficient, since electronic pulses are traversing much shorter distances between synapses. Placing this in a conventional vernacular context, our resource functions physically way beyond any Olympic decathlon participant in history and does so with an IQ of around one seventy."

"A superman," said Tallon.

"No," said Finkel. "A human being artificially enhanced and maintained through advances in biotechnology."

"But if these characteristics can be passed on genetically..." said Tallon.

"They can't be," said Finkel. "They must be constantly maintained through bio-engineering mechanisms provided at the Holy Innocents monastery. Otherwise the resource would return to his normal performance levels, which in his case was sixty percent physical and fifty five percent mental. He was chosen with relatively high measurements initially, so we had a good running start toward the enhancements. I should add that he is highly trained in military performance elements. His initial training was based on Navy SEAL training evolutions and was undertaken at the Naval Special Warfare Operations Command in Coronado, California in addition to other NSWOC locations. The normal SEAL training cycle averages thirty months. Our resource completed the training cycle in six months breaking every training parameter by at least forty percent. He was then sent through additional specialized training for another six months. As you might surmise, it is extremely costly to train and maintain someone at this heightened level of physical and mental competence so it is not practical to extend this kind of training to very many individuals. One additional thing. Our resource, once in the field, has extremely heightened mission focus. He will do absolutely anything necessary to accomplish his mission. For example, he did in fact, eliminate each of the Iraqi insurgents and Al-Qaeda operatives I referred to earlier, including Abu Musab al-Zarqawi and the Hussein brothers, Uday and Qusay.

"I thought those were Special Forces operations," said Makin.

"Quite the contrary," said Finkel. "The resource engaged and eliminated each of the individuals. Special Forces were brought in for appearances' sake to make it look as if they executed the mission. The resource is now used sparingly for exceedingly delicate operations requiring highly surgical, military intervention."

"How many of these resources are there?" asked Tallon.

"There are three fully operational resources, including the one you will be working with, and two more in "training" so to speak," said Finkel.

"Does the resource have a name?" asked Makin.

"His name is Jacque Anquer, which is the French form. We call him Jake Ankyer. He is a first generation American. His father was a French national naturalized as a US citizen, and his mother was from the Basque region in Spain," said Finkel.

"How do we work with him?" asked Tallon.

"Initially, Jake will provide you and George with information he acquires regarding the whereabouts of Doctor McGinty. The three of you will then go to McGinty's location and interview him regarding his nanotechnology VX discovery. You will then establish the link between McGinty and Saddam Hussein, if one exists. If one does exist, you will then find Saddam and obtain information on the location of the Iraqi VX supply. At that point, you, Doctor Tallon, will take over and determine through a field DNA test, that you have in fact encountered the real Saddam Hussein and not another double. You will convey the information back to the N.S.A., which will attempt to certify the location of the VX. Once that is determined, Saddam Hussein will be dispatched...for the second time."

"You mean kill him," said Tallon.

"Yes," said Finkel. "Although that part of the plan will be the responsibility of Jake Ankyer. Once that is accomplished you will take charge of the body and make changes to it consistent with the photographs we have of Saddam, post hanging, including dissecting his neck to simulate the gash from the rope's noose in the actual hanging. It won't be perfect but considering the decomposition of the corpse in Tikrit it will probably be good enough at that point. The body will then be flown to Holy Innocents where it will be chemically processed to approximate a reasonable level of putrefaction consistent with the duration of death. The body will then be transferred to an N.S.A. aircraft and you and Ankyer will continue on to Iraq. Jake will exit the plane with the corpse, replace the remains in the Saddam Tikrit grave with the real Saddam, and remove the corpse of the double to a distant location for disposal."

"You can't be serious," said Makin.

"I would lose count of the things that could go wrong in the scenario you just described."

"I am mindful of the Erwin Rommel quote in World War II, "Every plan is good until the first shot is fired"," said Finkel. "However, you are at a disadvantage, having never been associated with Jake Ankyer. He has not come close to failing in a mission, even though mission parameters have often changed due to unforeseen variables. His enhanced intellectual ability gives him the wherewithal to dynamically adjust his ability for problem solving in real time. I envy you your opportunity to work with him in the field. Ordinarily he works independently, but your and Doctor Tallon's involvement is necessary due to the special circumstances surrounding our Mr. Hussein."

"I suppose there's the possibility that Saddam is dead even though the body in Tikrit is not his," said Tallon.

"That is a possibility," said Finkel. "However, our analysis, based upon what we know at this point, suggests that the probability of Saddam being dead is 30% at best. Not high enough to forego the process I described earlier. Then there is the issue of the human remains contaminated by the VX. This is as troubling as the issue of Saddam. If there is a connection between the two we need to find it."

Finkel turned to Neil seated at the end of the table. "Neil, please bring the cases here."

Neil got up, brought the cases to the end of the table where Makin and Talon were seated, and placed one case in front of each of them.

"When you left the FBI you left your service weapons there. While I don't expect you will need them, prudence suggests that we provide you with replacements. We have tried to match the weight and overall configuration of your former side arms, but have improved the quality of the weapons."

Tallon and Makin opened their respective cases. In each case was a semi-automatic pistol. Also included, was a silencer designed for the threaded barrel on each pistol and two magazines.

"Neil, would you give them a brief summary?" asked Finkel.

Neil began. "Mr. Makin, you have been issued a Heckler & Koch Mark 23, semi-automatic weapon. It is a 45 caliber and comes with a sound suppression attachment and a laser-aiming module. Doctor Tallon, you have been issued a Heckler & Koch semi automatic USP Combat Tactical 45 caliber, also with a sound suppression attachment. We tried to come up with weapons somewhat similar to your former weapons. They are a little heavier and larger than what you're used to but I think you will like them after working with them a bit. Doctor Tallon, we know you had a 9 mm caliber bore with your FBI weapon. However, we believe the stopping power of the 45 mm compared to the 9mm is important. You shouldn't see too much of a difference as HK semi-automatics have an integrated recoil reduction system. The weapons incorporate high profile, target sights, nine trigger firing modes, ambidextrous magazine release lever, and an adjustable trigger stop. We will also supply you with Winchester Ranger T-Series hollow point ammunition. We have a range on the premises that our SEAL team uses. We can check you out there."

"A few other house keeping details," said Finkel. "When we are finished here Neil will take you to our security office and have each of you sit for a bi-ocular eye scan. Each of the rooms here requires a dual eye check for entrance. Each eye scan is personalized to the individual for entrance into specific authorized locations in the Constable Club. We will also take you to your respective residences to pick up sufficient belongings for two weeks, since you will be either traveling to Holy Innocents or staying here. If our activity exceeds two weeks, we'll cross that bridge when we come to it. Any questions?"

"When do we start?" asked Tallon.

"We already have," said Finkel. "Jake Ankyer has been mobilized to visit Mr. Rodrigues-Zappa's location and to interview our friend Doctor McGinty. He should arrive there around three in the morning."

"What if McGinty's not there?" asked Makin.

"I hope for Mr. Rodrigues-Zappa's sake McGinty is," said Finkel.

JAKE ANKYER
PILATUS U-28A MILITARY SPEC SINGLE TURBOPROP AIRCRAFT
23,000 FEET, 20 MILES EAST OF TAXCO MEXICO
FEBRUARY 14, 2012
3:20 AM CENTRAL STANDARD TIME

The crew chief checked the fastenings one more time on Ankyer's parasail flight suit, and insured that his oxygen mask and helmet were secured. Once in the suit, Ankyer was difficult to see in the dim cabin. The parasail utilized molecular camouflage, the same as was used to camouflage Ankyer in his tactical body wrap underneath. The molecular camouflage material was similar to a squid or octopus biocamouflage, but operated more efficiently. It incorporated ambient light molecules and reflected them back. This neutralized the difference between the light reflected from the object and the light surrounding it. Ankyer wasn't completely invisible but you had to know where he was and intentionally look for him. The parasail flight suit itself was controlled with arm and leg movements and designed specifically for high altitude/low opening descents. The suit incorporated a modified drogue chute, which opened automatically at 100 feet above the ground and adjusted for sea level differences calculated via an integral altimeter. The suit also incorporated a GPS computer currently programmed to identify a location 17 miles outside of Taxco in the desert. The target was projected on the heads-up display in Ankyer's helmet, permitting him to adjust his body movements to place him on the ground two miles southeast from Arturo Ramon Rodrigues-Zappa...exactly.

Ankyer gave the combat pack attached to his left leg a final check. The combat pack contained a titanium combat knife with a two-micron thick ceramic blade, two white phosphorus incendiary grenades with timers, two portable C4 explosive packs with timers, one acid bath canister and a number of other mission-specific items. On his right leg was strapped a Heckler & Koch UMP 45 caliber submachine gun with a sound suppression attachment.

A green light next to the side cargo door was illuminated.

"Ten seconds to cabin depressurization. Twenty seconds to exit," the pilot's voice announced into the crew chief's and Ankyer's helmets.

The crew chief pulled an oxygen mask from a side panel and Ankyer twisted a dial on the side of his helmet activating the integrated oxygen re-breather and heads-up display. The cargo door of the Pilatus slid open.

"Ten seconds to exit," the pilot said.

The crew chief gave Ankyer thumbs up, the pilot banked the Pilatus hard right, and Ankyer dove through the cargo door opening.

The terminal velocity of a falling object is the velocity of the object when the sum of the drag force and buoyancy equals the downward force of gravity acting on the object, or stated differently, all other things being equal, the fastest an object can drop is on average 122 miles per hour. Except of course if the falling object assumes a heads down aerodynamic profile. Ankyer's high altitude/low opening descent speed was 225 miles per hour. His drogue chute deployed ten minutes into the jump 105 feet above the desert floor. He circled once and landed in the desert two miles from Arturo Ramon Rodrigues-Zappa's hacienda…exactly. Ankyer released the fastenings for the combat pack and H&K UMP 45 assault rifle, lowered them to the ground, and then stepped out of the parasail flight suit. He pulled a tab on the collar of the flight suit and it immediately began dissolving from chemical heat elements in the lining.

Ankyer's infrared helmet display revealed a jackrabbit and two scorpions a short distance away. There was a soft glow in the distance, which Ankyer surmised was the hacienda. He removed the knife from the combat pack and inserted it upside down into a specially designed scabbard integrated into the chest of his tactical camouflage body wrap. His helmet display indicated he was 1.99 miles from the GPS location of the hacienda. The time/distance would automatic re-calculate as he moved toward the hacienda. He picked up the combat pack and hoisted it on his back through the arm straps. He then locked the H&K UMP 45 on the swivel mechanism attached to his leg. Ankyer started running toward the soft light at a fast jog.

ARTURO RAMON RODRIGUES-ZAPPA'S HACIENDA
15 MILES SOUTH EAST OF TAXCO MEXICO
FEBRUARY 14, 2012
4:00 AM CENTRAL STANDARD TIME

Five hundred yards out from the hacienda Ankyer's helmet infrared cam revealed two images. Esteban Morales and Juan Garza were assigned outside perimeter guard duty for the hacienda that night. Morales was thirty yards from a jeep, urinating on a cactus. Garza was sitting in the jeep with his iPhone ear buds in listening to an iTunes selection.

Morales thought he saw some kind of grey image in the distance but it disappeared. A moment later Morales was struck in the shoulders and knocked backwards fifteen feet, still urinating. Had Morales been an NFL quarterback it might have been similar to standing straight up and getting hit by a middle line backer going full tilt. In Morales' case, however, it was more like getting hit by a freight train with failed brakes. The whiplash caused Morales' cervical discs to explode and his neck snapped. He laid on the ground without a sound, his penis still in his hand leaking urine and, if you looked closely, now a little blood. Ankyer moved on toward the jeep.

Juan Garza was enjoying the music "Enamorado Por Primera Vez" by Enrique Inglesias traveling through his ear buds. He felt a slight pinch in his neck, an insect maybe. He then felt wetness around his collar. He moved his hand toward his collar to investigate and it came away wet and sticky.

A knife came into his field of vision and a voice said in perfect Spanish, "Do not speak. I have cut your right carotid artery. I have my fingers on it and if I remove them you will die. Nod if you understand."

Juan thought for a moment. His AK-47 was in the back seat of the jeep. His pistol was in its holster. If he could even get to it and shoot this person he would bleed to death. Juan decided to live and nodded.

"Good. I have just one question for you and you must answer truthfully. How many people are in the hacienda? You may speak now, but quietly."

Juan said, "Si Senior. Mr. Rodrigues-Zappa, the padrone, is the only one in the house tonight. There is a bunkhouse to the right and there are ten hombres there. Some are guards and some are bosses. Two come out here every three hours to relieve the guards."

The voice asked, "When are the next guards due?"

Juan replied, "in thirty minutes."

"Good," said Ankyer.

He looked over at the bunkhouse. His heads-up infrared display showed twelve images. "Are you sure there are ten people in the bunkhouse?" he asked.

"Si senior" said Juan.

"It appears you are mistaken," said Ankyer. The combat knife moved across Juan's field of vision. Juan's head separated from his neck and fell to the ground, his ear buds still attached, and Enrique Inglesias holding a long note at the end of the song.

Ankyer removed the Hechler & Koch UMP 45 from the swivel on his right leg. He attached the sound suppression unit from the combat pack and started jogging toward the bunkhouse with the H&K at port arms. As he approached the bunkhouse, Ankyer's infrared display showed two people walking about 20 yards from the building. Probably the replacement guards for the two guards he dispatched a few minutes before. Without changing his stride Ankyer brought his H&K around to shoulder firing position and fired two shots. The first shot hit one of the infrared images in the throat, almost severing the head. A gout of infrared blood gushed from the top of the image. The second shot hit the other image in the forehead exploding bone and brain matter through the back of the skull and dropping the image instantly. Silence. Ankyer dodged around one body and leapt over the second. The bunkhouse was a rectangular structure with one door in the front and a side window. Ankyer looked in the window. The only light visible inside the bunkhouse was a small glow coming from a room at the end. Probably the head guard's room. The rest of the bunkhouse was an open bay with infrared images occupying beds on each side of a corridor. Four beds were empty, two for the first two dead guards and two for the next two Ankyer killed outside the bunkhouse. The count was correct.

Ankyer entered the front of the bunkhouse. As he walked down the aisle, he shot each infrared image in the head, one on each side of the aisle, insuring that no one would get up behind him. Ankyer stopped outside the room at the end where a faint light showed through the doorway. Just as he reached the room a door in front of Ankyer opened outwards and a figure hoisting its pants emerged. The head guard.

Ankyer said, "Stop and stay silent if you want to live."

The guard stopped, buckled his belt and squinted to see the face behind the helmet shield. He could not.

"Your compadres are all dead," Ankyer said. "You are alone. The only reason you remain alive is to answer these questions. First, how many people are in the hacienda? If you are not truthful I will know and you will die."

"The only one in the hacienda tonight is the padrone," said the guard.

"Second question. Does the hacienda have a security system?"

The guard paused. Ankyer pushed the barrel of the silenced submachine gun into the guard's stomach. "Yes."

"Is there a keypad to enter a security code into?"

"Yes."

"Where?" Ankyer asked.

"There is a keypad next to the front gate," said the guard.

"Is there another one inside the house?" asked Ankyer.

"Yes, but the keypad at the gate will disarm the one inside the house at the same time," the guard replied.

"What is the code?" asked Ankyer.

"I don't know," said the guard, his voice wavering.

"That code is the only thing keeping you alive," said Ankyer.

"The padrone will kill me if I give it to you!" the guard said.

"I will kill you now if you don't. Give me the code quickly!" said Ankyer.

"17889," answered the guard.

"Arms behind you," said Ankyer. Ankyer then pulled a plastic cufflink tie from his belt and secured the guard by his wrists. Ankyer stepped aside and said "Now, walk slowly in front of me down the aisle and out the front door. There is a lot of blood on the floor and if you slip and go down I will shoot you."

They walked down the aisle, the guard looking from left to right.

"You killed them all in their sleep!" said the guard.

"Every single one," said Ankyer. "You are the only one who is awake and I will kill you if you don't shut up and keep moving."

The guard and Ankyer walked out the front door and thirty yards to a ten-foot high gate connected to a twelve-foot high black steel fence surrounding the hacienda. A keypad was next to the gate as the guard said. Ankyer pulled the guard over to the keypad by the entrance. He unbuckled the guard's belt, pulled his pants down and ripped the guard's shirt open. Ankyer then pulled the combat knife down and out from its scabbard and using his left hand stuck it two inches into the guard, right above his pubic bone. The guard's eyes opened wide and tears started welling up in his eyes.

"Now, here is what is going to happen", said Ankyer. "I am going to enter the numbers you gave me into this key pad. If anything happens other than this gate opening silently, I am going to pull this knife up to your breast bone and spill your guts all over the sand at your feet. Then I will take your guts, wrap them around your neck, and strangle you with them."

The guard's lip was quivering and tears were running down his cheeks. Ankyer started pressing the numbers on the keypad speaking each one as he went.

"One, seven, eight, eight."

"Stop!" exclaimed the guard in a forced croaking voice. "The last number is two, not nine!"

Ankyer pressed the number two and the gate slid open silently, exposing a rectangular courtyard with a large four-tiered fountain. The guard breathed a sigh of relief.

"You were not truthful with the initial pass code," said Ankyer as he ripped the combat knife upwards. He removed the knife and spun the guard around, at the same time, pulling the knife across his throat and decapitating him. He wiped the combat knife on the back of the guard's shirt and returned it to its scabbard.

Ankyer entered the courtyard. The hacienda was a two-story structure and looked to be roughly seven thousand square feet. Ankyer opened the cover on his 511 H.R.T combat watch. 4:32 AM. He walked around a fountain, crossed the courtyard and approached the front door. The front door had opened when the steel gate opened. Not a good security system. Ankyer walked in the door, stopping short as two Presa Canario mastiffs stood ten feet away. Maybe the security system was better than he thought. The dogs were confused, issuing low growls as they saw only the helmet but smelled something larger in front of them. Ankyer's camouflaged tactical body wrap presented the image of a floating head and nothing else. Ankyer took advantage of the mastiffs' indecision and placed a shot in each dog's head.

"A waste of superior canines, but necessary," he thought. Ankyer's helmet infrared revealed no additional images. As he entered the hacienda's foyer he encountered a double curved staircase to the second floor where he assumed the hacienda's master bedroom was located. He ascended one side of the staircase. The doors to rooms down the corridor were open except for one at the end. Only the ticking of a grandfather clock could be heard. Ankyer unfurled a sling from the bottom of the H&K and attached it just below the sound suppressor. He opened his combat pack and retrieved a syringe. He then slung the H&K over one shoulder, took the plastic protective cap off the syringe, walked down to the closed door, opened it, and came face-to-face with Arturo Ramon Rodrigues-Zappa.

During his briefing at Holy Innocents Monastery, Ankyer had been given a digitized picture of Rodrigues-Zappa reproduced from a police photo taken several years earlier. He also had one of Angus McGinty taken from a photograph in his employment file at Nalco Pharmaceuticals. The man standing in front of Ankyer was definitely Rodrigues-Zappa. Without hesitation Ankyer swung his right arm holding the syringe and plunged it into Rodrigues-Zappa's neck under his jaw. Rodrigues-Zappa dropped as if poleaxed.

When Rodrigues-Zappa awoke he was sitting up naked against the headboard of his round king sized bed. His wrists and ankles were bound with plastic handcuffs.

The bed was covered with what appeared to be a white sable bedspread. A crystal chandelier hung from a twenty-foot ceiling. The rest of the room was furnished with French period chairs, tables and two lounges next to the windows leading out to a balcony. As Rodrigues-Zappa focused, he noticed some kind of rifle lying on the end of the bed, and what appeared to be a man seated in a chair next to the bed. The man's body seemed to waver in the dim light. He had black hair and curious eyes that seemed to shift color from dark blue to green to blue.

"Who the fuck are you?" asked Rodrigues-Zappa.

Ankyer answered with a question. "Where is Doctor Angus McGinty? I came here to see him."

"When my guards find you they will carve you into pieces," spat Rodrigues-Zappa.

Ankyer replied, "Your guards are dead, your dogs are dead, and that will be your condition if you don't answer my questions."

"Fuck you," said Rodrigues-Zappa.

"While you were taking your nap I had a self-guided tour of your hacienda," said Ankyer. "You have a beautiful home. The basement leaves something to be desired though. Those cells with the hooks suspended from the ceiling don't help the décor much. Decorated in torture modern are they? I did not encounter Doctor McGinty from which I infer he is not here. I'll ask you again, where is he?" asked Ankyer.

"Fuck you," said Rodrigues-Zappa, spittle flying from the force of his invective.

"Ok Arturo. We have to move along. I am leaving in ten minutes or so." Ankyer stood up, walked to the bottom of the bed and picked up a second syringe that was lying next to the H&K. He walked to the foot of the bed, removed the cap from the needle and injected the contents of the syringe into a vein in Rodrigues-Zappa's left ankle.

"Arturo, I've just injected you with a form of curare. Curare is used as an anesthetic but in this form it will paralyze your body, except your brain and your heart. It's fast acting and will leave you aware of your surroundings and able to think but that's about it. You have about 9 minutes to tell me what I need to know. I do have an antidote that will reverse the effects but we have to move fast. What do you say?"

"Bullshit," said Rodrigues-Zappa.

Ankyer pulled the combat knife from its sheath and plunged it into the top of Rodrigues-Zappa's thigh and out the other side. Blood spurted and soaked into the white sable bedspread.

"Arturo," said Ankyer. "I bet you did not feel that did you?"

Rodrigues-Zappa's eyes grew large and his lower lip started to quiver.

"You have about seven minutes left after which you'll be reduced to a vegetable."

Rodrigues-Zappa said, "McGinty was here around March, 2011. He wanted me to help turn cocaine into some kind of scientific version that packed the same punch with a lot less product. It would have destroyed the value of my drugs if it hit the market in the quantities he was talking about. I decided to kill him. At the last moment I called a guy who works for another guy who helps me launder money through a bank in Switzerland. I told him about McGinty and the next day I was instructed to take McGinty to General Aviation at the Benito Juarez International Airport in Mexico City. I did what I was told and that's the last I saw of McGinty."

"What was the name of the person you called and the phone number?" asked Ankyer. Rodrigues-Zappa paused. "The clock is ticking Arturo," said Ankyer.

"Mother of God! The number is 719 666 5553. I always leave a voice mail message and the guy returns my call the next day."

"What is his name?" asked Ankyer.

"If I tell you they will kill me," said Rodrigues-Zappa.

"If you don't, welcome to your new life as a vegetable," said Ankyer.

"His name is Ibram el Farsi."

"That's it?" said Ankyer.

"That's all I know!" screamed Rodrigues-Zappa.

"What about the other guy this el Farsi works for?"

Rodrigues-Zappa was losing sensation in his face and starting to drool.

"El Farsi refers to him as 'the Emir' and that's the truth!" said Rodrigues-Zappa through the bubbles of saliva forming at the front of his mouth.

"The phone reception here is poor. Is that your cell phone on the nightstand?" asked Ankyer.

"Yes!"

Ankyer walked over to the nightstand, picked up the Apple iPhone and opened it. He selected the Contacts utility and input the phone number. "Ibram" appeared.

"Ok Arturo. What is the name of the bank your associates launder your money through?"

"Oh god, please. No!"

"Hurry Arturo. Time's almost up." Ankyer inserted the combat knife about two inches into Rodrigues-Zappa's shoulder. "No pain?" said Ankyer.

"It's INF Banque Nationale," said Rodrigues-Zappa.

"Passcode," said Ankyer.

"I can't remember," screamed Rodrigues-Zappa.

"Hurry Arturo. Time is almost up."

"It's 4545321. No wait! It's 4547321."

"Ok Arturo. I think I'll believe you," said Ankyer.

Rodrigues-Zappa said: "I can't feel anything! Please…" he whimpered.

"Pleee…" An inch of Rodrigues-Zappa's tongue protruded from the front of his mouth. His face turned grey and the muscles sagged.

"It looks like time has run out Arturo. I must run along as well. Blink if you still can." Rodrigues-Zappa blinked, tears streaming from his eyes. "Ok Arturo. I'll do you a favor. Blink if you want me to save you from remaining a vegetable."

Rodrigues-Zappa stared back at Ankyer for a moment and blinked once.

"You don't deserve it but I will help you."

At 5:25 AM Jake Ankyer exited the hacienda of Arturo Ramon Rodrigues-Zappa.

He prepared the hacienda grounds for when his visit was discovered. He then pressed the key on the Falcon IV Tactical radio. A black dot overhead quickly grew larger and landed blowing dust over most of the bunkhouse. Ankyer climbed in the open bay door of the UH-60 Black Hawk. The helicopter powered up and took off. Rodrigues-Zappa's head rested on the ground in front of the hacienda gate, its eyes partially rolled up, unfocused, and pointed toward the black dot receding into the Mexican sunrise.

LIBRARY
EMIR'S RESIDENCE
GOLD COAST, LONG ISLAND NEW YORK
FEBRUARY 16, 2012
2:45 PM EASTERN STANDARD TIME

The rain sounded like gravel hitting the window. Rainstorms this time of year were unusual but the East coast weather had been atypical the past few years. It definitely was not like the dry, hot climate of the Emir's homeland. After the nano VX matter was concluded, it might be pleasant to relocate to Hawaii. Perhaps Hawaii should be spared. Something to think about.

Abu Mactar Kahn entered the library with a tea service. The Emir had become accustomed to Irish tea and preferred it now over the strong coffee he had grown up with. Abu Mactar Kahn placed a cup on a mahogany end table next to the leather wing back chair the Emir was sitting in. Kahn placed another cup on a table next to a wing back chair opposite the Emir. At that moment, Zainab Malibi entered the room carrying a sheet of paper, which she handed to the Emir. Malibi sat down opposite the Emir and watched the flames from the fire in the 6 foot by 5 foot marble fireplace, one of her favorite architectural elements in the library.

The Emir took a sip of his tea and started reading the document.

United Press Wire Service
February 15, 2012.
Mexico City, Mexico

Zappa Drug Cartel Taken Down

In what Mexican drug enforcement authorities are saying is a major blow to illegal Mexican drug trafficking, it was revealed today that Arturo Ramon Rodrigues-Zappa, the head of the Zappa drug cartel and 14 of his main drug distributors were found dead yesterday. The bodies were located in and around Zappa's hacienda compound about 15 miles from Taxco, a historic silver mining area and now a tourist destination. The crime scene was particularly gruesome. A pyramid of 14 heads was piled next to the front gate of the hacienda. In front of the gate was the decapitated head of Arturo Ramon Rodrigues-Zappa. Captain Emilo Ruiz of the Mexican Federal Drug Enforcement Agency said, "This was clearly the result of two warring drug cartels trying to wipe each other out." The Zappa cartel can only be described as one of the most ferocious and brutal drug organizations in Mexico. It would have taken a large, well-armed force to bring this cartel down. The amount of munitions found in the compound was sufficient to supply a small army. Investigators also found an estimated 10 million dollars in street value of cocaine, marijuana and heroin, which appeared to be in the process of being shipped the United States." Mr. Fredrick Moorehouse, US Ambassador to Mexico said, "The elimination of the Zappa cartel leadership by another drug cartel is yet another example of the competitive cannibalism rampant in these crime organizations, which will be their ultimate downfall."

© 2012
United Press Wire Service

The Emir placed the paper on the table and took a sip of his tea.

"What do you make of this Zainab?"

"I must say I'm surprised," said Malibi. "Rodrigues-Zappa's cartel was not the largest, but it was the most vicious. The others would leave them alone to avoid incurring their wrath. Perhaps a new cartel has emerged and was not familiar with the Zappa cartel's reputation."

The Emir gazed into the fireplace. "Perhaps," he said.

"How much was in their account at our bank?" asked the Emir.

Malibi pulled an iPhone5 from her pocket and touched an icon.

"$ 35,000,000 as of yesterday," she said.

"How much did they pay us last year for processing their money?" he asked.

Malibi touched more icons. "$ 50,000,000."

"A significant sum," he said "... and he was useful as well."

"He gave us McGinty," Malibi replied.

"True," said the Emir.

"Leave the money in Rodrigues-Zappa's account. If someone tries to access it they might be the ones who took down the cartel. Maybe we could do business with them. After the Americans are destroyed, the remaining drug cartels will be looking for new markets. Speaking of McGinty, what is the progress of the project?"

"He has converted roughly half of the VX nerve agent to nano VX. We have moved it to staging areas where we will place the steam generators. It has taken some time to determine the best locations based on wind currents but we have made good progress."

"Excellent!" he said. "When will we be ready?"

"Within two months at the latest, assuming McGinty keeps up his pace," she said. "McGinty has also asked about his money. He wants to confirm it is in his account."

"Have Ibram call our bank along with McGinty and have the bank tell McGinty the amount in his account. Add $ 2,000,000 more to the account before the call. Ibram can tell McGinty it is a bonus for his hard work. That should give the infidel bastard incentive to finish the work quickly."

"I will contact Ibram immediately," replied Malibi

"One more thing," said the Emir. "Where are the steam generators for dispersing the nano VX to be located?" Malibi removed a folded piece of paper from her suit pants pocket and handed it to the Emir. He scanned the list. "Excellent!"

LABORATORY FACILITY BLACK FOREST, COLORADO FEBRUARY 16, 2012

Ibram el Farsi finished the call with Malibi. He was pleased that he would be calling the bank in Switzerland. Doctor McGinty, when he was not working on converting the VX to nano VX, was constantly badgering Ibram about his money. Where was it? When would he be paid? He would not continue his work without seeing the money and so on and so on. Ibram thought that if enough nano VX was made they could then just kill McGinty and be done with him. Malibi suggested not. They might still need McGinty. Calling the INF Banque Nationale with Ibram's cell phone and the speaker on, and asking the INF director to confirm McGinty's account balance would mollify McGinty, at least temporarily. After all, they owned the bank and the bank would comply with whatever they said. Also, when McGinty discovered that his bank account had $ 2,000,000 more in it than he thought, he would calm down. Ibram had to use his cell phone for the call, as the Emir's laboratory was in an old abandoned industrial district where the landline service had been disconnected years ago.

The actual laboratory facility was in a subbasement, and Ibram stepped into a freight elevator and pushed the 'SUB 1' button. The large door shut with a clank and the elevator started down in a jerking motion with a loud mechanical sound. It came to an abrupt stop and the doors opened into an anteroom with glass walls. There was an airlock, beyond which Ibram could see a large area containing what appeared to be a series of connected vats not unlike a brewery processing plant. In among the vats was McGinty in a HAZMAT suit accompanied by three others also wearing HAZMAT suits.

Ibram pressed an intercom button and said "Doctor McGinty could you please step out of the laboratory. I have something to discuss with you."

McGinty turned and said something to the HAZMAT suit next to him. The HAZMAT suit walked over to a control panel and started adjusting dials. McGinty walked over to the airlock and opened a door. He entered the room, stepped out of the HAZMAT suit and hung it on a hook. He then pressed a button on the wall and a mist filled the airlock. After a moment a loud vacuum noise filled the area and the mist cleared leaving McGinty standing in the middle of the airlock wearing nothing but a swim suit which did nothing to compliment his dumpy physique. McGinty opened the door and stepped into the anteroom.

"Where is my money!" exclaimed McGinty.

Ibram had a vision of strangling McGinty. However, he managed to suppress the image and replied, "That's what I want to talk to you about. The Emir has instructed me to call his bank in Switzerland and have them confirm for you over the phone what the balance is in your account."

"It's about goddam time," McGinty said.

Ibram fought to control his temper. "We need to go upstairs where I can get a cell phone signal, Doctor."

They entered the freight elevator and went to the first floor. Ibram took his cell phone from his pocket and touched a speed dial button. The phone rang three times.

"Guten Tag. Wie kann ich Ihren helfen?" said the female voice in German.

"I wish to speak with Mr. Hans Greffen please," said Ibram.

Switching seamlessly to English, the female voice replied: "May I have your name, please?"

"Ibram el Farsi," he replied.

"One moment sir."

After a pause, "Ibram my friend, how are you?" inquired Greffen.

"Very well thank you" said Ibram.

"How can we help you today?" asked Greffen.

"I have you on a speakerphone," said Ibram. "With me is Doctor Angus McGinty for whom we recently established an account."

"I am familiar with that account," said Greffen.

"Doctor McGinty would like to know the account balance if you would be so kind," said Ibram.

"Would you please confirm the account number for me," said Greffen.

"The account number is 8723669Z," said el Farsi.

"Thank you. Doctor McGinty's account balance was $ 5,000,000 US dollars as of February 14th. An additional $2,000,000 US was added on February 15th making the account balance $ 7,000,000 US as of today."

"When can I get the money?" asked McGinty.

"The money is available now but the account requires you to appear here in person for withdrawal," said Greffen.

"Goddamn it!" exclaimed McGinty.

"I'm sorry sir but that is the bank policy for this type of account," replied Greffen.

"Thank you Mr. Greffen. That's all we need for the moment," said el Farsi.

"You're welcome Ibram. Please give my regards to the Emir," said Greffen.

"I will," replied el Farsi and pressed 'end' on his phone.

"What the hell is the personal appearance crap at the bank all about?" asked McGinty.

"It's our insurance that you will stay here to complete your work," said el Farsi.

"Also, as you probably noticed, you have $ 2,000,000 more in your account than our agreed upon arrangement. That's an additional bonus for all your hard work on our project."

McGinty stared at el Farsi. "Ok. But how do I get the fucking money when I'm done?"

"When your work is complete you will be flown to Switzerland where you can either withdraw your money or have it switched to an account that permits electronic funds transfer to any account you want. You will then be flown to any destination of your choice. And that will be the end of our relationship." McGinty appeared to calm down.

"Ok. But just don't try to fuck with me. By the way, there's a serious problem with the steam generator operation."

THE CONSTABLE CLUB EMBASSY ROW WASHINGTON DC FEBRUARY 17, 2012 1:00 PM EASTERN STANDARD TIME

Asher Finkel, Margie Tallon and George Makin sat in the Constable Club dining room. The menu changed daily and included a "Personal Request" item, which was just about anything one could wish for. The dining room was open twenty-four hours a day. The ceiling of the room was carved plaster and the walls beechnut wood paneling.

"How are you two finding your accommodations at the Club?" asked Finkel.

"Superb," replied Tallon. "I feel as if I should be paying to stay here but am glad I am not since I could never afford it."

Makin added, "Neil has been very helpful getting us acquainted with the facilities. The shooting range is first rate, as is the exercise equipment."

"No surprise there," said Finkel. "The range and workout rooms have all been designed to Joint Special Operational Command specifications."

"I'm glad you are both comfortable here. But don't get too comfortable. It's time for you two to go to work," said Finkel. "Jake Ankyer completed his mission at Rodrigues-Zappa's hacienda a few days ago. He did not find McGinty but he did acquire actionable intelligence. It turns out that McGinty left the hospitality of our Mr. Rodrigues-Zappa around March 2011. He was flown out of Mexico City on a private jet, which had a flight plan that brought it into Denver International

Airport. It seems that McGinty originally went to meet with Rodrigues-Zappa to propose converting Zappa's raw cocaine to nanotechnology-processed cocaine. Zappa felt that the new version of high performance cocaine would significantly devalue his product. He reasoned that the best way to eliminate the problem would be to eliminate McGinty. Before doing so, however, Zappa called someone named Ibram. The number he gave Jake was 719 666 5553. We checked the number against the N.S.A. database and it matched to Ibram el Farsi, who, as it turns out, hails from Iraq. The area code is for Black Forrest, Colorado, which is 64.03 miles from Denver. We think that McGinty may be, or may have been, at that location. Zappa explained to Jake that Ibram el Farsi was his link to a bank in Geneva Switzerland, the INF Banque Nationale. It seemed that Zappa had an arrangement with el Farsi to wash the Zappa cartel's drug proceeds through an account in this bank."

"It would sure be nice if we had that account number," Makin said. "Mr. Rodrigues-Zappa was accommodating in that regard as well," Finkel said. The account pass code is 4547321. We have confirmed that this is a legitimate account at that bank. All this information has been uploaded onto your N.S.A. smart phones."

"...And you're telling us that Jake Ankyer obtained this information from Zappa voluntarily?" asked Tallon.

"Not exactly," said Finkel. "There's more."

Finkel handed copies of the United Press Wire Service article to Tallon and Makin. Finkel continued as they read. "Jake has been specifically trained to elicit information from resisting subjects quickly and accurately. Essentially, Rodrigues-Zappa perceived that the consequences of not giving Jake the information he requested would be much worse than any resulting problems he might endure from giving the information out."

"Waterboarding?" asked Tallon.

"No. It is much more effective than that. It includes both physical and psychological stimulation over a very short period of time. Suffice it to say that Rodrigues-Zappa asked Jake to kill him at the end, which Jake had to do in any event."

Makin finished reading the news story. "Ankyer eliminated an entire drug cartel by himself!" he exclaimed.

"Not the entire cartel, but essentially the entire management structure," said Finkel.

"Jake also realized that creating the illusion of a competing cartel might cause the person behind the money laundering scheme at the Swiss bank to emerge and to lead us to…"

"Ibram el Farsi or even Saddam Hussein," said Tallon completing Finkel's sentence.

"Exactly. It may not play out exactly like that, but our analysts have computed the probability at between 60 and 75 percent," said Finkel.

"Which explains the decapitated heads. Drug cartels decapitate the heads of their enemies to send a message," said Makin.

"Yes. And in this case Jake was sending a message from us to whomever is behind the bank's arrangement with the cartel," replied Finkel.

"This couldn't have been planned as part of his initial mission," said Makin.

"It wasn't," replied Finkel. "We give Jake one hundred percent field flexibility to permit him to adjust mission outcome depending upon variable circumstances."

"He must really be something," said Tallon.

"You can judge for yourself," replied Finkel. "You and George will be flying out to meet with him at our facility on the grounds of the Holy Innocents Monastery in the Gila National Forest in New Mexico. We need the three of you in one place so you can deploy as a team. Apart from finding and neutralizing Saddam, if he is in fact alive, this business of the VX is troublesome. During the Iran/Iraq War several tons of VX were placed at the disposal of Saddam. The nanotechnology form of the VX found in the body part of the person in Colorado was from that batch. If the person killed by the VX was some form of test and the balance of the VX, or even a part of it is in the United States, that would be a very vexing issue indeed. So much so, that your mission has been expanded from finding Saddam Hussein to include determining the source of the VX found in the Colorado remains. We must know how or if Saddam is linked to the VX and, if so, what plan if any is in place. I have also activated Neil and the rest of our SEAL Team to provide the three of you backup as necessary."

"What's the next step?" asked Makin.

"You need to meet Jake at Holy Innocents Monastery and fly to Switzerland. You will be traveling under US diplomatic passports. Once there, you will meet with Doctor Heidi Riekert, Chair of the Swiss Financial Markets Authority's Executive Board in Berne. Doctor Riekert has been requested to cooperate with you and can delicately facilitate our inquiries regarding the INF Banque Nationale. Based upon the information that emerges, you and Jake will adjust your mission strategy and proceed from there. You will need to pack both business and 511 tactical clothes. Anything you don't have you can acquire from the SEAL team stores here. Ask Neil. You leave for Joint Base Andrews in Maryland in an hour. You can contact me via your secure tactical phones with anything that comes up during your deployment. If something occurs that changes your mission profile we will contact you through Ankyer immediately. Time to go."

Neil approached the table and looked at Makin and Tallon.

"Please follow me," he said. They got up from the table leaving Asher Finkel talking on his secure tactical phone.

"Father Bruno! It's nice talking with you. Yes. They are just leaving. Is Jake ready? Excellent."

HOLY INNOCENTS TRAPPIST MONASTERY GILA NATIONAL FOREST NEW MEXICO FEBRUARY 17, 2012 6:17 PM MOUNTAIN TIME

The Learjet C-20B twin engine, turbofan, military version of the Learjet C-20 initiated its descent from the 46,000 feet military air space corridor. The cabin steward, if you could call a 6'3", 240 pound male in camouflage fatigues with a 45 caliber semi-automatic strapped to his leg a "steward", approached Makin and Tallon seated in the mid section of the plane. "We have started our decent into the Holy Innocents' air space. You will have to buckle up tightly. The pilot executes several sharp maneuvers over mountains as we approach the Monastery runway."

"The Monastery has its own runway?" asked Tallon.

"The Monastery has its own everything," said the steward as he sat down and strapped in. Five minutes later a window next to Tallon was filled with a fighter jet. "That would be the Monastery's F/A-18F or Super Hornet for short," said the steward.

"You have got to be kidding!" said Makin.

"Not kidding. It's also got a second seat for a weapons officer," said the steward.

"You have just entered air space that is as secure if not more so than the White House. The pilot sent a transponder signal into Monastery Air Control about ten minutes ago. That signaled the Monastery to send up the Super Hornet for another transponder signal and visual confirmation. Green means "come on in boys!" and red means we get blown to smithereens, no questions asked. We make damn sure those transponders are working."

At that point they saw the Super Hornet pilot give a salute through his cockpit window. The C-20B decelerated, banking sharply several times, and dropped nose down and the flaps deployed. A few minutes later the Learjet C-20B touched down, flaps extended for braking, causing the bodies of Tallon, Makin and the steward to jerk forward with the momentum of the rapid deceleration as the plane rolled to a stop. The pilot's voice came on over the intercom. "Thanks for flying Holy Innocents Air. Hope you enjoyed the landing!"

The steward looked at Tallon and Makin. "I didn't mention all the banking coming in. No point in causing you undue anxiety for your first Holy Innocents' landing. You'll get used to it."

The front hatch of the plane opened and a short person with a somewhat disproportionately large, bald, head wearing a brown tunic over a white cassock came in.

"Hey Fred, how's the family?" the head said.

"Family's great," replied the steward.

"How's by you Brother William?"

"Can't complain. You and the boys up front should drop by the refectory. We've got steaks tonight."

"You've got a deal!" said Fred.

Brother William waved to Makin and Tallon. "Glad to see you guys have recovered from the landing more or less. Hurry up now. I'll drive you over to the Monastery."

They followed Brother William from the plane and into a black Hummer. Makin climbed into the front seat and Tallon slid into the rear. Brother William started the Hummer, put it in gear, and raced down the runway quickly reaching sixty miles per hour.

"I love driving down the runway!" he said. "No traffic!"

"Are you a priest here?" asked Tallon.

"Definitely not!" exclaimed Brother William laughing. "That's way above my pay grade, Doctor Tallon. No, when I'm not driving the Hummer, I work with Jake Ankyer in various aspects of his training. He is really something!"

"So we've been told," said Makin.

Brother William slowed the Hummer and executed a sliding right hand turn onto a trail leading from the end of the runway, but not before the Super Hornet screeched over their heads landing at the opposite end. "You two are going to love this place. I'll see if I can talk someone into giving you a ride in the fighter. It's a blast! The Monastery is about thirty minutes into the forest."

"Is Holy Innocents an actual Trappist monastery?" asked Tallon.

"You bet it is," said Brother William. "I can even arrange to have a couple of fruit cakes mailed to you courtesy of our Kentucky brothers in Gethsemani Abbey in time for Christmas, if you give me your addresses!"

Brother William negotiated several curves as they went deeper into the forest.

"The Monastery occupies about 3,000 acres including the runway and hangars for the planes. The Gila forest itself occupies 3.3 million acres and we're in the center of it. When the Monastery was built they intentionally constructed a lot of curves in the road to prevent a vehicle from rapidly accelerating in a straight line. My personal best is 14 minutes from the runway to the Abbey. It's sort of like driving at Le Mans but not as much fun. The Abbey caught me on its radar and he was not pleased."

"How many Trappists are here?" asked Makin.

"There are seven of us at the moment. That doesn't include Jake of course. We tease him a lot about joining us but he has resisted so far."

"I gather Jake is not married," said Tallon.

"Definitely not," replied Brother William.

"He once said he would consider joining our group if the Church let priests marry. There's a fat chance of that happening. I think when it comes to persuading Jake to joining up we're screwed...so to speak."

As Brother William was talking Tallon thought she saw some shadows moving in the woods but then they disappeared leading her to conclude the shadows were the result of dappled sunlight shining through the trees or possibly deer. Brother William decelerated, and as the Hummer emerged from the turn, they came upon a large irregularly shaped lake. On the other side of the lake was the Abbey, behind which there were mountains with snow-capped peaks.

"Your tax dollars at work!" exclaimed Brother William. "What do you think?"

"Its breathtaking," said Tallon.

The Abbey was a four story stone structure, with at least ten gables that Tallon could see. Three four-story wings radiated from the main structure. The building was set among a large stand of Ponderosa pines. Five minutes later Brother William started around the lake and the road eventually turned into a gravel driveway. The Hummer stopped in front of two large wooden doors.

"Here we are, safe and sound," said Brother William. At that point, a helicopter landed on a helipad partially obscured by one of the Abbey wings. "We could have brought you here by helicopter but we wanted to give you a sense of the place from the ground."

One of the large wooden double doors opened and a Trappist walked out. He was about 6 feet 3 inches tall and was wearing a white robe covered by another sleeveless dark brown robe, with a cowl. He wore glasses, had white hair and a full white beard, and a kindly smile. "Hi. My name is Father Michael Bruno and I am the Abbot here at Holy Innocents. Welcome! Doctor Finkel has told me all about you. Your bags are being taken to your rooms."

"Brother William. You didn't promise our guests a ride on the fighter plane did you?" asked Father Bruno. Brother William got a sheepish look. "You did, didn't you? We've talked about that. Brother William would be happier if we were located in Disneyland, since he thinks a lot of what we have around here is an A Ride," said Father Bruno with a twinkle in his eye. "He probably also said we will have holiday fruit cakes sent to you from the Gethsemani Abbey in Kentucky."

Tallon laughed. "I'm beginning to think we are not the first ones."

"No indeed. The Abbot at Gethsemani sent me a Christmas card last year thanking us for being among their best customers."

Brother William started the Hummer and waived. "See you later! I'll give you a tour!" The Hummer turned around in the driveway and accelerated toward the helicopter's landing pad in a cloud of dust.

"Well, come on in. We have a lot to talk about," said Father Bruno.

Makin and Tallon followed Father Bruno past the entrance into a stone corridor. The ceilings were vaulted and about 30 feet high. The corridor extended about 200 feet, and diffuse light emanated from sconces sunk into the wall. Periodically there were stained glass windows with rounded tops letting dappled, filtered light into the hall. Midway down the hall was a leaded glass door opening out on to a large rectangular garden. Just past the glass door on the left side of the corridor was another wooden door opening into a room into which Father Bruno led his visitors.

The room was furnished with prairie style chairs and tables, a fireplace at one end, and a wall to wall, floor to ceiling bookcase at the other end, with a large flat screened television in the bookcase's center.

As they were standing in the room, Father Bruno said, "While you are here you will notice that there is a high degree of technology present at the Abbey. For example, we use the same type of optical recognition equipment you were registered with at the Constable Club. You are already in the system here, and have access to most parts of the Abbey and grounds except for the cloistered areas, which we Trappist brothers keep to ourselves. Every place else, including the shooting range, refectory, and meeting rooms for example, is accessible. Doctor Finkel is an absolutely lovely man and close friend, but he is always trying out new technology on us. We prefer a simpler life but Asher is hard to turn down."

At that moment a man entered the room. Tallon noticed he was about 6 feet 4 inches in height and had black medium cut hair. His eyes seem to change in color from deep blue to green. He had prominent cheekbones and his facial features reminded Tallon of a prizefighter, but somehow softer. He didn't walk as much as he seemed to glide toward them. He wore a dark blue, long sleeved, tunic-like shirt outside dark grey slacks.

"Ah. I would like you to meet Jake Ankyer. Jake this is Doctor Margie Tallon and George Makin, both late of the FBI and now transferred to our clutches for the moment," said Father Bruno.

Ankyer shook hands with Makin and then with Tallon. Tallon noticed his wrist was unusually thick. His handshake was firm...but in a way almost gentle.

"I'm delighted to meet you both," said Ankyer. Tallon also noticed his voice was without any inflection which might give away his origin. "Doctor Finkel has told me all about you."

"We've heard quite a bit about you as well," said Tallon.

"I spoke with Doctor Finkel earlier and he will be calling in to us shortly with some new information," said Father Bruno.

As they walked toward the chairs, a large four-legged shape centered itself in the doorway. It walked into the room and stood next to Ankyer.

"I'd like to introduce you to Varna."

"That has got to be the largest German shepherd I've ever seen," said Makin.

"That would be true if he was a Shepherd," said Ankyer.

"Varna is a Mackenzie Valley wolf, which is a strain of Canadian Timber Wolf. The males weigh in at an average of 170 pounds. Varna is slightly larger at 185 pounds. George, Doctor Tallon, please hold out a hand. Varna, meet our new friends," said Ankyer. The wolf walked over to Tallon, sniffed her hand and then licked it. He went over to Makin and did the same. "Varna now recognizes each of you, and considers you an accepted resident of the Abbey."

"I would not want him to think I was not an accepted resident," said Makin.

"You would be on the mark there, George," said Ankyer. "Varna is the Alpha male of the wolf pack that guards the Abbey. If Varna and the pack don't know you, well..."

"Brother William is always trying to teach Varna tricks and tries to bribe him with meat treats from the Refectory. Learning tricks goes against Varna's instincts but he does enjoy Brother William's treats."

I expect Doctor Finkel will be calling in a few minutes," said Father Bruno.

They walked over to the chairs and sat down. Tallon watched Ankyer out of the corner of her eye. Ankyer seemed to move like flowing water. He was incredibly graceful but his thick wrists suggested considerable power. What she could see of his body structure looked perfect. Once Ankyer was seated, Varna padded over and lay down next to his chair. Not "on guard" but ready nevertheless. At that moment a chime issued from a small speakerphone on a square, burled walnut coffee table located in the center of the grouping of chairs.

"Father Bruno, are you there?"

"Yes, Doctor Finkel. I'm here with Doctor Tallon, George Makin and Jake," he replied. "Excellent. I'm glad everyone has met. After Jake's recent visit to Rodrigues-Zappa during which Zappa provided the phone number to his money-laundering colleague, N.S.A. began tracking the usage of the number called. We are using Radio Frequency Pattern Matching algorithms for tracking the location of both the outgoing and receiving cell phones. Using RFPM we can locate the exact latitude and longitude of the specific cell phone making the call as well as the location of cell phones answering calls from the target phone. The accuracy of the location is within one meter. As we now know, the target number is a cell phone, which is registered to one Ibram el Farsi, who is an Iraqi. Our analyst picked up a conversation between el Farsi and someone named Zainab Malibi who referenced McGinty in the conversation. The N.S.A. transcript is being sent to your screen now."

The flat screen in the bookcase flickered and a document started scrolling slowly down the screen.

> N.S.A. Secure Transmission. Level desig. Priority Red Protocol
> -----Eyes Only Finkel and auth.----
> Encryption/Decryption: Activated
> 17 February 2012....1500 hrs. Eastern Time Zone
> Tracking Phone No.: 719 666 5553
>
> <u>Date: 16 February 2012 Time: 1520 EST</u>
> Phone 1: 719 666 5553 [Registration: el Farsi, Ibram]
> Phone Type: Cell; Tower 90KL821;Loc: Black Forest, CO
> Phone 2: 631 781 5567 [Registration: Malibi, Zainab]
> Phone Type: Cell; Tower 67HD332; Loc: Long Island, NY
> ...Analyst ID:YNT567
>
> Phone 2 [Incoming]: Ibram this is Zainab. We have added another $ 2,000,000 to McGinty's account. Please call the bank today and have them confirm for McGinty his account balance. We have to keep him under control until he finishes his work.
>
> Phone 1 [Outgoing] : I will do as you ask Zainab. McGinty is working diligently and the conversion process is well underway.
> Call Terminated: 1524 EST.
>
> <u>Date: 16 February 2012 Time: 1600 MST</u>
> Phone 1: 719 666 5553 [Registration: el Farsi, Ibram]

Phone Type: Cell; Tower 90KL821;Loc: Black Forest, CO
Phone 2: 011 41 31 888 7888 [Registration :INF Banque International]
Phone Type: Land; Tower: N/A; Loc: Berne Switzerland
....Analyst ID:YNT567

Phone 1: [Outgoing]: Connected
Phone 2: [Incoming} Guten Tag. Wie kann ich Ihren helfen?
Phone 1: I wish to speak with Mr. Hans Greffen please.
Phone 2: May I have your name please?
Phone 1: Ibram el Farsi
Phone 2: One moment sir.
Phone 2: Ibram my friend, how are you.
Phone 1: Very well thank you.
Phone 2: How can we help you today?
Phone 1: I have you on a speakerphone. With me is Doctor Angus McGinty who we recently established an account for.
Phone 2: I am familiar with that account.
Phone 1: Doctor McGinty would like confirmation of the account balance if you would be so kind.
Phone 2: Would you please confirm the account number for me?
Phone 1: The account number is 8723669Z.
Phone 2: Thank you. Doctor McGinty's account balance was $ 5,000,000 US dollars as of February 14th. An additional $ 2,000,000 US was added on February 15th making the account balance $ 7,000,000 US. as of today.
Phone 1: When can I get the money?
Phone 2: The money is available now but the account requires you to appear here in person for withdrawal.
Phone 1: God dammit!
Phone 2: I'm sorry sir but that is the bank policy for this type of account.
Phone 1: Thank you Mr. Greffen. That's all we need for the moment.
Phone 2: You're welcome Ibram. Please give my regards to the Emir.

Phone 1: I will.
Call Terminated: 1620 MST.

After the scrolling stopped Finkel came back on the line. "I'm sure you have questions, but let me take a few minutes to give you our initial review at this end. Based on the second phone call with the INF Bank, it is clear that Doctor Angus McGinty is a complicit and active participant in whatever is going on. Up until now, we thought the principal person dealing with both Rodrigues-Zappa and McGinty was Ibram el Farsi. However, we now believe that based on the passing comment made by Rodrigues-Zappa during his interview with Jake and these phone calls, that the person referred to as the 'Emir' may in fact be controlling events."

"You think he is Saddam don't you," said Makin.

"We think it is a possibility," said Finkel. "However, we now are equally concerned about what McGinty is doing. The distance between Texas Creek, Colorado where the VX infected partial corpse was found, and Black Forest, Colorado, where we now believe McGinty to be located, is only 90 miles. If McGinty has developed a process to convert VX through nanotechnology to an enhanced form using a process similar to his cocaine proposal to Rodrigues-Zappa, the human remains found in Texas Creek might be the result of a test run. And remember, the VX particle found in the cadaver was from the VX stockpile in Iraq. There are just too many coincidences."

"Originally our plan was to have you Jake, and George and Margie go to Switzerland to try to isolate the source of Rodrigues-Zappa's funds. With this new information from the monitored phone call we think it essential to quickly investigate the activity in Black Forest, Colorado and Long Island, New York as well. Jake, I would like you to fly to Black Forest tomorrow and determine exactly where Angus McGinty is, using the RFPM location from el Farsi's cell phone we will provide when you arrive."

"If I find McGinty and el Farsi, should I place them under our control?" asked Ankyer.

"Ordinarily I would say yes," replied Finkel. "However, apprehending them might signal to Malibi and the Emir that something has occurred and they may take evasive action and be more difficult to reacquire. Our best strategy at this point is to locate McGinty and initiate surveillance while we try to sort out the 'Emir' part of this problem. Margie, I would like you to fly out to Long Island and make visual contact with Malibi, also using the RFPM location we provide. Initiate a clandestine surveillance and try to track her to wherever the Emir is located. We'll decide what to do at that point. George, I would like you to go to Switzerland and meet with Doctor Heidi Riekert who is Chair of the Swiss Financial Markets Authority. They have legal oversight responsibility for Swiss banks. She has been given limited information regarding the INF Bank Nationale and has been informed that you are a US State Department investigator looking into a possible drug scheme. She has indicated that she will cooperate any way she can and will be expecting you to call on her at her office tomorrow. That's about it. The major problem before us is time. We simply don't know what these people intend on doing and when. On the side of caution we must assume time is short and we must move as quickly as possible. If we generate any additional information from the phone surveillance we will have Father Bruno contact you through your secure tactical radio links. Good luck."

The light on the speakerphone changed from green to red and the monitor on the bookcase faded to grey.

"I will have the aircraft prepared for your flights tomorrow," said Father Bruno. George, you will be going out on the Lear jet."

"Jake, I assume you will be wanting the Pilatus for your trip," continued Father Bruno.

"Yes. Thank you," said Jake.

"Margie, there is a second Lear on the way which should be here around 10:00 AM."

They all got up from their chairs. Varna rose and stood next to Ankyer.

"One thing," said Tallon. "I haven't had a chance to exercise on this trip. Can I jog around the grounds before I leave tomorrow?"

Father Bruno looked at Ankyer. "Absolutely," said Ankyer. "Why don't you join Varna and me for a morning run? We will meet you in front of the Abbey at 6:00 AM."

"Great," replied Tallon.

Father Bruno said to Makin and Tallon: "Dinner is now being served in the Refectory, if you will follow me. After dinner I suggest you retire early. You will have a long day tomorrow."

"Will you be joining us Jake?" asked Tallon.

"I'm afraid I am scheduled with Brother William for the next three hours so I'll see you in the morning." Ankyer left the room with Varna padding next to him.

After Ankyer had left, Father Bruno, Makin and Tallon walked down the hall and approached a door on the left. Father Bruno looked into a glass panel imbedded in the wall. It flashed once and a sliding door opened. The interior lighting was subdued. There were ten tables, each with four chairs. The tables were separated from each other and along one wall there was a cafeteria-like serving station.

As they walked in, Fred, the "steward" from the Lear jet, passed them holding a tray piled up with two large steaks and various salads. He said, "Glad to see you guys made it for dinner. The food here is great." Turning to Makin he continued: "The Lear will be ready for you around 0900 hours tomorrow George. See you then."

As Fred walked by, Father Bruno said: "I think we will have to have another talk about the sin of gluttony, Fred."

Fred replied, "Big guys need big meals Father. Besides, any time me and my friends have an opportunity for something to eat besides military snacks we grab it!"

"You can't tell me that Fred is just a 'steward' on a plane," said Makin.

"Must be your FBI investigative training," said Father Bruno. "Actually Fred Bell is a chief petty officer with the N.S.A. SEAL team at the Columbine Club. He's detailed to keep track of you in case you should run into any trouble in the field. Even though you folks are trained FBI agents, Doctor Finkel tends toward being on the over protective side when it comes to his colleagues. We keep asking who would want to bother a bunch of Trappist monks, especially with someone like Jake Ankyer around, but Doctor Finkel keeps telling us to humor him. He is our boss in a secular sense, but also has come to be our good friend so we like to make him happy."

"Speaking of Jake Ankyer, he mentioned that he had three hours of time scheduled with Brother William," said Tallon. "What's that all about?"

"It's part of his training," replied Father Bruno. "I imagine Doctor Finkel gave you an insight into Jake. In order to keep his performance levels up he needs to be stimulated. On the physical side of things, he works on his martial arts skills with Brother William three hours a day, at least when he is here. Brother William is the only one here who can keep up with him."

"Brother William?" said Makin.

"Yes. Underneath that jolly countenance is one of the most accomplished martial artists in the world. He showed up at our New Melleray Abbey in Iowa one day and asked if he could stay awhile. Fifteen years later he's here causing his own special brand of chaos, but we love him. He actually invented a new form of karate-based combat, which has been adapted for use by Jake and they practice it for three hours every day. Doctor Finkel is worried that they might hurt each other, but so far so good. By the way Margie, its unusual that Jake invites someone to join him on his morning run," continued Father Bruno. "I hope you are in good condition since no one around here can keep up with him. In any event, I have a feeling you are in for an interesting time."

LABORATORY FACILITY BLACK FOREST, COLORADO FEBRUARY 16, 2012

Ibram el Farsi looked at McGinty and repeated McGinty's words: "A serious problem with the steam generators? They are critical to our plan. What kind of serious problem?"

"I was testing a generator with live nano VX to determine the rate at which the nano VX precipitates from the steam cloud. I placed a mouse in the steam chamber to assess how quickly it would die. The mouse died before I turned on the steam machine. I rechecked all the connections to the nano VX canister attached to the steam generator and everything was as it should be. I then set up the test again, and the mouse died as soon as the nano VX canister was attached to the generator, but before it was turned on. To make a long story short, the nano VX particles are so small, some are escaping through the steam generator seals. The nano VX is so effective, it kills any air breathing entity before the steam generator is even turned on."

"How do we fix this problem?" asked el Farsi.

"You can't," replied McGinty.

"Water vapor can penetrate a Tyvex suit so the VX particles in water vapor will still get in the suit and kill the operator. A full HAZMAT suit with an external air pressure system is not practical. We're screwed."

El Farsi looked at McGinty and contemplated. "How much time would the steam generator operator have after attaching the nano VX canister before he died?" asked el Farsi.

"It should take a little longer than with a mouse. Maybe ten seconds. But that would not make any difference. The nano VX particles would almost instantly seek out air breathing organisms and kill them."

"But the operator would still have enough time to turn on the steam generator, would he not?" asked el Farsi.

"Yes," replied McGinty.

"But the nano VX would escape into the area around the steam generator and kill the operator," said McGinty.

"What about using a remote control device?" asked el Farsi.

"Won't work," replied McGinty. The problem is not starting up the steam generator. The problem is connecting the nano VX containers to the steam generators. Also training is required to test the pressure in the nano VX containers so that it equalizes with the pressure settings in the steam generation equipment."

"Ok," said el Farsi. "Go back to your work and I will discuss the problem with the Emir and let you know what we will do."

El Farsi took the elevator up to the ground floor and stepped outside. He took his cell phone out and called Malibi.

"Yes Ibram."

"Zainab. I have just completed a meeting with McGinty. He says the canisters with the nano VX leak when coupled with the steam generator because the nano particles are so small. The result is to kill the operator within about ten seconds."

"Is there enough time for the operator to start the machine?" asked Malibi.

"According to McGinty there is. He also says that the operators have to be trained to use the equipment because of pressure issues with the containers and the generators."

"The Emir and I have been discussing McGinty. How much time is left before he is finished converting the VX to nano VX?"

"He is almost finished. It is going faster than we anticipated. Also, the nano VX is much more potent and we do not need to convert as much VX as we first thought."

"Excellent," replied Malibi. "Tell McGinty that we will take care of the problem ourselves and he is to train you in the operation of the equipment. After that when he completes the VX conversion and your training, his work will be done and he will be flown to Switzerland to collect his money as we agreed."

"But what about the leakage problem?" asked el Farsi.

"We can deploy some of the martyrs to the task. They are awaiting instructions for suicide bombings but they will obey us and accomplish this task instead."

"Good thinking!" said el Farsi. "Then the plan is to pay McGinty and release him?"

"Not quite," said Malibi. "As we have discussed, there is something very special in store for our Doctor McGinty. Please call me when he has completed his task."

HOLY INNOCENTS TRAPPIST MONASTERY GILA NATIONAL FOREST NEW MEXICO FEBRUARY 18, 2012 6:00 AM MOUNTAIN TIME

Tallon walked out of one of the front doors of the Monastery. She was dressed in dark green running shorts and a sweat shirt with "You got a crime I've got the time" printed on the front and FBI printed in block letters on the back. She wore an orange headband that said Girls Rule. According to a wireless thermometer in her room it was 55 degrees Fahrenheit outside, so a sweatshirt seemed best for a jog.

As she walked down the stone front steps, the early morning fog separated, and then she saw them. Varna was sitting next to a stone bench twenty yards to the right of the Abbey entrance. Standing next to Varna was an image dressed only in navy blue running shorts and wearing unusual dark grey colored shoes. Steam curled from the image's back and shoulders. Tallon had seen many bodies, both intact and dismembered, in her medical career, but nothing remotely like what stood in front of her. It was clearly Ankyer, but the trunk, shoulders and legs appeared to be perfectly symmetrical chiseled granite. His wrists were unusually thick, something she had noticed in their meeting the day earlier. His forearms were also large and his upper arms well defined with his triceps revealing exceptional definition. It wasn't a muscle builder's body though. It looked... unbreakable. As she got closer she noticed his eyes again which seemed to fluctuate from green to dark blue. Varna stood up and padded over to her. He rubbed his head and shoulder against her thigh.

"Good morning, Margie," said Ankyer. "Varna just rubbed his scent on you. It helps him find you from a considerable distance. Call it a wolf trait. He likes you."

Tallon stopped in front of Ankyer. Even at her height of 5' 10" she only came up to his shoulder.

"I apologize if I stared at you. I've never seen anyone like you, and as a physician I've seen a lot of bodies."

"Don't worry about it," he replied. "I'm the product of N.S.A.'s and Doctor Finkel's little science project. I was in pretty good shape before but they knocked off the rough edges and the training program here at the Abbey keeps me tuned up. By the way, I was speaking with Doctor Finkel after our meeting yesterday. He wants to talk with us again before we go our separate ways later today. Another change based on updated intelligence. I mentioned we were going jogging this morning and he sent you a gift in the overnight resupply flight. Have a seat on the bench and I'll get it."

Tallon sat on a stone bench next to Varna while Ankyer retrieved a box over by the front door. He knelt in front of Tallon and before she could say anything her running shoes were off. He opened the box and removed two grey shoes. He reached around her leg just above the ankle and slipped on a shoe. As he touched her, an electric thrill coursed through Tallon and she had to catch her breath.

"I'll have to get over this guy some how," she thought. "Or maybe I won't!"

Ankyer slipped the second shoe on. "Now stand up and walk around a little," he said. As she walked she couldn't believe the feeling.

"These are incredible!" she exclaimed.

"The N.S.A. labs produce all sorts of surprises," he replied. "You are wearing a combat running shoe that is a composite of carbon and titanium with a malleable cork lining. The shoes are now a perfect fit for your feet and will stay that way. And if your foot changes they will change."

"I'm not going to give these back!" she exclaimed laughing.

"That's exactly what I said when Doctor Finkel gave me my pair," said Ankyer.

"Are you ready for our run?" he asked. Tallon was still jogging up and down.

"I am. I definitely am. From the steam coming off your shoulders it looks like you have been out for awhile," she said.

"Varna and I do a training run every morning when I'm at the Abbey. Today we did 20 miles up the mountain and back," he replied.

"20 miles is incredible!" she exclaimed.

"Actually I misspoke," he said. "It was 20 miles up the mountain and 20 miles back. 40 miles. You ready?" Tallon was speechless and could only nod.

They started jogging down the Abbey driveway toward the lake. Varna was in front and pulling away. Tallon could tell Ankyer was intentionally moderating his pace so she could keep up. She followed him to the shore of the lake and then to a trail that connected from the lake to the woods. The fog had started to clear and the clean air and pine aroma were exhilarating. Twenty minutes into the run Tallon lost sight of Varna around a curve. Ankyer slowed down so she could catch up. She noticed he ran like a well-oiled machine, each muscle and tendon in perfect harmony.

When she caught up to him, he said, "There's a clearing about a mile up. We can stop there and take a break," and he pulled away again.

Tallon entered another curve where she lost sight of Varna. During the run she thought she saw vague shapes beyond the tree line similar to the ones she saw when Brother William drove her and Makin to the Abbey, but they were gone before she could focus. As Tallon came out of the curve the path opened wider, the shapes were back and keeping up with her and Ankyer ahead of her. Suddenly the shapes exploded from both sides of the path and were pacing them.

"Wolves!" her mind shrieked. There had to be at least fifteen of them and they were huge!

"Jake!" she yelled.

Ankyer looked back and waved his arm in a "follow me" motion. A particularly large wolf Tallon recognized as Varna detached from the group and ran up to Ankyer. Another fifty yards and they had entered a clearing surrounded by maple trees. The wolves bounded into the clearing running up to Tallon and rubbing her legs or licking her.

Ankyer walked over. "I apologize. I should have mentioned the wolf pack might be joining us. When Varna rubbed against you back at the Abbey he put his scent on you so the wolves would recognize you. Varna is the pack's Alpha male and they take their cue from him. The good news is that you are now officially a member of the wolf pack. Congratulations!"

"If you weren't so damn big I'd punch you!" Tallon exclaimed, and then started laughing. "When I accepted this assignment Doctor Finkel never said anything about being inducted into a wolf pack."

"There's a serious side to it," said Ankyer.

"The pack patrols the 3,000 acres of the Abbey, which is quite large but actually smaller than their normal hunting range which can be as much as 1,000 square miles. A few months ago two poachers decided to ignore the "keep out" signs. Varna and three other wolves deposited two arms, a leg bone and what appeared to be groin parts in front of the Abbey entrance. Father Bruno was not pleased and asked that the pack be removed. Doctor Finkel said that the security afforded by the wolf pack was much more cost effective than armed guards or the commercial service with their little blue signs popping up all over. The wolf pack stayed."

"But what if someone from the Abbey goes out at night?" Tallon asked. "The wolves have the scent of everyone who is legitimately here. If they don't have an individual's scent, body parts start showing up."

Tallon looked around the clearing and noticed a round table with two chairs. On the table were carafes of orange juice and coffee along with an assortment of pastries. "It appears we were expected," she said.

"That would be Brother William," Ankyer replied. "It looks like he has adopted you along with the wolves."

As they walked over to the table, she said, "If you don't mind I'm going to take off my sweatshirt. It's soaked from keeping up with you and Varna."

With that she pulled the sweatshirt over her head revealing a pink running bra.

"Pink suits you," Ankyer said.

They sat down and Ankyer poured the juice and coffee. Two of the wolves padded over to where Tallon was seated. One put its head on her lap and the other licked her leg. The other wolves were either play fighting or rolling around on the ground making noises like dogs. "They are like big puppies," said Tallon.

"That's how Brother William describes them," replied Ankyer. "The next time we're out I'll take you to their den. There are five pups, all sired by Varna."

"And they will turn out to guard the Abbey as well?" she asked.

"Absolutely. Once in the pack you're in the pack. No exceptions. And the pack will defend you to the death."

"But you're in the pack as well," she said.

"I am indeed," he replied. She took a sip of coffee and considered his last comment. And realized that there was no one she could think of whom she would want to watch her back more than Jake Ankyer.

"So how did you come to all this and have an entire Abbey all to yourself focused on your training and support?" she asked.

"Most of this is classified but since you signed the N.S.A. "non disclosure agreement from hell" I guess I can give you the "Cliff Note" version. After I graduated from the University of Chicago's undergraduate business school I joined the Marine Corps. It was just after September 11th and I decided, like a lot of other guys, to join the military to wreak some payback on the people who destroyed the people in the Twin Towers. I was half way through Marine Corps basic officer training at Brown Field at Quantico, Virginia, when I was called into the Commandant's office. No trainee, and I mean no trainee, was ever called in to meet with the Commandant. I walked into the office in my physical training gear no less, moved into the middle of the room and stood at attention."

"Candidate Ankyer reporting as ordered sir!"

"At that point a man in a three piece suit with glasses and a beard said: "Colonel you may leave Candidate Ankyer and me now. Thank you."

"Yes sir," replied the Colonel who left the room closing the door behind him.

"Over the next two hours I had my first encounter with Doctor Finkel. He proceeded to explain that I had an opportunity to serve the United States in a way not made available to anyone before me. It involved enhanced mental and physical conditioning at a variety of closed, secure N.S.A. site locations. My orders would come directly from Doctor Finkel. I would not be commissioned through the Marine Corps but my pay grade would be at the level of a full colonel. At the end of the two hours I agreed to become part of Doctor Finkel's program. No, that's not accurate. I agreed to become Doctor Finkel's program. There was a knock on the door and the Commandant entered the office. I snapped to attention. The Commandant said "At ease, Mr. Ankyer. You are no longer in the Marine Corps. And then he saluted me!"

"Good luck in your new assignment," he said.

"The next four years I trained with the Israeli Sayeret Matkal commandos and British Special Forces, and received additional specialized training. On the intellectual side, I was enrolled in a PhD program in the London School of Economics and graduated in two years. The mental and physical stimulation program the N.S.A. labs have developed is incredible."

Tallon interrupted. "What's your thinking like?"

"The best way to describe it is total clarity. One day I woke up and everything was clear in my mind. Complete understanding. I talked about it to Doctor Finkel and he just said that my mental processes had just come into alignment."

"Then what?" Tallon asked.

"I was sent to the Navy SEAL training base at Coronado, California. At that point I was pretty much trained through my British Special Forces and Israeli Sayeret Matkal commando units. I would be periodically working with SEALS so Doctor Finkel thought I should go through a SEAL training cycle. The SEAL training cycle averages 30 months. I went through it in 6 months as an individual, not with a training group. They did make me go through "Hell Week", which I found to be not very challenging. They have a plaque somewhere in Coronado, which attests to someone breaking all the training records. They did award me a SEAL Trident pin in a private ceremony. It was a bit awkward since they didn't know my name. Doctor Finkel told the Base Commander not to change the SEAL trainee performance criteria based on my metrics since I reflected training not available through normal military channels."

"I understand what makes you physically and mentally different," said Tallon. "But what about operationally?"

"Ah. Good question. The basic difference between me, and a Navy SEAL team, is that the SEAL team operates according to a tactical protocol for a specific mission. They can tactically adjust for changing circumstances, but the mission itself remains unchanged. If the mission parameters change, the SEAL team will disengage for new orders. In my case, I can design new tactics and strategies and define a new mission in real time. I never redeploy. One example I can give you is the recent events regarding Rodrigues-Zappa. My initial mission was to find and retrieve Angus McGinty. When I determined he was not there, I changed the mission to identifying the money-laundering conduit for the drug cartel and designed the illusion of a competing drug cartel wiping out Rodrigues-Zappa's operation. It has worked out well for us. Not so well for Rodrigues-Zappa and his associates."

"Some illusion. Perfect operational flexibility. Incredible," said Tallon. "But why you?"Tallon continued. "How did they select you?"

"That's interesting," Ankyer said. "I asked Doctor Finkel that and he said..."

At that point the wolves went on alert and looked toward a thicket of trees. A large, bald, head became visible. "I though I'd find you guys here," said Brother William as he threw the contents of a box of large dog biscuits in the middle of the wolves.

"You know you're not suppose to give them dog biscuits," said Ankyer. The wolves pounced on the biscuits, each wolf grabbing one and running off to a side of the clearing to protect their food.

Brother William reached in a bag he was carrying and threw sweatshirts to both Tallon and Ankyer. "It's too cool out to be running around in a pink bra," said Brother William to Tallon.

She looked at the sweatshirt. Printed on the front was "Loose Lips Sink Trappists". As Tallon and Ankyer put the sweatshirts on, Brother William said, "I was sent to collect you and get you back to the Abbey. It seems that there is a development that Doctor Finkel needs to discuss with you right away. Margie, you can bring your other sweatshirt with you and I'll have it cleaned. I have the Hummer parked on a fire trail in the woods."

At that point one of the wolves howled and they all disappeared, merging into the woods, except Varna. He padded over to Ankyer and sat next to him.

"We need to hurry," said Brother William as he turned and started running into the woods, his robe flowing behind him.

"I don't think my morning jogs will ever be the same again," said Tallon smiling, as she and Ankyer hurried to catch up with Brother William.

The Hummer pulled up in front of the Abbey main entrance. Ankyer and Tallon exited the back seat. Ankyer opened the front passenger door and Varna jumped out.

"It would be a lot easier to drive if this wolf didn't constantly lick the side of my face," Brother William said.

"You don't suppose it's because of all the dog biscuits you give him?"Tallon said.

"I doubt it," replied Brother William as he threw a large biscuit out the door opening and Varna caught it in mid air.

"He's hopeless," said Ankyer as he, Tallon and Varna entered the front door.

They went directly to the room that they had been in the first time Tallon met Ankyer. George Makin and Father Bruno already occupied the room. Tallon expected to sit around the speakerphone again, but instead was greeted by Doctor Asher Finkel in a dark blue, Gieves and Hawkes, three-piece suit and a blue and green-striped bow tie.

"Doctor Finkel. You are looking your usual sartorial best," said Ankyer.

"Good morning, Jake and to you, Margie. I would return the compliment but from your attire I see that Brother William has you modeling his latest clothing items from what he hopes will be approved as his Trappist boutique. Do you know he actually submitted a funding proposal to the N.S.A. to finance a Web site design and operation? Jake, what shall we do with him?" asked Finkel.

"I'd give him the money. He's not going away, that's for sure," said Ankyer, laughing.

"As a matter of fact, we just approved his proposal but don't say anything. I want to surprise him."

"Isn't there a problem with US taxpayers funding Trappist web sites?" asked Makin, chuckling.

"There might be, except the N.S.A. budget is not subject to Congressional oversight; and if he were to charge us commercial rates for his services it would cost a great deal more than developing a web site. Besides, we want to keep Brother William happy. But let's get to business."

They walked over to chairs surrounding a rectangular table. Finkel sat down where there was a small stack of papers.

"The last time we spoke it was decided that based upon cell phone intercepts between Zainab Malibi and Ibram el Farsi, we would initiate a surveillance operation in which Margie would observe Malibi, Jake would observe el Farsi, and George would travel to the Swiss Financial Markets Authority to discuss the activities of the INF Banque Nationale. We have since obtained another intercept which changes the dynamics of the situation dramatically."

He then distributed a single document to each of the others seated at the table. Finkel gave them a few moments to digest the N.S.A. intercept.

"As you can see from the latest call from el Farsi to Malibi, what has started out as a curiosity regarding the continued existence of Saddam Hussein, has developed into a full fledged terrorist plot. Hussein or not, this is something we must act on immediately. N.S.A. has alerted the Center for Disease Control, and Homeland Security. N.S.A. continues to run the overall operation and the other agencies are designated as backup. But I have to tell you, that Homeland Security is not thrilled with suicide bombers running around the United States. Saddam Hussein was not mentioned of course, but we gave them the general idea. We asked the CDC if this idea of distributing what the terrorists refer to as nano VX through a steam generator is practical. They said the concept is brilliant. The idea of using suicide bombers to overcome the leakage issue is also inspired. These individuals, who are already committed to killing themselves for a cause, are perfect to activate the steam generators. The CDC and N.S.A. scientists are unsure as to how far the steam laden nano VX could spread, but however far it spread, the casualties would be massive."

Ankyer leaned forward: "It would appear that rather than observing these people we need to be more proactive."

"Exactly," replied Finkel. "Thanks to the "competing drug lord" ruse you staged at Rodrigues-Zappas, we may be able to flush these people out, capture McGinty, who has obviously thrown in with the terrorists, and, if we are lucky, throw a net over Hussein assuming he's still alive, or at least neutralize this Emir fellow who ever he is. I have to admit I was not excited with your pyramid of heads outside the hacienda, but it appears your usual insight into a problem has given us this opportunity. Margie, this situation has also escalated beyond what we initially had in mind for you."

"Before you go on Doctor Finkel, I am all in. I may be a physician, but I'm also, or was, an FBI agent capable of taking care of my self. I would not miss this for anything."

"Excellent!" exclaimed Finkel. "I was hoping you would want to stay involved."

"George, you are the point person for the Emir part of this. You still need to fly to Switzerland tomorrow and meet with Doctor Riekert at the Swiss Financial Markets Authority. Your flight was originally scheduled for today but we need time to get Margie to Long Island where Malibi is located. Your operating identity is Phillip Black with the United States State Department. During your conversation with Doctor Reichert, she will be advised that the US Government is officially requesting that all accounts of the INF Banque Nationale be frozen as part of an Interpol international terrorism investigation. Doctor Reichert will then make a call of introduction for you to Hans Greffen who is the Director of the INF Banque Nationale. Greffen will be advised that you are associated with a very large international financial organization interested in depositing substantial funds in the INF Banque Nationale. When you arrive for your meeting with Greffen, here's what you will tell him...."

When Finkel had finished explaining Makin's role he turned to Margie.

"Once you have arrived in Long Island, we will send you the real time coordinates of Zainab Malibi. The tactical smart phone you have will convert the coordinates to street locations in real time. When George has finished explaining the situation to Greffen, Greffen will place a call to Malibi and George will get on the line. He will explain to Malibi that his organization needs to meet with the Emir and that you are the organization's representative. You will then make contact with her and tell her the following..."

"After that you will insist on a meeting with the Emir. It will be important that you make two assessments. First, you will need to evaluate the extent of Malibi's personal influence. She is clearly the principal interface between el Farsi and the Emir. When you talk with her, try to determine if she exercises independent judgment or is simply a conduit that passes information from the Emir to el Farsi and back. Second, and more importantly, if you do manage to meet with the Emir, you will do a facial recognition evaluation based on Saddam's facial and other body structural parameters you can review on the flight to Long Island. This is based on the facial recognition work done by Brother Arlot here at the Abby, with whom you will meet shortly. We have to assume that Saddam has had some facial reconstruction. However, unless his skull has been completely altered you should be able to at least make an inferential anatomic comparison to determine how close the Emir matches up with the Saddam parameters. Of course a DNA sample would be ideal. but obtaining that is probably a stretch. Fred Bell will accompany you on the flight and will provide additional security. You may be able to take care of your self, but Fred is trained to take care of everything else. Your operational name will be Eileen Bach. You will be given supporting identification in case you are pressed."

"Jake's mission to Black Forest, Colorado has now been adjusted as well. Jake, now that we know that McGinty is directly involved in a terrorist conspiracy with potentially dramatic consequences, we need to disrupt his involvement if at all possible. We also need to ascertain how much nano VX has been produced and the distribution points. Based on the cell coordinates generated from the call el Farsi made to Malibi, we have a good idea of the location of the nano VX manufacturing facility. We expect there to be extensive security around the grounds. The part of the last phone intercept in which it is said, "...The Emir will deploy some of his martyrs to the task. They are awaiting instructions for suicide bombings but they will obey the Emir and accomplish this task instead" is instructive. Based on this, we think it is conceivable that the Black Forest site might be protected by suicide bombers."

"We have added a transponder to your combat pack, which can send a sympathetic signal to the suicide vests. Assuming the radio wave length is the same, the transponder will arm the vests and explode them. Unfortunately, you will have to somehow obtain a sample vest so that the transponder can register itself to the suicide vest's radio wave length. You may not need it but we don't want to take any chances. I have also activated Neil and the SEAL team and they will be available on site should you need them. There is an Army Reserve unit at an airfield just outside Black Forest, Colorado and the SEAL team is there now. They should be able to deploy to the facility within fifteen minutes after you contact them."

"We have also arranged for decontamination support from the CDC. After you have neutralized the site, and assuming there is residual VX or converted nano VX at the location, CDC personnel will be sent to clean it up under the direction of N.S.A. with the appropriate security protocols in place. It is important to emphasize that the technology being used to manufacture the nano VX is exceedingly dangerous and none of the people involved there, especially McGinty, can be allowed to escape. It would be advantageous if we could apprehend McGinty alive, but as usual, you have complete discretion to adjudicate the situation and act accordingly. Once you have completed your mission you will leave and the SEAL team will assume control of the site."

Finkel paused, then continued.

"Let me be clear on a few things. So far, our Doctor McGinty has been quite difficult to pin down. I believe this has been coincidental and that McGinty, el Farsi, and this Emir person are not aware of our interest in them. This could change, however, and we must be able to adjust our activities rapidly. N.S.A. has obtained the necessary

Foreign Intelligence Surveillance Court warrants and we have entered the cell phone numbers for el Farsi and Malibi into the NASA pattern matching algorithms. All their calls are now being monitored by our contractor's analysts."

"It appears that Malibi is the communications nexus for this conspiracy and, assuming she remains the coordinating element, we are hoping that we will be able to isolate the locations of these nano VX steam generator sites. Depending on our success, as well as the number of sites identified, we may have to expand our counter terrorism resources to include the CDC as well as the FBI. Should that occur, everything would be coordinated through the N.S.A. However, and most importantly, the Saddam connection must remain completely transparent to our sister agencies involved in the terrorist threat aspect of this problem. If somewhere in all this activity the Emir appears and turns out to be Saddam, we must be prepared to act independently from the terrorism part of the equation. That's it. You all have my secure line. I will remain here at the Abbey until we have neutralized this situation. Good luck. Brother William is outside and will take it from here."

EMIR'S RESIDENCE
GOLD COAST, LONG ISLAND NEW YORK
FEBRUARY 18, 2012
1:00 PM EASTERN TIME

Malibi entered the Great Room. The Emir had just dropped a mouse into a large saltwater tank located next to a leaded glass window, overlooking a rose garden. One of three moray eels in the tank nudged the furiously paddling mouse. The second eel struck biting the mouse in half while the third eel darted after the entrails. The remaining half of the mouse floated toward the bottom of the tank and the eel, that had initially nudged the mouse, dove down and swallowed the remaining half. The roiling water turned pink then disappeared as it entered the tank's filtration system.

"Feeding your pets I see," said Malibi as she approached the Emir.

"There is a lesson here," replied the Emir. "Which of the eels demonstrated the most intelligence?"

"The second," replied Malibi.

"Why the second?" asked the Emir."

"It waited until the first eel determined if the mouse was food by pushing it, and then moved in for the kill."

"That's a reasonable conclusion but would be incorrect."

"Which one then?" Malibi asked.

"The first one," said the Emir. "It not only did the initial research to determine if the mouse was food; it also waited until the second eel expended the energy to make the kill and it waited further until the food came into its reach. The third eel was impatient and had only the entrails to eat. The lesson is therefore clear. Initial caution and patience provide greater rewards at less cost and effort. Instead of rushing around attacking the Americans in one place or another, we were patient and awaited an opportunity for much greater destruction which McGinty and his science has provided for us."

"In the spirit of your lesson, I have some good news," said Malibi.

"McGinty completed his work yesterday. According to our prearranged plan, Ibram el Farsi has left the Black Forest laboratory facility with Doctor McGinty and they have flown to the town house in Chicago. The remaining nano VX is being transported to the final steam generator location. Your martyrs will sacrifice the laboratory workers as you instructed to prevent capture and information extraction by the Americans. They then will blow up the factory with the unconverted VX at the time when the steam generator sites are activated at your command."

"Excellent!" exclaimed the Emir. "Not only will we destroy millions of Americans with the nano VX, if we are fortunate and it is God's will, we will also destroy many more Americans with the unconverted VX as well!"

BERNE, SWITZERLAND AIRSPACE
17,000 FEET
FEBRUARY 18, 2012

The Learjet C-20B flew along a slope of the Jura Mountains, crossing Geneva and Lausanne, Switzerland on a direct heading to Berne. The flight had been uneventful, providing Makin an opportunity to review the current Priority Red Protocol's operational history to date on an iPad supplied by Doctor Finkel. It also gave him time to become acquainted with his US Department of State credentials, as well as the credentials for his new identity as Phillip Black, Executive Vice President of Advantis Financial Industries. He had not conducted any undercover operations during his tenure with the FBI, but he had come to realize that Doctor Finkel was a hard man to say no to.

The plane executed a sharp bank and in ten minutes had been cleared to land at Bern-Balp Aeroport. After they rolled to a stop at the General Aviation hangar, the pilot came back into the cabin.

"Doctor Finkel instructed us to wait for you to return. When you are ready, hit '22' on your secure phone. An N.S.A. team is in place at the US Embassy and can get to you if things get a little weird. You can't carry your piece with you into banks here. We don't expect any problems but if something arises and you need the N.S.A. team all you need to do is hit '33' and they will come a running. Just don't lose that phone."

"You guys are all over this," replied Makin.

"Doctor Finkel advised us, it would be our collective asses if anything happens to you, so call it self preservation," the pilot said. "There's a helicopter outside which will take you within a mile of the Swiss Financial Markets Authority. A N.S.A. car will take you over there."

With that, Makin shook hands with the pilot, exited the plane, walked over to the helicopter and was on his way.

SWISS FINANCIAL MARKETS AUTHORITY
BERNE, SWITZERLAND
FEBRUARY 18, 2012

Thirty minutes later Makin was sitting outside of Doctor Heidi Riekert's office for his 2:00 PM appointment. Riekert's assistant motioned to Makin and he was escorted into an office with floor to ceiling windows offering a panoramic view of the Berne River. A slender woman, five feet seven with greying hair, stepped over from a conference table extending her hand.

"Mr. Makin, I am Doctor Riekert. Nice to make your acquaintance."

"Nice to meet you as well, Doctor."

"Would you like a beverage?" asked Riekert.

"Water would be fine," replied Makin. Riekert turned to her assistant.

"Horst, would you kindly get both Mr. Makin and me some water?"

"Yes, Doctor," and he turned and walked into an alcove. Riekert extended her hand to a chair at the conference table.

"Please, make yourself comfortable." She walked over to her desk, picked up a thin folder, and sat down at the conference table opposite Makin. "Before we proceed, could you please show me your credentials?" asked Riekert.

Makin handed over his diplomatic US State Department passport along with a US State Department ID, which identified him as Director, International Investigations Division. Riekert returned Makin's credentials.

"How can we help you?" Riekert asked.

"As I understand it, you have been given a general idea regarding our interest in the INF Banque Nationale. Is that correct?"

"It is," replied Riekert.

At that point Horst returned with two glasses of water. He placed two coasters on the table and set the glasses down.

"Will there be anything else, Doctor?"

"No. Thank you, Horst."

The assistant walked out of the office and closed the door. Makin noticed a 'hissing' sound. "This office is hermetically sealed. We are quite serious about our confidentiality here in Switzerland," Riekert said.

"So I've been told," replied Makin.

Riekert continued, opening the folder in front of her.

"We reviewed our records on INF. The bank has roughly $ 5 billion US dollars on deposit. That is not a great deal from our perspective, but it is large enough to function as a financial institution according to Swiss banking laws. Their charter and regulatory documentation appear in order. There is one curiosity. It looks as if INF is wholly owned by a Cayman Islands holding company, INF Holdings International. We also discovered that virtually all of the depositors are of foreign origin. No Swiss clients. They are operating like a bank but do not have many of the operating characteristics of a normal bank. That's what we have. I'm afraid it's not much."

Makin took a sip of water. "Doctor Riekert, what I am about to tell you is highly confidential and is covered by our countries' mutual, interlocking security agreements."

"I understand." replied Riekert.

"INF Banque Nationale is a money laundering operation for large drug cartels. It is also quite possible that they provide financing for several international terrorist organizations."

Riekert's eyes narrowed. "This is outrageous. They must be shut down immediately!"

Makin replied, "That would be my immediate reaction, as well. But we are requesting that you don't do anything yet. If you shut them down they will simply move somewhere else. At this point we have identified several persons of interest but the head of the organization eludes us. The purpose of my visit here is to go the INF and portray myself as a senior representative of a large financial organization interested in retaining their services. What we are asking the Swiss Financial Markets Authority to do is to contact them today and confirm my bona fides. I will be representing myself as Phillip Black, Executive Vice President of Advantis Financial Industries. We are hoping that once we have what appears to be a very lucrative business opportunity for them, we will be able to uncover the ringleader of the operation."

"But we must be able to do something!" exclaimed Riekert. "The entire Swiss banking system relies on the fidelity of its banking members. Being subverted by drug cartels and terrorist organizations is absolutely intolerable!"

"There may be something you can do," replied Makin. "We managed to infiltrate an INF account for a drug lord named Arturo Ramon Rodrigues-Zappa and remove several million dollars. Rodrigues-Zappa is now deceased and his associates may believe a competing drug cartel managed to obtain the funds. Is there some way you can freeze the INF assets based on what happened to the Rodrigues-Zappa account? This might force the head of the organization out into the open."

Riekert thought for a moment. "While it has not been used except to protect our banks from the Nazis in World War II, each bank in the Swiss banking federation must agree to have all its monetary funds moved by the SFMA into an escrow account maintained by the SFMA in the event there is an attempt to illegally access a bank's financial systems. Each bank provides the SFMA with a master account number, which enables the SFMA to transfer all the funds at once. It takes seconds. This is particularly important now with the advent of Internet crime where tens of millions in currency can be electronically stolen, in which case the funds are frozen in the SFMA escrow account until the breached system is repaired and stable. The Rodrigues-Zappa situation, if it came to our attention, would certainly qualify as a trigger for this action. How would you like to proceed?"

"After I leave here, call Hans Greffen at INF and tell him that Phillip Black, Executive Vice President of Advantis Financial Industries is on his way over to discuss a substantial deposit. Give me half an hour from when you make the call and then transfer the INF accounts to the SFMA escrow account. I am sure you will get a call back from Greffen. Tell him that you have become aware that the Rodrigues-Zappa's account has been electronically compromised and that you have invoked the SFMA master account transfer process to protect the balance of the INF funds, as well as to protect the other banks in the Swiss banking system from being infected by the illegal hacking. Tell him that you will be sending technical auditors to his location to evaluate the INF bank's systems for additional infections. When I'm finished with Greffen I will call you and let you know what to do with the escrowed funds."

Riekert stood up followed by Makin. Riekert said, "I have to tell you that Greffen and the INF Banque Nationale have broken more Swiss banking regulations than I can recite, not to mention criminal conspiracy violations. The Swiss government will want to mount extensive criminal proceedings against Mr. Greffen and god knows how many others."

"I can assure you that the United States government will cooperate with your government fully. However before we do anything, it is critical that we come to terms with the terrorist activity the INF bank is financing," Makin replied.

"I absolutely agree," said Riekert.

"Horst will see you out and I will make the call to Greffen."

"If for some reason you can't reach Greffen, here's my card with my cell phone number. Please call me immediately."

"I will," said Riekert.

"Thank you for bringing this matter to our attention. This is a cancer on our system and we must eradicate it as soon as possible."

With that Makin left the office.

INF BANQUE NATIONALE BERNE SWITZERLAND FEBRUARY 18, 2012

The N.S.A. car pulled up in front of the INF Banque Nationale.

The driver said: "If you run into difficulty hit 11 on your phone."

"Thanks," said Makin, exiting the car and walking up toward the bank. The bank itself was a five story concrete structure with a marble facade and three story marble columns bracketing the front door on each side.

As Makin walked through the front door he was greeted by a slightly overweight man who appeared in his fifty's and was dressed in a dark grey, pinstripe suit with a vest.

"You are Mr. Black?" he said.

"I am indeed," replied Black.

"How do you do!" said the man. "My name is Hans Greffen and I serve as the Director of the INF Banque Nationale. Doctor Riekert called me a short time ago and said that I should be expecting you. Please follow me." Greffen led them to a private elevator with oak paneled doors and pushed the button for the fifth floor. As they ascended Greffen remarked, "It's rather unusual that Doctor Riekert calls me to recommend a client. You must have made quite an impression on her."

"I think you could say that," replied Black.

The elevator doors opened soundlessly and Black followed Greffen through doors into a substantial, paneled, corner office replete with a large fireplace, what appeared to be a solid onyx desk, and a conversation area flanked by four wing back leather chairs.

"Please have a seat," said Greffen. "I do not wish to be impertinent Mr. Black, but as we have not met before could I see some identification?"

Black extracted a business card from his vest and handed over a passport from his inside suit pocket. Greffen handed the passport back, picked up a cordless phone from a side table and dialed the number on Black's business card. The phone rang three times.

A voice answered: "Advantis Financial Industries, executive offices, Mr. Black's office. Can I help you?"

"Is Mr. Black in?" answered Greffen.

"No sir. Mr. Black is out of the country on business for the balance of the week. Would you care to leave a message?"

"No, that will not be necessary. Thank you." Greffen disconnected and replaced the phone on the table. "I apologize for that. We tend to be overly cautious in our part of the world."

"I can appreciate that," said Black.

"Well, on to business then," said Greffen. What can I do for you today?"

As Black surveyed the office he concluded that Greffen displayed a passion for creature comforts and fine art. There were two Picasso's on one wall and a Renoir on another wall in a recessed alcove. There was a model of Rodin's Thinker on Greffen's desk as well as a variety of other sculptures displayed around the office.

"I see you have a replica of Rodin's Thinker on your desk," commented Black.

"Actually it's one of the original models Rodin created for use in creating the larger sculpture," replied Greffen. "Very impressive," said Black. "Well, as you said, on to business."

"When I spoke with Doctor Riekert she indicated that INF Banque National is a relatively small, efficiently run institution and that you are a serious and well respected person. Based on my conversation with Doctor Riekert as well as some additional due diligence we have undertaken, my firm, Advantis Financial Industries, is interested in making a sizeable deposit in your bank."

"How sizable?" Greffen asked.

"To start with we were thinking of depositing four billion euros, with additional periodic deposits of three to five billion euros. There would of course be withdrawals during the course of a year, but the account balance would not decrease below five billion euros for any given twelve month period."

Greffen's mouth hung partially open. "Good lord. That's more financial wealth than many countries have," Greffen sputtered.

"Actually it's not even half of the organization's resources, but we like to disperse our assets and we have identified your bank as a possible repository for some cash."

"Some cash indeed. INF will do whatever is necessary to accommodate your needs," said Greffen. Black smiled.

"I was hoping you would be interested in our business."

"I would be insane not to be," said Greffen. "By the way, exactly what is your business?" asked Greffen.

Black looked around the office. He reached into his suit coat pocket and removed a small rectangular box with a single flashing red light.

"There is a device in this office recording this conversation. Turn it off," directed Black. Greffen's complexion flushed red. He picked up the phone and pressed a button twice. The red light on the small rectangular box changed to green.

"Confidentiality is important to us. As I said before, you appear to be a serious man Mr. Greffen and one whom I would hope would respect my organization's privacy."

"I apologize Mr. Black. I am embarrassed and can assure you that our conversation will be held in complete secrecy."

"A moment ago you asked what kind of business Advantis Financial Industries was in," said Black. "Advantis Financial Industries is a holding company with organizations throughout South America, Asia, Mexico, Russia and a variety of locations within the United States as well as a few in China. Among our array of interests are drugs."

"You mean pharmaceuticals of course," said Greffen.

"No. I mean illegal drugs including heroin, methamphetamine, opium, cannabis, cocaine and a variety of other designer formulations. We coordinate manufacture and distribution. We also resolve internal disagreements. You are familiar of course with the untimely passing of Arturo Ramon Rodrigues-Zappa?"

"Yes," said Greffen. "He was one of our depositors. He was murdered recently. His accounts at INF were also cleaned out. We are still trying to determine how."

"You can stop trying now," said Black. "We visited Mr. Rodrigues-Zappa for two reasons. First, he was in the habit of supplying tainted cocaine at depressed prices causing market fluctuations and a number of deaths in the user population. The second reason had to do with a houseguest of his named Doctor Angus McGinty, who has devised a way to process cocaine into a much more robust product that we are interested in. Mr. Rodrigues-Zappa refused to reveal the location of Doctor McGinty and was unhelpful regarding the tainted, price depressed drugs he was selling. Being of no use to us at that point, we eliminated Mr. Rodrigues-Zappa and all his associates. Before he died, he did however, reveal his arrangement with INF Banque Nationale, a relationship we will find useful. This is the reason I am here today."

Sweat had formed on Greffen's upper lip and he felt a tightening in the pit of his stomach. "The arrangement you are suggesting is beyond my portfolio with INF Banque Nationale," said Greffen. "I could not approve your proposed arrangement, even if I wanted to."

Black replied, "I know that. We have done our due diligence on you and INF. What you can do, however, is call Doctor Zainab Malibi. I will explain the situation and she will arrange a meeting with our representative and the Emir, who can approve the arrangement I am suggesting."

"The Emir? You know about the Emir?" said Greffen with a tremor in his voice.

"We know a great deal," said Black.

"The Emir may not do business with you in any event," replied Greffen.

"That has occurred to us and we are providing a little incentive."

The phone on the end table next to Greffen issued a low chime. He picked it up. "Yes, what is it?"

Greffen listened intently and turned white, his lip quivering. He placed the phone down.

"They will kill me," he said. "How did you persuade the SFMA to freeze all our assets?"

"That's irrelevant at this point," replied Black. "But I agree with you when you say they will kill you. They will also likely kill your family. The only way for you and your family to survive this is to do exactly what I say."

"Anything!" said Greffen.

"Good. What you are going to do is to call Doctor Zainab Malibi right now. You will tell her that all of the Emir's funds held in INF have been frozen and that Mr. Phillip Black is here and needs to speak with her to resolve this situation. You will then hand the phone to me and sit quietly. Can you do that?"

"Yes," replied Greffen.

"Make the call," said Black.

HOLY INNOCENTS TRAPPIST MONASTERY
GILA NATIONAL FOREST
NEW MEXICO
FEBRUARY 18, 2012

Asher Finkel and Father Michael Bruno sat in the library waiting for the secure speakerphone to ring. The N.S.A.'s FISA request for a tap on Zainab Malibi's phone had been approved and, if Makin's meeting with Greffen went as planned; Malibi should receive a call at any time. The N.S.A. wire tap had synchronized Malibi's cell phone with the N.S.A. direct connect data base, which also linked in the Holy Innocents secure phone in the library.

"Should we condition Brother William's Trappist boutique Web site on him not giving the wolves dog biscuits?" wondered Father Bruno aloud.

"We could try but he would probably feed them anyway," said Finkel.

At that the light on the secure speakerphone started blinking red.

Malibi "This is Doctor Malibi."

Greffen "Doctor Malibi, this is Hans Greffen at INF."

Malibi "I was going to call you as a matter of fact. We tried to transfer some funds from the bank a short time ago and the message we received was funds unavailable."

Greffen "That is why I am calling. The Swiss Financial Markets Authority has frozen all of INF's assets including your accounts."

Malibi "How did this happen!" Malibi exclaimed.

Greffen "There is a man named Phillip Black here in my office who says he can explain everything."

Black "Doctor Malibi, my name is Phillip Black and I am the Executive

Vice President of Advantis Financial Industries. It was our organization that eliminated the Rodrigues-Zappa drug cartel and removed the funds from the cartel's INF accounts. We are interested in developing a multi billion dollar, ongoing financial arrangement with the Emir to facilitate the movement of substantial drug-related revenues."

Malibi "How did you know about the Emir?"

Black "Mr. Rodrigues-Zappa enlightened us regarding his financial arrangements with the Emir and INF before he died.

Malibi "What exactly do you want?"

Black "We want to meet with the Emir and discuss the financial arrangement I mentioned. We also want to discuss using the services of Doctor Angus McGinty who is an associate of the Emir."

Malibi "What does McGinty have to do with this?"

Black "We are aware of Doctor McGinty's ability to convert cocaine to a much more concentrated form. We have some designer drugs which we believe will benefit from this technique. We will of course compensate the Emir for the use of Doctor McGinty's expertise."

Malibi "When do you want to meet?"

Black "We have an associate in your area who can meet with the Emir tomorrow."

Malibi "Why did you have the INF banks assets frozen?"

Black "We thought it might be necessary to get your attention and provide an indication that we are serious people."

Malibi "You managed to achieve your objective on both counts. What if we are unable to reach an agreement?"

Black "We are not unreasonable. The INF assets will be released and we will look elsewhere for an arrangement."

Malibi "I will call you back at Greffen's number in fifteen minutes."

The line went dead. Finkel immediately picked up a portable phone on the table and dialed a number. "This is Asher Finkel. Do you have a location for the cell phone that just hung up on the tracked call?" A moment later Finkel wrote on a pad and hung up.

"The call came from 7 Early Bird Lane, Long Beach, New York. It's a mansion in Nassau County. We may have found the location of the Emir."

Father Bruno said, "The trick is going to be to get Margie and Fred out of there when she's ascertained the identity of the Emir."

"That's why I sent her. Apart from the facial recognition process, Margie appears non- confrontational and is talking about a financial deal so large that the Emir will let her out to confer with her superiors on any deal that starts to develop. Once she has left the premises we can go in. Fred can also run interference if necessary."

"Keep in mind there are only two of them," said Father Bruno.

"I've considered that. Two people are non-threatening psychologically. Once you get to three or more the perceived threat level goes up in people's minds," replied Finkel.

At that point the light flickered on the table's speakerphone.

Malibi "Mr. Greffen. Are you there?"

Greffen "Yes."

Malibi "Let me speak to Mr. Black please.

Black "Yes Doctor Malibi."

Malibi "The Emir will meet with your representative, but not tomorrow. He asked that I meet with your representative tomorrow and review the elements of an arrangement and he will then meet with your person on February 20th."

Black "That is acceptable."

Malibi "Are you familiar with Elmer's Fruitopia Emporium and Café in downtown Long Beach, Long Island?"

Black "No, but we'll find it. "There will be a man wearing a Chicago Cub's baseball cap seated at a table. Sit down across from him. He will expect you at 10:00 AM."

Malibi "I will be there."

Black "Thank you."

The call disconnected.

"What do you think?" Finkel asked Father Bruno.

"I think Fred had better be on his game. Fred and Margie are walking into a pit of monsters."

"I agree," replied Finkel. "I'll call them and review the arrangements our Mr. Black has just made with Doctor Malibi."

INF BANQUE NATIONALE
BERNE SWITZERLAND
FEBRUARY 18, 2012

Black handed the phone back to Greffen. "They will still kill me," said Greffen.

"There is no doubt about it," said Black. "But not until their funds are again available and they have a replacement for you. I would say you have three or four days. We can protect you but we will want complete access to all INF bank clients, contacts, accounts and the actual set of financial books you use to operate INF."

"I will do whatever you say," said Greffen.

"Good," said Black. "I'll call you in a day or so. In the meanwhile, you should prepare to move your family out of the country. I will make arrangements to fly you into the United States and get permanent visas for you and your family. I can get your family specifics when I call. You are very fortunate Mr. Greffen. Ordinarily we let nature take its course, as in the case of Mr. Rodrigues-Zappa. Since you will be helping us we will make an exception and let you live."

"Thank you Mr. Black. Thank you!"

DENVER INTERNATIONAL AIRPORT
US ARMY RESTRICTED RUNWAY AND HANGAR
FEBRUARY 18, 2012
7:00 PM MOUNTAIN TIME

The Pilatus U-28A landed on the restricted runway, reversed its engine, and taxied into the large hangar, which had just opened its doors. As soon as the Pilatus came to a stop the doors closed. The plane pulled into a space behind two Sikorsky MH-60 Black Hawk stealth helicopters and one MV-22 Osprey combat helicopter with a .50 caliber GAU-19 three-barrel Gatling gun mounted below the MV-22's nose.

The forward door to the Pilatus opened. Varna padded down the steps and sat at the bottom of the stairway, on alert. Ankyer filled the doorway, paused and descended to the floor below. His camouflage tactical body wrap caused him to blend into the dim light in the hangar. The N.S.A. SEAL team surrounded Ankyer shaking his hand and giving him pats on the back. Varna emanated a low growl until Ankyer said, "Varna, friend", at which point Varna walked around each SEAL and put his scent on them.

Neil said: "One of these days you have to get us some of these camouflage wraps."

"Your ship has come in. There's a crate of them in the Pilatus courtesy of Doctor Finkel," said Ankyer.

"We'll make Finkel a SEAL," said one of the SEALs.

"I doubt if he could do a pull-up," replied Ankyer.

"No problem," said another SEAL.

The pilot came out of the door with Ankyer's combat pack, H&K, and helmet. The SEALs walked over to the Pilatus cargo hatch and started to unload boxes. The pilot walked to a table alongside a hangar wall and deposited Ankyer's gear.

"It's great to see you again Jake", said Neil. "Doctor Finkel briefed us on the mission. I have to say it's good to have some activity. Duty at the Constable Club is ok, but it's nice to get into the field again. It helps us to keep our edge. So how do you want to proceed?"

"They want me to neutralize the nano VX production facility over at Black Forest," Ankyer said. "They have an idea where it is but are not sure exactly. They also think McGinty may be there."

"You missed him the last time in Mexico," said Neil.

"Finding McGinty is turning out to be problematic. If I do find him, I'll have to decide what to do with him. This technique he's developed to make nanotechnology substances intrigues N.S.A. On the other hand, they don't want him running around making other nano VX-like weapons, so I'll have to play that one by ear."

"What about site security?" Neil asked.

"That's where you guys might come in. N.S.A. has some intercepts which suggest that this Emir fellow may have suicide bombers protecting the facility."

"Those must be the 'martyrs' Doctor Finkel referred to in our briefing," said Neil.

"Their the ones," replied Ankyer. "We don't know how many there are or what they're deployment is around the site." As they walked over to the table with Ankyer's gear Ankyer continued. "We are guessing that these martyrs, if they are there, might be wearing explosive vests. Once a martyr is sufficiently screwed up in his head, his non-martyr handler likes him to wear the vest all the time to reinforce the martyr's commitment. The non-martyr handler also has one more trick up his burka. If the Muslim martyr decides that seventy two virgins in Paradise after the explosion is not incentive enough, a crude cell phone link is usually integrated into the vest to allow the handler to override any yellow streak which may develop down the martyr's back."

"The Kamikaze who survived World War II… so to speak," said Neil.

"Exactly," said Ankyer.

"So how do you stop one of these martyr guys from blowing you up?" Neil asked.

Ankyer reached over and opened a box on the table with a red band around it. Inside were two objects. The first was a small, black, rectangular device with a short antenna and yellow, black and red buttons. The second object was a small model Jeep also with an antenna. "Do me a favor and walk the car model out about thirty feet and push the black button on the top," said Ankyer.

Neil did as he was asked. One of the headlights on the model jeep started to blink. Neil walked back to Ankyer.

The other SEALs stopped what they were doing and watched.

"If the car was a suicide vest and it was activated, and my transponder here was synchronized to the radio frequency of the car, I could interrupt it and stop the car's signal," said Ankyer. Ankyer pushed the black button on his device. The flashing headlight on the car stopped. "On the other hand, if I push the red button on my transponder, it will activate the object."

Ankyer pushed the red button. The car started up and rolled toward Neil and Ankyer, picking up speed. At that moment a large grey body bounded toward the oncoming model car and pounced on it. Varna seized the model car in his jaws, crunched down on it, and hurled the car toward the Osprey. He then howled, padded over to Ankyer and sat down. The SEALs were clapping and yelling "Hooyah, Varna!"

"Varna also got pissed the first time we tried this", said Ankyer.

"So if you run into some martyrs, which button are you going to push, the start or the stop button?" asked Neil.

"I haven't decided," said Ankyer.

"You also mentioned that you had to synchronize the transponder," said Neil.

"That's the yellow button," replied Ankyer. "I have to get close enough to a martyr to synch the transponder with his vest. That assumes of course that each vest is on the same radio frequency. I can't shoot him. Even the sound suppression system on the H&K might give away my position and I may not be able to get close enough for the combat knife before he ignites the vest."

"An insolvable problem?" asked Neil.

"Not quite," replied Ankyer who opened another rectangular box on the table. "I'll have this along." He lifted out what at first glance appeared to be a long semi automatic pistol with two handles under the receiver, one centered and one at the back, and a short, curved front horizontal bar. "Meet the latest toy from the Holy Innocents Abbey's armory. It's a combat crossbow that operates at three hundred pound-feet of kinetic energy using a pneumatic, CO2 gas firing mechanism. It also has a ten bolt magazine and an integrated, motion reactive laser sight. Ankyer handed it to Neil.

"God, it's light," he said.

"It's titanium and aluminum alloy and weighs in at three pounds fully loaded, said Ankyer. Neil handed the cross bow back to Ankyer as the rest of the SEAL team walked over.

"How about a demo?" Neil asked.

"See the Gatorade bottle on the ledge at the other end of the hangar? That's about sixty yards or so," said Ankyer. The moment Ankyer stopped speaking he raised the cross bow and pulled the trigger. Almost simultaneously the plastic bottle exploded showering a workbench with Gatorade.

"The crew chief is really going to be mightily pissed off," said Neil.

"I'll buy him a steak at the Holy Innocents' refectory," replied Ankyer.

"In theory if I can take out one of the martyrs with the cross bow I'll be able to synchronize his vest with the transponder. And then, if the vest's wavelength is the same for his other martyr buddies' vests, I can neutralize the whole bunch of them."

"That's a lot of 'ifs'," said Neil.

"Right," replied Ankyer. "If this doesn't work and I'm up to my ass in AK-47s you guys will have to come to the rescue. In any event, you'll have to come and secure the site so I can get out of there. You'll also be coordinating the CDC techs' entry into the facility so they can disarm the equipment or do whatever is necessary to clean up the site. I also brought along Dräeger rebreathers modified to counteract nano-sized particles. You'll have to wear these within a one-mile perimeter of the facility. We're not sure how small the nano VX particles are, but Doctor Finkel wanted to be able to handle a particle as small as four microns. He doesn't want to take any chances with his N.S.A. SEAL team. He even tried to have a rebreather designed for Varna, but Varna wasn't buying it."

"So when's lift off?" asked Neil.

"I'd like to get within two miles of the industrial park around Midnight. I'll use one of the Black Hawks and then send it back for you guys. If I can't get things resolved by 0300, I'll contact you with my extraction coordinates."

"We would be happier if we were going in with you," said Neil.

"Ordinarily I'd agree with you," replied Ankyer. "But this is more of a modified reconnaissance mission since we really don't know what is going on in there. I'll let you know the status when I get a handle on things."

"By the way, I understand that Fred Bell and Margie Tallon are headed to the East coast," said Neil.

"Doctor Finkel has engineered a meeting with someone involved with the Emir guy, who we think is behind all of this and who might in fact be the cover for Saddam. I'm actually more concerned for Fred and Margie than I am for my mission. At least I'm pretty sure I'll be running into some resistance. They are going in blind," said Ankyer.

At that point a pilot walked up to Ankyer.

"We've finished our pre flight. As soon as you get your gear on board we're ready to go."

ELMER'S FRUITOPIA EMPORIUM AND CAFÉ LONG BEACH LONG ISLAND, NEW YORK FEBRUARY 19, 2012 9:00 AM, EASTERN STANDARD TIME

The black SUV was parked across from Elmer's Fruitopia Emporium and Café.

"I wonder how this place was picked for the meeting?" speculated Tallon, out loud.

"Malibi told Makin that she was familiar with it," replied Bell.

"It's just a strange name…Elmer's Fruitopia?" said Tallon.

"It could also be Doctor Finkel's weird sense of humor. He has me wearing a Chicago Cubs baseball hat, and he knows that I'm a rabid White Sox fan."

"That's torture!" laughed Tallon.

"No, that's Doctor Finkel. He likes to hang out with Brother William."

"That explains it," replied Tallon.

"So tell me, how are you going to figure out if the Emir is actually Saddam Hussein?" asked Bell.

"Good question," replied Tallon. "Before I left Holy Innocents I sat down with Brother Arlot. It turns out that Brother Arlot is a neuroanatomist. Where Trappists get these guys is a mystery, but well, there you are. Anyway, my medical training and practice have given me access to a large number of heads, both dissected and undissected, so I have a good grasp of the overall structure of the human skull, internal anatomic structures and so on. Brother Arlot sat me down in front of a computer terminal and we analyzed a number of photographs and videos of Saddam Hussein from a variety of angles. By memorizing various aspects of his face, I was able to extrapolate variations in age, facial expressions, and so on. This allowed me to create a structural model of Saddam's face in my mind reflecting how his face changes during certain actions such as talking, frowning, or chewing, for example. Its somewhat like facial recognition software but much more efficient since instead of trying to match his facial pattern to lots of different faces, my memory is comparing differing facial angles and characteristics to one face."

"But what if he's had plastic surgery?" asked Bell.

"Another good question," replied Tallon. "The genius of Brother Arlot is that he applied a computer program he designed to visualize the movement of flesh on the skull as it migrates across the contours of the surface. The underlying skull features of the skull essentially control what the skin movement looks like when Saddam has different expressions, when he is speaking and from different angles. He had me memorize what skin movement on Saddam's skull looks like so I can now make comparisons, watching him when he is talking, or chewing gum, and so on. Even if he's had plastic surgery, its unlikely, if not impossible, that he's had a complete skull reconstruction. So a nose job, lips or cheek alteration, for example, will not completely change the identification configuration. In a sense, Saddam's head is in my head now. Bottom line, when the Emir is speaking to me I will be comparing the skin movement on his skull with the skin movement over Saddam's skull that I've memorized. We'll have to get a DNA sample at some point of course, but I should be able to establish a reasonable front end confirmation."

"I don't think I've ever run across Brother Arlot at the Abbey," said Bell. Tallon laughed.

"I think he hangs out with Brother William," she said.

"I wonder. Is there is anyone who does not hang out with Brother William?" replied Bell.

"We had better get ready for Malibi," said Tallon.

"Right," replied Bell. "Doctor Finkel texted me a picture of her they found on the Internet. I'll check to see if she's the one we are expecting. If it turns out not to be her or if there's something weird like bodyguards, I'll just get up and leave. Otherwise, I'll take this goddamn Cubs baseball cap off, which is your signal to come in. When you get to the table I'll get up and leave and you've got the ball with Malibi. I'll go back to the car, call Doctor Finkel, and tell him 'game on'."

"The plan works for me. Lets do it," said Tallon.

Bell got out of the car, crossed the street, and walked into the Fruitopia. The next thing Tallon saw was Bell, with his 'goddamn Cubs baseball cap' on, seated at a table for two in the glass-enclosed annex, with the windows facing the street. The restaurant was fairly empty and there was no one else in the glass annex. A waiter approached Bell's table. "Hello sir. My name is Ralph. We have a special on Fruitopia mocha latte laced with raspberry pomegranate and caramel orange melon for $ 7.85."

Bell said: "Sounds great. How about a light black coffee with a couple ice cubes to go instead?"

Ralph gave what Bell thought was a somewhat haughty sniff and said:

"As you wish, sir," and left the table.

Tallon checked the time. It was 9:55 AM. She noticed an Indian or Pakistani or possibly an Iraqi woman get out of the passenger side of a black Mercedes 500 SEL, which was parked down the street. She was about five feet, seven inches tall, dark complected, slim in stature and wore a light blue, silk business suit. She walked toward the Fruitopia, looked at Bell, and entered the café. She walked directly to Bell's table and sat down. Tallon got out of the car and started walking toward the café. She could see Bell, and whom she assumed was Malibi. They appeared to exchange a few words. Bell removed his Cubs hat. He intercepted Ralph on the way back with the small light coffee. Bell gave him some bills from his wallet, took the coffee and walked out. Tallon walked into the Fruitopia and sat down where Bell had been seated. She was dressed in a jet-black pants suit, a red blouse and a pendant displaying a great white shark's tooth. The ensemble perfectly complimented Tallon's 5 foot 10 inch frame topped with perfectly coiffed blond hair.

Malibi seemed stunned.

Tallon said: "My name is Eileen Bach and I assume you are Doctor Zainab Malibi."

Malibi replied: "You are not what I expected."

"And what did you expect?" asked Bach as she removed a business card from her dark green, Hermes Matte, Crocodile Birkin bag and handed it to Malibi.

The card read 'Eileen Bach, President & Executive Director, Advantis Industries'.

Malibi examined the card and looked up at Bach.

"Is that a Hermes Birkin bag you have?" she asked.

"Its one of several I've collected," said Bach.

"Those bags run over $ 100,000," said Malibi.

"This one was actually $ 150,000. It was custom made for me," said Bach.

Ralph appeared to take their orders. Malibi extended her hand to Bach and shook it.

"I'll have a Fruitopia clear marmalade latte with mulberry whipped cream and one ice cube," said Bach.

"Excellent choice madam," said Ralph.

Malibi ordered: "I'll have the same."

Ralph left to place the drink order.

"Your colleague Mr. Bell will not be joining us?" asked Malibi.

"Mr. Bell has a conference call he needs to attend to for me. But he is available if I need him," replied Tallon.

Malibi said: "I appreciate your willingness to meet me today."

"Ordinarily I only meet with principals. However, I can understand, given the Emir has not been exposed to our organization previously, that he would want to vet whomever was going to meet with him. I believe that in meetings of consequence it is both necessary and appropriate that co-equals be present," replied Bach.

"I am sure the Emir will appreciate your sensitivity and courtesy," said Malibi.

Malibi cocked her head slightly and looked at Bach. "Have I made your acquaintance before? You look vaguely familiar. Perhaps we encountered each other at some point."

"I doubt it. I would probably remember," said Bach.

"If I may say, you are quite striking," continued Malibi. "I'm sure we've met somewhere."

Ralph returned with the drinks and left.

"So tell me, said Malibi, how does your influence extend so far that you are able to freeze the assets of an entire Swiss Bank?"

"My organization moves substantial funds through the Swiss banking system. This enables us to exert considerable influence on individuals, including several Board members of the Swiss Financial Market's Authority. When our contacts became aware of the money laundering relationship Mr. Rodrigues-Zappa's organization had with the INF Banque Nationale and the implications for the larger Swiss banking system, they were inclined to freeze the assets of INF. We suggested that we look into the situation informally for them and advise the SFMA as to whether or not INF funds should be unencumbered."

"Amazing," said Malibi.

"It would be an honor to be associated with an organization such as yours," Malibi continued. "We will of course, enter into a very competitive agreement with your organization and will instruct Mr. Greffen to construct an exceptionally advantageous arrangement for your organization with our bank."

"I expected you might," replied Bach with a passing smile.

"I can understand why you would be interested in working with INF, said Malibi. Mr. Black also mentioned that your company is curious about Doctor McGinty's work and how it may apply to some designer drug projects your organization is interested in."

"That's correct," said Bach. "Our organization is diverse in its holdings and eclectic in its pursuits. We also hold patents on a variety of legitimate medications. Those patents are expiring and, to obtain new patents, we need to radically change the drugs' formulations. It appears that Doctor McGinty's nanotechnology conversion process may provide the technology we require. We would, of course, have to try it out to test its scientific and legal efficacy."

"What would be the advantage to the Emir?" asked Malibi.

"There would be a substantial financial advantage in which we would propose a revenue sharing arrangement for those drugs that are successfully converted and their patents extended."

During the Tallon [Bach]/Malibi conversation, both Bell and Finkel were listening in real time courtesy of a high gain transmission unit installed in Tallon's Hermes Birkin bag. "For a moment I was afraid that Malibi was going to ask to see the bag," said Bell.

"That occurred to us as well so we had the transponder and listening devices sewn into the bottom. Malibi would have to dig through the bag's contents, something a woman would never do as it would be considered an invasion of privacy," said Finkel.

"That bag was a great idea," said Bell.

Finkel replied: "We tried to figure out what would cement Margie's bona fides with Malibi and concluded a very expensive, high end hand bag would confirm Margie's importance and position. It's the equivalent of a man bringing a Howitzer into a meeting with other men. It immediately makes a statement."

"Well whatever it did it sure worked. It looked through the field glasses like Malibi's eyes almost popped out of their sockets," said Bell. "By the way, she showed up in a Mercedes S500 and the guy driving looked like two of me."

"I expected she would have protection," said Finkel. "The way things are going it doesn't look like you will have to deal with him."

"It would be interesting if I had to," replied Bell.

Malibi took a sip of her drink and said: "How large would the incentive be for the use of Doctor McGinty?"

"Tallon said: I will discuss the specifics of the arrangement directly with the Emir."

"Fair enough," replied Malibi. "The Emir can meet with you tomorrow, the 20th, at 9:45 AM at his residence. The address is 7 Early Bird Lane in Long Beach."

"Can I expect that you will brief the Emir regarding our conversation? I don't want to waste time reviewing information he already has."

"I definitely will brief him," replied Malibi.

Bach rose from the table, as did Malibi. They both shook hands.

"I appreciate your directness and your interest in our INF Banque," said Malibi.

"We are always interested in forming new business relationships," replied Bach.

"I am looking forward to meeting the Emir tomorrow. Will you be there as well?"

"Most assuredly," replied Malibi.

Bach left the table and walked out the front door of the Fruitopia, crossed the street and got in the passenger side of the black SUV.

"Mission accomplished!" said Bell. "Way to go kid!"

Finkel's voice issued from Bell's secure phone.

"Good job, Margie."

"I think the Hermes bag sealed the deal," said Tallon chuckling.

"By the way, I don't suppose..."

"No, you can't keep the bag," said Finkel.

"Ok. But I had to try. How do you want to handle tomorrow?" Tallon asked.

"We've located the residence," said Finkel. "It's very large, on about 50 acres, with a secure front gate. We pulled satellite images 20 minutes ago. There appear to be guards of some kind at the front gate as well as roving patrols on the grounds. I'm assuming that when you pull up to the gate the guards will want some ID from both of you. The driver's licenses we issued you both should suffice. I also assume that you will be escorted to a meeting room of some kind. The estate is very large so it's hard to determine where exactly you will be. They must have enhanced the walls with some type of material to block radio waves so we will be unable to track your transponder signal. Fred, you can't let Margie out of your sight. Margie, if they try to split you up tell them that Fred is your personal assistant and that you will not attend the meeting without him. There probably will not be an issue since you have made a very compelling proposal and the Emir's greed will likely override his caution. Once you see the Emir and have made your physical assessment of him, move the conversation along as quickly as you can without raising suspicion and exit the premises. As soon as you are out of the building and off the grounds we can reconnect via your secure smart phone and you can debrief us. We will have Brother Arlot available who will discuss your facial evaluation of the Emir with you. Any questions?"

Tallon replied: "We're all set. You can track us until we enter the residence. If something occurs before we go in let me know. Otherwise I'll contact you as soon as I leave the building."

"Ok," said Finkel.

"Thanks," said Tallon and terminated the call.

"I don't know about you," said Bell, "but I could use a steak." "You read my mind," replied Tallon.

After Tallon/Bach left the Fruitopia, Malibi reached in her bag and removed an iPad.

She entered a search term in Google and read the results. She entered another search term and studied the displayed list. Ralph stopped by the table and asked if she wanted a refill. She said she did, and Ralph returned a few minutes later with the drink.

Malibi continued to enter search terms. Five minutes later she gave a sigh of frustration. She sat back and took a sip of her Fruitopia clear marmalade latte with mulberry whipped cream and contemplated the iPad screen. Finally, she entered a search term, a Boolean 'and' connector and another search term. The Google results list appeared. Malibi clicked on the second link. The screen appeared. She then did another search. The screen appeared. A faint smile flickered across Malibi. She replaced her iPad in her purse, left a $ 20 bill on the table and walked out of the Fruitopia. She waived at the black Mercedes 500SEL down the street.

The car pulled up in front of her. Malibi got into the front passenger seat and turned to Sheik Abu Mactar Kahn. Abu Mactar Kahn was so large he almost could not fit into the driver's seat of the Mercedes. "Its time to talk to the Emir."

"As you wish Doctor. Your meeting went well?" Malibi just looked ahead.

"You could say the meeting went better than expected."

Malibi pulled her iPad out of her bag and rechecked her Google search. The page displayed as it had done before. "I think the Emir will be as interested in the results of the meeting as I am," she said. Malibi then closed her eyes. The smile appeared briefly across her face once again.

STAATSGRENZE UTAH/COLORADO INTERSECTION 40 DEGREES 15 MINUTES 31.12 SECONDS NORTH 109 DEGREES 01 MINUTES 39.40 SECONDS WEST ELEVATION: 6,078 FEET FEBRUARY 19, 2012 1:00 AM MOUNTAIN TIME

The UH-60 Black Hawk stealth helicopter descended from 27,000 feet crossing the Staatsgrenze Utah/Colorado intersection. The pilot came on over Ankyer's helmet link.

"Jake, we're about fifteen minutes from a flyover of the objective. Doctor Finkel is on COM Channel 2."

Ankyer pressed his throat mike twice.

"Doctor Finkel, this is Ankyer."

"Jake, we have a N.S.A. low earth orbit satellite image of the industrial park. We also have the infrared filter activated. At the moment it looks like there are between ten and fifteen guards positioned from a minimum of twenty yards from the complex to five hundred yards out. The numbers apparently vary as shifts change. I also spoke with Mary Hendricks over at the CIA. They've launched a General Atomics MQ-9 Reaper UAV and armed it with Hellfire missiles and a BLU-113 Super Penetrator bunker buster bomb. The Reaper should be on station over the complex in about twenty minutes. I suggested to Mary that it might be overkill. She is concerned, that if something happens to you, they want to be in a position to completely incinerate and sterilize the site eliminating any residual VX or nano VX."

Ankyer replied: "I agree with her concern, but if there is a chance of taking McGinty alive we should do so. As to the guards, I feel confident that Varna and I can neutralize most, if not all of them. Once I determine which building houses the production facility I can decide how to deal with the occupants."

"Ok," said Finkel. "We will also be watching you in real time, so if we see anyone coming up behind you or flanking you we can advise you via your satellite helmet com link."

"That will be helpful," said Ankyer. "I think Varna can handle most of that for me. But if he is otherwise distracted or engaged, having that additional input available will be useful."

"Oh, by the way, Margie had her meeting with Malibi," said Finkel.

"How did that go?" asked Ankyer.

"It sounded as if it went well. You'll have to ask her about the Hermes Birkin bag."

Ankyer laughed. "At $ 150,000 a copy I'll bet she tries to keep it."

"If we pull this off I might let her," said Finkel. The Black Hawk jerked and started a descent.

"It looks like we are closing in on station for the flyover. I'll let you know if anything appears unusual," said Ankyer.

The stealth-equipped Black Hawk UH-60 flew over the industrial park at 10,000 feet in virtual silence. Ankyer watched a television monitor, which provided a close-up, stereoscopic image of the facility in infrared. The buildings occupied about ten acres. Ankyer could see the images of guards that Finkel referred to. They did not look as if they were on alert, and three of them were actually sitting down around a tree about thirty yards from the facility. He flipped down his visor to check the monitor's infrared images against his heads-up infrared display. The images on the heads-up helmet display and the Black Hawk monitor coincided. While there were infrared images visible outside the abandoned industrial complex, there were no images visible in the complex itself.

Ankyer commented to the pilot: "It looks as if the buildings are deserted. That doesn't make sense. Either one or more of the buildings' walls are shielded or they are just guarding building contents."

"I don't want to go any lower," replied the pilot. "The rotors on the Hawk are sound suppressed, not completely silenced."

Ankyer replied: "I'm going to assume the walls of the buildings are shielded just in case. I might also be able to keep one of the guards alive long enough to extract some kind of confirmation."

"Sounds good to me," said the pilot. "I'm going to start evasion maneuvers in case these guys have some kind of unmanned aerial drone floating around. Is Varna secured back there?"

"No problem," said Ankyer. "He's taking a nap."

"I love that goddam dog, oops. Sorry, wolf," said the pilot. The Black Hawk jinked left and then right a couple times, climbed and then dove again.

Ankyer rechecked the contents of his combat pack and found a large Milk Bone Brother William had snuck in for Varna. He then checked the bandoleer with the crossbow attached. The bandoleer and crossbow scabbard were made of the same molecular camouflage material as Ankyer's tactical body wrap. Four ten bolt projectile magazines were integrated along with four CO2 cartridges, in addition to the one in the cross bow. Ankyer had a Heckler & Koch UMP 45 with a spring loaded folding stock attached to a swivel leg harness, with two thirty round clips also attached to the harness and one inserted into the receiver. This gave Ankyer immediate access to the H&K with the stock automatically unfolding as he pulled the weapon from the harness without interfering with his running ability.

The cabin lights flickered, the red night vision lights came on, and the Co-Pilot said: "Jake. We're approaching the LZ, which is about 2.5 miles out from your objective. It's a little farther out than the designed infiltration route but there is a stand of trees and some boulders, which were not initially evident on the satellite images. There are also a few inches of snow on the ground, which may have screwed things up somehow. You ok with that?"

"Not a problem," replied Jake. "It's actually better. It gives me a little more maneuvering room to deal with the security."

Ankyer scratched Varna behind the ears. "Time to go to work, partner."

Varna yawned, shook, and sat up looking to Ankyer for his cue. The Black Hawk pulled around in a tight arc and settled down. The cabin door slid open and the pilot's voice came on in Jake's helmet.

"You're outa here. If you run into trouble give us a holler and we'll show up with the Reaper and blow their collective asses back to Mecca."

Ankyer jumped out of the Black Hawk and Varna jumped out right behind him. The Black Hawk pulled up and away, rapidly gaining altitude into the darkness.

Ankyer's heads-up display indicated an air temperature of 41 degrees Fahrenheit and a wind chill of 37 degrees, all within the operating range of his equipment. There was a light snow blowing and the ground had patches of white. Ankyer started jogging along the tree line. His helmet's time/speed/distance calculator indicated he would be at the industrial complex within forty minutes at the current north, northeast direction. Varna ranged thirty yards ahead of Ankyer, moving in and out of the tree line. The light snow covering gave both Ankyer and Varna the advantage of complete silence as they progressed forward.

Ten minutes into the advance Varna dodged into the tree line as Ankyer ran by several large boulders. As he passed the last boulder, his heads-up display projected two infrared images of guards thirty yards out. One guard was facing Ankyer and the second was behind the first. Ankyer pulled the crossbow from his combat vest and fired two bolts in quick succession at a dead run. The guard facing Ankyer stood for a moment and then slowly crumpled to the ground. The second guard remained standing next to a tree. Ankyer released a third bolt from the cross bow, which hit the standing figure in the upper torso. As Ankyer approached the first guard, he saw a mass of blood in the mouth and brain matter hanging from a jagged hole in the back of the head. The second guard's body was directly behind the first. Ankyer realized that the first bolt entered the mouth of the first guard now on the ground, and continued on out the back of the skull into the left ear of the second guard pinning his head to a pine tree which left the body suspended.

Ankyer returned the crossbow to its retainer on his vest. He quickly knelt down, pulled the titanium/ceramic combat knife from its sheath and carefully slit open the first guard's coat. He pulled the coat apart. No exploding vest. He stood up and examined the second guard pinned to the tree. The second guard's body was starting to sag from the weight of the body on the neck but was still upright. Ankyer slit the guard's coat down the side being careful not to penetrate the coat too deeply and to avoid inadvertently hitting the exploding vest. He replaced the knife and pulled the slit coat apart. No vest.

"Shit," he thought. "This transponder idea may not fly and I will have to neutralize the guards individually. So much for economy of operation."

As Ankyer was turning from the body, a third guard whose infrared image had not appeared on Ankyer's display moved out from behind a boulder and started walking toward Ankyer while leveling an AK-47 at him.

"Are you some kind of ghost or what?" the guard asked in Arabic.

Ankyer realized that the image projected in the snow from the molecular camouflage of his body wrap made him look like a diffuse, grey being. Ankyer's helmet with its integrated rebreather only added to the effect. As the guard looked around he saw the two bodies and jacked a round into the chamber of the AK. "Put up your fucking hands!" exclaimed the guard in Arabic.

At that moment a grey mass launched itself from the boulder. One hundred and eighty five pounds of snarling Mackenzie Valley Canadian Timber wolf hit the guard square in the chest, knocking him to the ground. The guard tried to raise the AK-47, but Varna's weight pinioned his arms. The guard looked up into Varna's open jaws with the lips pulled back into a slavering, fanged nightmare and started to scream. Too late. Varna's head dove down into the guard's neck and ripped out the guard's throat disconnecting the guard's carotid arteries on the way. Varna shook his head twice as the snow around the guard turned red, and dropped the remnants of the guard's throat at Ankyer's feet.

"I was beginning to wonder where you were," said Ankyer.

As Varna sat in front of Ankyer, Ankyer noticed part of the guard's trachea hanging from the side of Varna's blood soaked jaws.

"Brother William needs to give you a refresher on fine dining," said Ankyer as he pulled the trachea remnants from Varna's mouth and threw them on top of the guard's body, which, by that time, had stopped gurgling. Varna rubbed up against Ankyer wagging his tail.

"Ok. Let's see what we have here." Ankyer slit open the guard's jacket and pulled it apart. Bingo! An exploding vest. Leave it to a wolf. Ankyer located the cell phone on the vest. He then removed his transponder from a pocket in his combat vest. He pushed the yellow button. A yellow light flashed three times indicating that Ankyer's transponder was now on the same radio frequency as the guard's phone. Ankyer then pushed the black button on his transponder and a red blinking light on the guard's cell phone went out.

"I'll bet the vests for the other two guards are in that Ford Explorer over there," Ankyer said to Varna looking out past another boulder. Ankyer walked over to the 4 X 4 with Varna at his side. There in the back seat were the two exploding vests. Ankyer checked the transmitters. The lights on the guards' transmitters were out. "They probably got tired of wearing the damn things. Are you catching all this?" Ankyer asked.

"Absolutely," came Finkel's voice in Ankyer's helmet. "We'll try our transponder idea on IEDs over in Afghanistan," said Finkel.

"You'll probably blow up half the country," replied Ankyer.

"Not a bad idea, but you didn't hear it from me," said Finkel.

"What's it look like in front of me?" asked Ankyer. Eight red dots and a green dot appeared in Ankyer's helmet's heads-up display.

"You're green and the martyr guards are red. It looks like there are eight of them spread out about a quarter mile from the buildings. You're now three quarter's of a mile away from them. A flanking maneuver appears to be in order," said Finkel.

"I agree," replied Ankyer.

With that Ankyer and Varna resumed running along the tree line closing the distance between the green and red dots on the helmet display. The snow flurries increased. Instead of ranging ahead of Ankyer, Varna positioned himself about two yards off to the right. Droplets of the martyr guard's blood combined with the snow collecting on Varna's muzzle as he ran.

Farook el Muffti was cold. Guarding the laboratory was not why he joined the martyr's brigade. He was loyal to the Emir, but el Muffti felt he was grossly underutilized. Better that he was in a car loaded with explosives blowing up people in a Bagdad market, advancing the cause of Islam and getting him in the company of his 72 virgins. He walked over to the Jeep Laredo and rested his AK-47 on the bumper. He took a thermos from the front seat and swallowed some tepid black coffee. He imagined that Zarbob, Saeed and Madhur felt the same way. They, too, were guarding the building in the wind and snow. There had to be a better way to Paradise than this.

As Farook contemplated his situation, the moon briefly emerged from the clouds and he noticed movement out of the corner of his eye. It disappeared and reappeared in the distance. A wolf! A big one. It was running out by the trees. It looked like there was some kind of grey outline with the wolf but Farook thought the snow and terrain were playing tricks on him. He grabbed his rifle from the side of the Jeep. He doubted he could hit the wolf from this distance but it would help break the monotony. Farook took aim and fired leading the wolf with each shot. He saw the wolf go down.

As soon as Ankyer heard the first shot he dropped to the ground, as did Varna. Three plumes of snow erupted, one ten feet from Ankyer and the other two twenty feet from Varna. Ankyer had the eight infrared images between 200 and 500 yards away spread out in various positions. Ankyer was surprised anyone saw them. One of them must have seen movement from Varna. Varna was conditioned to drop to the ground at a shot instead of continuing to run instinctively. He crawled over to Ankyer.

Ankyer said: "It looks like we are close enough to the guards where they can see you Varna. Maybe we should see if the transponder works. What do you think?"

"I'd be happier if you were a little closer," Finkel's voice responded in Ankyer's helmet. "The transponder was designed to operate at a thousand yard range but hasn't been adequately field tested. You may be too far away."

"I'm still a quarter mile from the facility. Getting into a firefight this far out could be a problem. I need to close the distance rapidly before they figure out what is going on and decide to evacuate. If Varna and I get pinned down that could be an issue."

"It's your call Jake," said Finkel.

"If you see anything going on around the buildings let me know," replied Ankyer as he took the transponder out of its combat vest pocket and pushed the red button.

Farook el Muffti was pleased with himself. Killing a wolf at such a great distance was a feat truly worthy of a superb marksman. He would have to drive out and bring the wolf back for all to see. Maybe this whole martyrdom idea was premature. There were many pleasures on this earth, such as killing the wolf, he thought. Of course, lying with seventy two virgins was nothing to scoff at either. Perhaps he could find two or three virgins here on earth before he decided to go to Paradise. He smiled at the thought and started to get an erection.

Not all Islamist martyrs are the same and neither are their exploding vests. There are differences in martyrs, including size, shape and commitment. Regarding the vests, there are different types of connections, explosive materials, and projectiles. After what he believed was his marksman-like shot for the wolf, Farook el Muffti was light on the commitment aspect. When he heard a buzzing and smelled smoke under his shirt he decided to delay his martyrdom. He ripped open his shirt... and exploded.

It is said that exploding vests are specifically designed to preserve the martyr's head so as to ensure the head arrives intact in Paradise (at least virtually) permitting him to enjoy his surroundings immediately and, not the least, his seventy two virgins. In Farook el Muffti's case, everything below his neck combined into a gelatinous mass with the only discernable parts left over being a foot attached to a partial ankle, a shoe and two fingers. His head on the other hand made the trip to Paradise and shot ten feet into the air on a gout of blood, coming back to earth with three bounces and resting under the left front tire of the Jeep Laredo.

After Ankyer pushed the red transponder button he waited for three or four seconds and was rewarded with six, sporadic, midsized explosions and two large explosions. Behind him he heard a large explosion followed by a smaller one.

"Probably the three martyr/guards we first encountered," he thought.

The auto imaging dimmed the infrared images in Ankyer's heads-up display and showed six explosions, each with a round projectile hurled at least fifteen feet straight into the air. 'Heads', he guessed. The two larger explosions came from two vehicles parked about eighty yards away from each other. When Ankyer's helmet display regained its normal visual light Ankyer could see no additional infrared images other than the fires from the explosions. "Doctor Finkel, I've got to get moving."

"Good job Jake. I'll let you know if we pick up anything on visual. The exploding martyrs were quite something to behold on the satellite cams. It was a little like the seventh inning fireworks at Wrigley Field in Chicago with the Cubs losing. I'm sure Fred Bell would be pleased. I'll get you a copy of the video when you return," said Finkel.

Ankyer did not respond as he and Varna ran toward the industrial site.

OUTSIDE OF BLACK FOREST, COLORADO
ABANDONED INDUSTRIAL PARK COMPLEX
FEBRUARY 19, 2012
3:00 AM MOUNTAIN TIME

As Ankyer and Varna ran forward, they periodically encountered smoldering heads and other body parts spread over a landscape illuminated by vehicle fires. Ankyer's external visual helmet feed had self-adjusted to almost normal to compensate for the intensity of the surrounding ambient light. Ankyer thought, "If there's anyone in those buildings, they must suspect something has happened by now."

The campus of the industrial park itself consisted of four, four story buildings positioned in a semi circle with a fifth, five-story building positioned ahead of the others in the center. There was a large number 1 on the upper right hand corner of the first building in the semicircle and the numbering continued clockwise ending with building number 5 in the center. The main driveway led to the center building and then split off into a circular driveway connecting to a circular driveway that connected with sidewalks to each of the four other buildings. There were scrub trees and bushes everywhere and the concrete walks were cracked. Each of the buildings was in disrepair, three in a substantially more advanced state than the others. From what he could see, most of the windows facing him were broken out and the concrete facades of each of the buildings showed cracking. Building number 2 was unusual. The building was as decrepit as the others, except all of the windows on the first floor were intact, as were most of the windows on the second floor.

Approaching the complex, Ankyer stopped, opened his combat pack and pulled out four booties, which he affixed to each of Varna's paws.

"There's got to be glass all over this place," Ankyer thought. As they approached the center building, number 5, there was a shaking in the lower branches of a large cottonwood tree. Ankyer reached to the side of his helmet to activate the infrared, which had automatically turned off with the flashes of the exploding martyr guards. Before he could activate the IR, a shape launched itself out of the tree and hit Ankyer in the chest knocking him on his back. Ankyer reached for his combat knife secured to his chest but the body of his assailant was over the scabbard. Ankyer heard a screeching and felt two fangs penetrate his shoulder through his body wrap. While he was trying to disentangle himself from his attacker, Ankyer heard a howl and felt the body on top of him move and then fall away. He sprang to his feet, swinging the H&K UMP 45 up from his leg swivel and looked around. Twenty feet away there was a ball of grey and tan fur furiously rolling around in the snow, which was rapidly turning black in the dim light. All at once there was a screech and the grey part of the fur ball detached itself trailing the guts of what had been an exceptionally large mountain lion. Varna threw the guts to one side, turned, and threw himself back at the mountain lion biting down and crushing its skull. The one hundred and ten pound mountain lion had not anticipated a one hundred and eighty five pound Canadian Timber wolf when it had started its hunt that night.

Varna padded over to Ankyer and lay at his feet. Ankyer immediately turned on his narrow beam helmet light and surveyed for damage to Varna, which appeared relatively slight. Aside from a gash on his side and a few scratches, the injuries did nothing to make him non functional. Ankyer pulled a combat antiseptic patch from his combat pack and applied it to Varna's gash. He removed another patch, presoaked with antiseptic and topical anesthetic, and applied it to his own shoulder. The patches adhered tightly to both Varna and Ankyer due to a 'crazy glue'-like substance, which bonded instantly with any kind of skin or fabric. The patches would have to be removed with special solvents when Ankyer and Varna returned from the mission. Both Ankyer and Varna stood up.

Ankyer spoke into his helmet microphone: "Doctor Finkel, I have an equipment update. It looks like the camouflage body wrap does not prevent animals from seeing me."

"We observed the encounter on the satellite cam," said Finkel.

"What was it?"

"It looks like a mountain lion. It punctured my shoulder so I'll collect some brain matter and have it checked for rabies back at the Monastery. Varna also sustained an open injury on his side when he fought the cat. I have a combat patch on it but he'll need stitches."

"Ok," said Finkel. "We'll also start checking animal sensitivity to the camouflage wrap. It may be the cat was sensitive to your body heat, movement, or possibly its retinal sensitivity somehow blocked out the molecular environmental synchronization of the wrap. We'll figure it out and adjust. Do you and Varna remain operational with your injuries?"

"Not a problem at this point. We are heading toward the entrance of the building complex. The second building in the crescent is curious. It's the only one of the buildings I can see which has some unbroken windows."

"We do not see any additional movement or infrared images on our monitors at this time. The transponder appears to have eliminated the external threats wearing vests at this point," said Finkel.

"Good. Now I have to determine which building the laboratory is in," replied Ankyer. "I have an idea for that," said Finkel. "Try the transponder again pointed at building 2."

Ankyer walked back to the mountain lion's corpse, took a Plexiglas vial from the combat pack and scooped up some brain remnants from the open crack between its eyes, and replaced the vial in a pocket in the combat pack.

The snow outside the building complex started to pick up. Ankyer and Varna jogged up the main driveway to the center building. The building looked as deserted as each of the others. They then ran to their left over the damaged circular driveway and stopped at the corner of building number 1. The building was missing its front door and appeared to have been scavenged for materials leaving a shell. They looked over at building number 2 about twenty yards away. "We're there, Doctor Finkel. We'll give the transponder a try." With that Ankyer took the transponder from his combat vest, gave Varna the down command and knelt next to him. Ankyer pointed the transponder toward building 2 and pressed the red button. Almost immediately there were two explosions on the building's second floor and two heads trailing smoke and sparks broke through two large windows at opposite ends of the building.

"Good idea, Doctor," said Ankyer.

"The walls of the building weakened the cell phone signals on the vests, which is why they didn't go off the first time. We can't visually track you inside. Let me know when you locate McGinty," said Finkel.

"Ok," Ankyer replied. He and Varna ran toward building 2 with Varna close behind. As they approached the building, Ankyer pressed the black button on the transponder hoping he would disable any remaining exploding vests on the same wavelength.

HILTON HOTEL/CIA SAFE HOUSE LONG BEACH LONG ISLAND, NEW YORK FEBRUARY 19, 2012

Hilton Hotel
February 19th, 2012
12:00 PM Eastern Standard Time

After Tallon's meeting with Malibi, Tallon and Bell were instructed by Finkel to spend several hours out of sight at a Hilton hotel in Long Beach. "Doctor Finkel decided to have the CIA set up a safe house for us which they are arranging for today," said Bell. "I was then given the address where we will meet two CIA operators at around 3:00 PM."

"Why are we killing time at a hotel?" asked Tallon.

"Long Beach is a relatively small community," said Bell. "Doctor Finkel didn't want to take a chance on us being spotted while we were waiting for the safe house arrangements to be made."

"Doctor Finkel doesn't take many chances, does he?" asked Tallon.

"I've never known him to take any chances at all. I'm usually in an operation and I don't get a chance to see Doctor Finkel that often. But I'm told that Doctor Finkel is one of the most meticulous planners in the entire N.S.A.," replied Bell.

CIA Safe House
February 19, 2012
3:00 PM Eastern Standard Time

"When Mary Hendricks called us from Langley she told us told not to ask you what's going on, so we won't," said the CIA operator after Bell and Tallon arrived.

"But if you guys get in the shit, we won't be able to pull you out."

"Understood," said Bell.

Two CIA operators, Oscar and Jason, had met them at the door. The safe house was barebones with four bedrooms, a kitchen and a living/dining room. Tallon and Bell had been told by Jason that they were having Chinese takeout, courtesy of the CIA, for dinner.

"We were thinking steaks," said Bell.

"Maybe on the N.S.A.'s budget, but not on ours," replied Oscar.

"Miss Hendricks had us obtain a change of clothes for each of you. I have to say that these clothes must cost more than Oscar and I make in six months," said Jason.

"Don't worry," said Tallon. "We don't get to keep them."

"There's some justice," said Oscar.

Jason continued. "We've been surveilling the location. The residence is very well guarded. It looks like they use a combination of human operators and dogs. X-ray images indicate the boys at the gatehouse are all packing. The dogs look like Dobermans and are fast as hell. Basically, if you have to make a run for it you're screwed."

"This is a business meeting," said Tallon. "I expect we'll be treated with courtesy."

"Well, just in case you're not," said Jason, "we have this for Fred."

Oscar placed a box on the table. Inside there was what appeared to be a light grey semi automatic with two clips in a quick draw belt holster. "With the level of security we've seen at this place, we are guessing that you might encounter a metal detector somewhere along the way. What we have here is a reinforced plastic automatic complete with ceramic bullets. It's undetectable in a metal detector and has an irregular surface, which creates an outline that confuses the shit out of x-ray machines. We got this from Mary Hicks, who got it from some guy named Finkel. Hicks said we couldn't play with it on pain of death so we don't know if it works, but Hicks assured us it does. The gun is for Fred since he's billed as your bodyguard, Margie. You don't get one because you're suppose to be some big deal executive and packing heat would screw up the illusion. The rounds are 45 caliber with 230-grain loads. We've been told that one of these bullets on impact acts like a hollow point on steroids. Fred, you've got a ten round magazine, one in the pipe, and two extra magazines."

Fred took the gun from the box and hefted it.

"This weighs almost nothing," he said.

"Just over two pounds," replied Jason.

"What about recoil," Bell asked.

"Beats me, but it has a standard 45 caliber load so I would expect a pretty good kick," said Jason. "Let's put it this way. If you have to pull this out you're going to be spraying lead, sorry… ceramic, all over the place so recoil should not be a problem."

"Gotchya," replied Bell.

A speakerphone on a coffee table buzzed. Oscar pressed the 'talk' button.

"This is Mary Hendricks. Who is in the room?"

"Miss Hendricks this is Oscar. Jason is here along with Doctor Tallon and Fred Bell."

"Oscar and Jason, could you excuse yourselves for a few minutes?"

Oscar and Jason walked into the kitchen and exited through a back door.

"Margie and Fred, wait one while I patch Doctor Finkel in."

A moment passed. "Margie and Fred…how are you both doing?"

"We're fine Doctor," said Tallon.

"I wanted to spend a few minutes bringing you up to date," said Finkel. "Jake has penetrated the external security system at the industrial complex in Colorado. He encountered some resistance but overcame it."

"How many?" Fred asked. "Last count was thirteen martyr/guards, now all deceased."

"Tallon thought: "My god, Jake has killed thirteen guards and he's not even inside the complex yet! He's unbelievable."

"I wanted to bring this to your attention, since you may run into something similar when you arrive at the Emir's residence. Fred, don't use your weapon unless it's absolutely necessary. Jake had the advantage of a transponder, which blew up their vests. If you encounter a martyr/guard you may get off a shot and even hit him, but he might still be able to fire off his vest. We thought about trying to get you a transponder like Jake's but their security would probably find it."

"Understood sir," said Bell.

"Jake also was attacked by a mountain lion just outside the complex. We don't think it was part of the security system. It was probably just hunting."

"Is he alright?" asked Tallon.

"He was bitten in the shoulder…"

"Rabies," said Tallon.

"That is a concern," said Finkel. "Varna dispatched the cat and Jake has collected some brain matter. We'll fly it back to the Abbey as soon as Jake returns to the Denver airport and have it checked. Varna also sustained a gash in his side from his battle with the mountain lion. Jake applied a combat patch, which has closed up the wound. We have a vet on call to take care of him when he returns. Jake said Varna continues to be operational, so it is probably not too bad. The bigger problem is Brother William. He is beside himself with worry. We may sneak a sedative in his tea to calm him down."

"There is a possibility that the Emir may be alerted to the current activity in Colorado prior to your arrival at his residence. He may not make the connection, but just be sensitive to the possibility," said Finkel.

"We will be," replied Tallon. "It's my intent to make the evaluation the second I see the Emir," said Tallon. I should have a reasonable idea if the Emir is Saddam almost immediately. I will finish the meeting as soon as I can, and Fred and I will get out of there."

"Ok," said Finkel. "We will have a N.S.A. satellite over the location giving us real time imagery, so we will be keeping close tabs on you two. Remember, the moment you leave the estate contact me. One more item," said Finkel. "George Makin did a spectacular job with his visit to the INF Bank Nationale. The Director, Hans Greffen, now understands the gravity of his relationship with the Emir, and is cooperating. The INF bank launders money for an extensive number of drug cartels and other criminal enterprises. Greffen provided George with a computer disk with names, account numbers, and contacts, which George has uploaded to a secure computer at the Abbey. Even if it turns out that the Emir is not Saddam, the Emir and his associates will disappear into some country's criminal justice gulag for the rest of their lives, and the INF bank will cease to exist, placing a huge dent into what may be hundreds of criminal enterprises. It's a dramatic breakthrough."

"It comes as no surprise to me. He certainly managed to get Zainab Malibi's attention," said Tallon.

Fred stuck his head out the kitchen door. "Ok boys. Secret meeting is over. Say, does that gas grill work?" "You bet it does," said Oscar. "We were shitting you about the steaks. That's what we're having for dinner," he said.

"Way to go, boys!" replied Bell.

The three men walked back into the living room. Tallon had disappeared into a bedroom. She came out fifteen minutes later having changed into the new suit Finkel sent.

"What do you guys think?" she asked as she turned in a circle.

The suit was light grey silk with subtle pin stripes with a tailored jacket and a skirt hemmed just above the knees. "I can see why Doctor Finkel didn't send a weapon for me. I don't know where I'd put it." The ensemble, completed with a pastel blue silk blouse with a hint of ruffles was stunning.

Jason walked up to her and asked: "Will you marry me and bear my children? Please?"

"I don't date spies," she said.

"Shit," he replied.

"Too bad, Jason," said Fred. "I would have been your best man."

BLACK FOREST, COLORADO
ABANDONED INDUSTRIAL PARK COMPLEX
BUILDING 2
FEBRUARY 19, 2012
4:05 AM MOUNTAIN TIME

Ankyer and Varna entered building 2 through the glass front doors, which had been shattered by the explosions. The interior of the building was filled with glass shards and overturned chairs and tables. Beams from emergency lights shone from corners of the twenty-foot ceiling, a further indication that the building was in use. As Ankyer walked into the center of the first floor, a door opened forty feet away in a corner of the room. A bearded man with a bandana around his forehead and baggy pants jumped out and leveled an AK-47 at Ankyer.

A maxim of military training is that if a soldier levels a gun at someone else with a gun, the soldier shoots his gun. The bearded man was likely absent from that class. Having the image of a helmet with the face covered by a Draeger rebreather floating over an amorphous body might have given him pause as well. The moment Ankyer saw the AK he pulled his H&K UMP 45 from its hip swivel and fired three rounds into the bearded man's forehead blowing the back of the man's skull in various directions. Ankyer ran up to the now partially headless figure and ripped open its shirt. Underneath was an exploding vest with the cell phone lights out. The transponder at work again! Varner padded up to Ankyer, sniffed the body and emitted a low growl. Ankyer pulled the leads from the cell phone, stood up and looked into the doorway. Empty.

With Varna in the lead, Ankyer and the wolf entered the doorway and descended down twelve steps to a landing and then to another landing twelve more steps down. A door was partially open at the second landing and a soft light emanated from the room. As Ankyer walked down the corridor he observed two rooms with glass windows. They looked like laboratories, each with a small decontamination room and a door opening to a larger room with laboratory equipment. The third room down the corridor was different. It did not have a decontamination foyer or a window. What it did have, when Ankyer carefully opened the door was seven or eight bloody bodies in white lab coats. The bodies, both male and female, were scattered around the room as if they were trying to escape. They had not succeeded. Ankyer reentered the corridor and continued down the hall. He saw another windowless room, its door partially ajar. Five more bodies, this time huddled in a far corner of the room. It was clear to Ankyer that the laboratory staff had completed its work and payday had been at hand. Not the payday they had imagined thought Ankyer.

Just past the second room there was narrow door, which appeared to be a utility closet. Varna was sniffing it and growling. Ankyer heard a shuffling sound behind the door. The door cracked open an inch and Ankyer saw an eye peering out about half way up. He pulled the door open and the eye pulled back into the recess of the closet. A white-coated shape sat on the floor with its arms around its knees.

"Please don't hurt me," it said. A woman. She was short with a slight build covered by a lab coat. She looked at Ankyer with large brown eyes. Ankyer detached a corner of the Draeger unit from the helmet so it hung down. He lifted the visor in front of his helmet exposing his face. The woman looked at the large figure in front of her and shook with fear.

"I'm not going to hurt you," he said.

"I'm here to save you."

"Your body looks strange," she said.

"Don't worry", said Ankyer.

"It's just a special uniform. I'm military."

She moved more toward the back of the closet when Varna came into her view. "Varna, stay," said Ankyer. The wolf shook once and sat next to the open door.

"He won't hurt you", said Ankyer.

"My god. Is that a wolf?" she asked.

"Yes," replied Ankyer. "But you will be alright as long as you are with me."

"What is your name?" asked Ankyer dropping to one knee in front of the closet.

"Its Emily Tyson," she replied.

"What is your job here Emily?"

"I'm a lab assistant," she said. "I work in a nano conversion lab."

"Why are you hiding in the closet?"

"After the explosions outside, the people guarding the building told everyone to go to a room. They didn't say why. As I was walking to the room I heard some 'bangs,' like shots. I got scared and dropped back and hid in the closet."

"You saved your life," said Ankyer. "There are people in rooms down the hall, all dead."

"Those bastards killed them!" she exclaimed.

"I'm sorry," said Ankyer.

"They held all of us prisoners here for months. They said they would release us when the project was completed."

"What project?" asked Ankyer.

"They said they were converting VX nerve agent to a specialized nanoparticle formulation to eradicate pests in third world countries. I'm not sure exactly what the process was. The nano VX formulation was completed in a locked bio level 4 containment facility one level below us. Doctor McGinty told us the final steps of the process were secret and only he could be involved."

"Where is Doctor McGinty now?" asked Ankyer.

"I don't know. Doctor McGinty and Mr. el Farsi left the facility yesterday, after informing us that the project was complete. Someone said that they heard that they had gone to Chicago, but that's just a rumor. I'm not sure."

Ankyer paused, looking at Tyson who was silently crying.

"Emily, these people, including Doctor McGinty are terrorists. Their plan is to release the nano technology form of nerve gas into locations throughout the United States and kill millions of people. I'm with US military special operations and I'm going to need your help to stop them."

"Anything," said Tyson, moving up to the front of the closet. "I still can't believe they killed everyone. Doctor Thomas was a wonderful man. Are you sure he's dead?"

"Is he about six feet tall with white hair?"

"Yes," replied Tyson.

"He's in one of the rooms down the hall with the others. They shot him several times in the head," said Ankyer.

Tyson started crying again.

"Emily, you need to get hold of yourself." Varna looked down the hall at a partially open doorway at the end and emitted a low growl.

A martyr/guard emerged holding an AK-47 waist high.

"Who the fuck are you?" the guard asked stumbling over the words.

Without responding, Ankyer released the crossbow from its holder and in one fluid motion shot a bolt into the guard's eye fifty yards away, dropping him instantly and causing the rifle to clatter several feet down the hallway. Tyson looked down the hallway with her mouth agape. Ankyer helped her to her feet.

"I'm sorry you had to see that. These people are wearing exploding vests and I can't take a chance of a shot hitting the explosive."

"I know," said Tyson. "The guards told us if we caused any kind of a disruption they would explode themselves, and us with them!"

"What is on the floor below us?" asked Ankyer.

"I'm not exactly sure," said Tyson. "Some of us were hired to create reagents that would enable Doctor McGinty to reduce the VX to nano particle size. All that work was done on the floor below, which was not accessible to the laboratory staff up here. Material we processed on this floor was loaded onto carts and the guards would move the carts onto a freight elevator down at the end of the hall. The material would then be moved down below from there."

"Ok Emily. We're going down stairs now. Do you have a protective mask you can wear?"

"Yes. There are masks in a small store room area by the freight elevator."

Ankyer, Tyson and Varna moved rapidly to the end of the hall. Ankyer checked the carotid pulse of the guard confirming his status as deceased. He then ripped open the guard's shirt revealing an exploding vest. Ankyer pulled the wires from the attached cell phone. Tyson opened a door next to the freight elevator, removed a safety mask, and put it on.

Ankyer said: "Varna…guard."

Varna walked two feet forward and sat, looking down the hall. Tyson looked quizzically at Ankyer. "Believe me," said Ankyer. I'd rather have him guarding my back than someone with a gun." "Now, open the front of your lab coat."

Tyson stood still. "I have to be sure," said Ankyer.

Tyson unbuttoned her lab coat and continued to unbutton her blouse. There was a brassiere but no exploding vest.

Ankyer opened the door the now deceased martyr/guard had emerged from earlier, reattached his Draeger rebreather, and started walking down the dimly lit stairwell. "Do you know how many guards there are?" Ankyer asked.

"I think I may have seen as many as fifteen but I'm not sure because I never saw them all at once and most of them have full beards," replied Tyson.

"Stay about two feet behind me," Ankyer instructed Tyson. "I may need a little room for movement in case we encounter a problem."

They continued their descent for about forty steps and stopped at a landing. There was a keypad next to a solid steel door. "Do you know the code?" asked Ankyer.

"Its 6774521," replied Tyson. "Doctor Thomas found it out somehow."

Ankyer pressed the digits on the keypad and heard a 'click'. Ankyer removed the H&K UMP 45 from its swivel hip leg harness with his right hand and pulled the door open with his left.

And then Ankyer and Tyson walked into hell.

FRONT GATE
EMIR'S MANSION
7 EARLY BIRD LANE
LONG BEACH
LONG ISLAND, NEW YORK
FEBRUARY 20, 2012
9:30 AM EASTERN TIME

The black SUV turned off Long Beach Drive onto Early Bird lane. Tallon and Bell had had a conference call with Finkel at 7:30 AM at the CIA safe house. Finkel reviewed the plan point by point. He reinforced the need for Tallon and Bell to leave the Emir's estate as soon as possible after Tallon had evaluated the Emir's skull structure and matched it against the skull configuration she had memorized. Oscar and Jason, the CIA security operatives, were to be following a half-mile behind. They would stop at the top of Early Bird Lane and wait for Tallon and Bell to reemerge. If Bell and Tallon were being pursued, the operatives had a M242 Bushmaster chain gun, mounted inside the back half of their extended black SUV, barrel pointing toward the back window. The cyclic rate of fire, coupled with the heavy metal depleted uranium incendiary rounds, would destroy any vehicle within 2500 meters. They also had a N.S.A. secure phone link and would be advised by N.S.A. staff, monitoring the area visually via a satellite feed, of any pursuit or other problem which could potentially compromise Tallon and Bell's exfiltration from the Emir's premises.

Early Bird Lane was a mile long and just wide enough for one vehicle. The sides of the road had steep drop offs making it impossible to turn around. Once on the road, the only way back would be to back up or somehow turn around up ahead in a wide apron in front of the mansion gates. The road also had frequent sharp curves making backing up highly problematic. Bell continued driving up the road for three quarters of a mile until he stopped at a ten-foot high, double, cast iron ornate gate. A small door was embedded in one side of the gate. One of four guards in black, single-breasted suits opened the small door, and walked over to Bell's window.

Bell lowered the window and said: "Eileen Bach and her associate Fred Bell to see the Emir and Doctor Malibi. We have an appointment."

The guard replied with a thick Arab accent: "Picture ID's."

Bell and Tallon had anticipated this and Bell had the ID's ready.

"Are either of you armed?" the guard asked.

"No," replied Bell.

"Please exit the vehicle," said the guard.

Bell and Tallon got out of the SUV. The guard who was slightly taller than Bell approached Bell and said, "Extend your arms."

Bell did as he was told and the guard waived a metal detector he was holding up and down the front and back of Bell. He then went around the front of the SUV, instructed Tallon to extend her arms and performed the same security procedure.

The guard said: "You can get back into your vehicle now."

Tallon and Bell got back in the SUV. All four guards entered a medium sized guard shack and closed the door. Once back in the SUV, Tallon noticed a guard in the shack speaking into a cell phone. The door of what appeared to be a very large kennel on the inside of the gate, across the driveway opposite the guard shack slid open. Tallon thought she heard a high-pitched whistle. While she was debating what she'd heard, five black figures came hurtling from different directions. The exceptionally large Doberman Pincers, with their teeth bared, but emitting no sound, ran up to the gate, reared up to the SUV, and then trotted into the kennel, the door sliding closed behind them. The dogs continued walking around the kennel snarling in silence.

"I've seen this before in a CIA "black detention site" in Asia," said Bell.

"Its surgically-induced canine laryngeal paralysis. The dogs have their larynx surgically altered to prevent any sound, but not in a way which restricts breathing. They are usually used for night security. You can't hear or see them coming. This place has exceptional security. Probably has extensive electronic security as well. Very hard to penetrate."

"We'll have to advise Doctor Finkel of this as soon as we're out of here," replied Tallon.

The gates opened and Bell slowly drove the SUV inside. The gates closed behind them. The guard walked out of the guard shack and motioned Bell to lower his window.

"Drive up to the front of the residence and park your vehicle in the parking bay off to the side. You will be met at the door."

Bell drove down the driveway and parked off to the left of the main entrance to the mansion. As they were exiting the SUV, Malibi met them.

"The Emir is quite security conscious. I trust you were not too inconvenienced, Miss Bach."

"The dogs…" said Tallon/Bach.

"Specially trained security animals," said Malibi.

"They will attack anyone, even the Emir or the guards. Once they attack they cannot be called off, even by the whistle which summons them to the kennel."

"That's why the guards went into the guard house when the dogs were called," said Tallon/Bach.

"Exactly," replied Malibi. "Don't worry. They will be placed in their kennel before you leave. Please, follow me."

Tallon/Bach and Bell followed Malibi up steps and through the main door. They found themselves in an exceptionally large, ornate, rectangular foyer with a curved, highly polished staircase on one side and an open mahogany door on the opposite side. The lighting in the foyer was subdued and paintings hung on the walls, each illuminated by a small light on the ceiling.

"The Emir leases his residences but likes to hang part of his extensive art collection where he resides so he feels at home. The Emir thought the solarium would be a comfortable surrounding for our meeting. We can take the lift to the fourth floor."

They entered the elevator noticing a small Matisse on the back wall. Malibi pressed the fourth button at the top of a column of buttons. The elevator door closed silently and Tallon/Bach felt the car move up. A moment later the door opened into a large room with an oval glass ceiling over a competition-sized swimming pool.

The area was decorated in a desert motif including tropical trees, flowers and furniture suggestive of Arabia. Bell and Tallon/Bach followed Malibi to a circular table at the far end of the pool. Tallon/Bach and Bell approached the table. The largest human being Tallon/Bach thought she had ever seen met them. He had to be at least seven feet tall and had massive proportions. He had black shoulder length hair and was clothed in a full-length robe. His hands were so large they were misshapen and his wrists were at least six inches in circumference. Bell went into instant alert.

"I would like to introduce you to Sheik Abu Mactar Kahn, the Emir's personal assistant. He would greet you but he speaks very infrequently. So I will speak for him. Mr. Bell, please remove the weapon from the small of your back."

"I don't think I will," said Bell. Mactar Kahn removed a semi-automatic handgun from a fold in his robe and pointed it at Bell's head.

"Give him the gun now!" exclaimed Malibi. "Mactar Kahn will shoot him between the eyes. We want to talk to you not him. Don't be foolish."

"Give him the gun Fred," said Tallon/Bach.

As Bell reached behind his back, Mactar Kahn cocked the semi automatic.

"Use two fingers and hand it to him," said Malibi.

Bell did as he was instructed and handed over the plastic automatic to Mactar Kahn who threw it into the pool.

"This is outrageous!" exclaimed Tallon/Bach.

"Mr. Bell serves as my security. What would you expect? Look at the security around here not to mention your friend."

"You told the guards at the gate you were not armed. You lied. You must think we are stupid people. A mistake often made by Westerners. The elevator we came up in also serves as the equivalent of an airport whole body scanner. We knew Mr. Bell was armed the moment you entered." "But let us not waste any more time," said Malibi.

"Why exactly are you here?"

"We've already discussed why I am here. This is a business meeting," replied Tallon/Bach.

"Kahn," said Malibi. At that Abu Mactar Kahn lowered his automatic and shot Bell twice, once in each shoulder dropping Bell to the floor with blood hemorrhaging from his wounds.

"You bitch!" exclaimed Tallon/Bach.

As Tallon/Bach reached for Malibi, Kahn reached over and pinched a nerve at the base of her neck. She went limp and Kahn caught her before her head hit the floor.

When Tallon/Bach regained consciousness, she tried to move and discovered she was naked with her hands and feet secured to a chair with plastic handcuffs. Malibi was seated in a chair opposite her. She couldn't see Kahn.

"Not exactly the meeting you had in mind, is it…Doctor Tallon?"

Tallon was stunned. "My name is Bach…"

"Stop it. You're insulting me," said Malibi. "Your name is Marjorie Tallon. You are a medical doctor and a pathologist. You are also an FBI agent."

"How could you…" started Tallon.

"Things have a way of coming out," said Malibi. "When we met at the Fruitopia I thought I recognized you from something we were both involved in professionally. And then it came to me. It turns out, Doctor Tallon, that you and I were both in the same anatomy class at Yale Medical School. I wouldn't have even remembered that except that you were awarded the Yale Prize for Excellence in head and neck dissection. I was a runner up for the same prize. And you know what? When I checked the Yale Medical School alumnae web site, there you were, picture and all! Imagine how excited I was. Margie Tallon MD, aka Eileen Bach, President and Executive Director of Advantis Financial Industries!"

Tallon could see that Malibi was gloating.

"And your colleague Mr. Black. Is he an FBI agent as well?"

"And you came up with a way to freeze all our assets at INF Banque Nationale. You almost had me convinced. Almost."

Malibi paused and looked at Tallon. Tallon stared back in silence.

"Well let's get to cases. You came here to meet with the Emir and so you shall. You may not think you are dressed appropriately for a business meeting, but I can assure you, your present attire is perfect for what we have in mind, getting to the naked truth, so to speak. I don't suppose you brought that Hermes Birkin bag with you today."

Malibi actually giggled.

Tallon felt a sharp prick in the side of her neck and she sagged in the chair.

“When will she be ready”, asked the Emir.

“In about ten minutes,” replied Malibi.

“I don’t want her dead, until we know what they know,” said the Emir.

“Oh, she will tell us everything she knows if for no other reason than to save Mr. Bell here.”

Fred Bell had been moved a few feet away from Tallon’s chair. The bullet holes in his shoulders had been stuffed with cotton soaked with a blood-clotting agent. “Can he attack us when he revives?” asked the Emir.

“No. Mactar Kahn’s shots were well placed. Both his humeral heads are broken,” said Malibi. “He will be in great pain, though, and we will have him secured to the floor.”

“Excellent,” said the Emir, a bubble of spittle forming on one side of his mouth. “Look, she is stirring. We can begin.”

HANS GREFFEN RESIDENCE 1257 SONNENBERGSTRASSE APARTMENT 5 BERNE, SWITZERLAND FEBRUARY 20, 2012 4:30 PM

Makin/Black had called Greffen later in the day on February 18th. He told Greffen he would pick him and his family up and to have his family packed and ready to depart by 5:00 PM on February 20th. Makin/Black also told Greffen not to tell anyone he was leaving.

Makin/Black arrived at the Greffen family residence at 1257 Sonnenbergstrasse. He was driving a Ford stretch SUV to accommodate himself, Greffen, his wife and two children, and their luggage. He parked the SUV in front of the building, walked in and pressed the button for Apartment 5.

Greffen answered: "Yes? Who is this?"

"Black" was the reply.

Greffen buzzed Black in, and he took the elevator up to Apartment 5 on the fourth floor.

The elevator door opened to a paneled corridor. Another door opened at the end and Greffen waived Makin down. "Mr. Black. I don't know how to thank you."

Black entered the apartment's foyer and followed Greffen to a large, well furnished living room. "We are sad to be leaving."

"Is your family ready?" asked Black.

At that moment a somewhat overweight woman, together with a boy about fourteen years old and a girl about twelve, entered the room each carrying a suitcase.

"Frieda, this is Mr. Black. Mr. Black, this is my wife Frieda, our son Rolf and our daughter, Heidi."

Black nodded and asked: "Are you all ready to go?"

"We are," replied Frieda. There was a knock at the door.

"Who could that be?" asked Greffen.

"I asked our neighbor Mrs. Blumquist from apartment four to come over to say goodbye," said Frieda.

"Don't open the door!" exclaimed Black as Heidi ran down the hall and opened the door.

Mrs. Blumquist had somehow been transformed into a bearded, black haired man pointing a Glock 31, 357, magnum automatic. He propelled Heidi forward toward Makin/Black. He ripped open his shirt yelling "Allahu Akbar" and pressed a button.

The ensuing explosion incinerated Makin and Heidi immediately and blew Frieda, Greffen and Rolf into pieces splattered around the walls. The black haired man's body dissolved below his head and the head bounced off the ceiling and came to rest in a corner of what was left of the room. The glass from the apartment windows showered the street and the fireball was seen two miles away. Mrs. Blumquist missed it all. She was sprawled in the living room of Apartment 4, a bullet hole between her eyes and the 'going away' gift box of Stam European Chocolates she had purchased for Heidi Greffen still in her hand.

Asher Finkel received a call on his private line at Holy Innocents Monastery. "Doctor Finkel, this is N.S.A. Communications. Mr. Makin's secure phone has stopped transmitting."

"Do you have a GPS fix on its final location?" asked Finkel.

"Yes, sir. When it stopped transmitting, it was located at 1257 Sonnenbergstrasse in Berne, Switzerland."

2ND SUBBASEMENT BUILDING 2 ABANDONED INDUSTRIAL PARK COMPLEX BLACK FOREST, COLORADO FEBRUARY 20, 2012 4:55 AM MOUNTAIN TIME

Ankyer, followed by Emily Tyson, entered the second subbasement of building 2. They were in an antechamber in front of which was a glass door. "This is a bio containment level four enclosure," said Tyson. "I heard there was one in the building, but I've never seen one. I know there is a similar lab at the CDC and at a government lab at Johns Hopkins Medical School. This is amazing. We are in a depressurization room that will equalize the pressure with the rest of the facility. I am assuming that there is negative pressure, which prevents any bio hazardous pathogens from escaping into the rest of the building. If I press that red button on the wall it should equalize the pressure with the rest of the containment area."

Ankyer pressed the red button. There was a whooshing sound and a click. He pulled at the door and it opened automatically. The door was about two inches thick and appeared to be made of some kind of clear plastic material. They found themselves in a very large room with more glass-enclosed rooms on each side and on the back wall. From what Ankyer could see, each room was about twenty feet wide and thirty feet long and had a door similar to the one they had just entered as well as observation windows made of the same material.

"What are these doors and windows made from?" Ankyer asked.

"If it's the same as the door we just went through, I'm pretty sure they are made from an acrylic resin which is exceptionally hard and non porous. It's pretty standard for a bio level four containment environment. This is amazing," said Tyson.

Ankyer walked up to the first room and looked in. Tyson came up to Ankyer's side, looked and then gagged. Inside the room were six gurneys, each containing a body. Each body was secured to its gurney by straps around the arms, legs and throat with a gag in the mouth. There was an instrument table at the head of each gurney. All of the bodies were in various stages of dissection, with the eyes open.

"I've read about this but have never seen one," said Tyson and paused to swallow.

"It is a vivisection laboratory," she said. "They were used in World War II to experiment on humans exposed to plague and other types of germ warfare pathogens. The German doctor Josef Mengele had a similar lab at Auschwitz to test exposure times to frigid water along with other experiments. The Japanese were worse. They had a whole system of facilities they called Unit 731 in China and Japan, which subjected people to terrible experiments with biological and chemical substances. At the end of the war the US and its allies let the German and Japanese scientists go, in order to get access to the experiments' results. Doctor McGinty must have been doing the same kind of thing here. Look. There are vents in the room's ceiling. He probably introduced a non-lethal level of nano VX into the room, which would have been inhaled by the people on the tables. The residual nano VX would have then been removed from the room through the other vent. Then he went in and dissected the bodies to determine the effects of the nano VX on the organs."

"Why did he dissect them alive?" asked Ankyer.

"He was probably determining the time it took for the nano VX to infuse into specific organs and destroy them. Look at the bodies. They are both male and female and different sizes and weights. I can't be sure, but he was probably trying to calibrate the formulation and dosage of the nano VX so that it would rapidly kill who ever it came in contact with regardless of size, age or gender. One thing is for sure. The pests Doctor McGinty is trying to eradicate are not insects. It is humans McGinty is trying to eradicate. If he is in fact calibrating dosage levels, there are probably a lot more bodies down here."

Ankyer walked rapidly down the hall, looking in each window on his left and right. Each room was similar. More dissection tables and bodies. One room had all women. Another room held all men. Still another room contained all children. Ankyer kept a mental count. Sixty bodies, and he was only half way down the hall. He stopped at one window. The room was piled with at least thirty charred bodies. Tyson caught up with him and looked in. "Jesus!" she exclaimed.

"Why are the bodies piled in here?" asked Ankyer.

Tyson looked at the room.

"It's different from the others," she said. "Look at the walls. They are metal. There are also metal shutters folded on either side of the window and ignition ports along the bottom of the walls. It also looks like there are ports for squirting flammable material into the enclosure. This room is for disposal. It's a crematorium!"

As they continued down the hallway they encountered a small office with a lab coat hanging from the back of a chair by a desk. Angus McGinty PhD was inscribed over a pocket on the front of the jacket.

"There's no doubt now that this was McGinty's domain," said Ankyer.

Ankyer quickly scanned the desk and pulled out the drawers. Nothing. Under the desk there was a small trash basket filled with pages of computer printouts. Ankyer dumped the contents of the basket on the desktop and quickly scanned the material. The papers were formatted as Excel spread sheets and contained numbers, times, and various cryptic notations. A wrinkled post-it note had attached itself to the back of a printout page. '1217 State' was scribbled on the note. Ankyer put the note in an arm pocket of his body wrap. As he left the office he heard:

"Mr. Ankyer! Down here!"

Ankyer walked quickly out of the office and trotted down to Tyson several windows away.

"Look" she said.

Ankyer looked in the window and saw what appeared to be some kind of small, rectangular air conditioner unit attached to a PVC pipe coming out of the wall. Two oxygen tank sized cylinders also had conduits, which were attached to another side of the device. Three decomposing bodies tied to chairs were also in the room looking out at them through empty eye sockets.

"I have no idea what this is," said Tyson.

"I know what it is," said Ankyer. "It's a steam generator, or at least a prototype of one. They are going to use them to disperse the nano VX into the human population."

"That's diabolical," said Tyson.

"It looks like McGinty tried it out, if the bodies are any indication," said Ankyer.

"I would say it worked," replied Tyson.

Down the hall an arm snaked out of a doorway and pitched a green oval object.

"Grenade!" yelled Ankyer, opened the steam generator room door, pulled Tyson in after him and closed the door. A bright flash and thunderous clap ensued. Inside the room there was a surreal quiet. The glass window flexed but did not break or even crack.

"This room is blast proof," said Tyson. "Standard issue for a bio level four containment lab."

"Stay down and keep your mask on," said Ankyer. "This room may still be contaminated."

Ankyer reached into his combat pack and took out a flash/bang grenade. As he was about to open the door, a second explosion rocked the corridor, but the room held. Ankyer opened the door and dove out into the smoke filled corridor. He lobbed the flash/bang grenade, from the prone position, down the hallway toward the source of the other grenades. He heard it bounce and then a vicious explosion followed by a horrendous thunderclap filled the hall. Ankyer sprang to his feet and sprinted toward the end of the hall. A martyr/guard was rolling on the ground with blood coming from his ears, nose and the sides of his eyes.

Ankyer brought the H&K UMP 45 around and placed three rounds in the martyr/guard's forehead, being careful not to deliver a center mass shot in case he was wearing a suicide vest, which it turned out, he was. Ankyer ripped open the martyr/guard's shirt and pulled the wires out of the cell phone detonator. Ankyer then looked up and stared in disbelief. He was in front of the window of the last room in the hallway. Behind the window were a beverage machine, a vending machine for sandwiches, and a refrigerator. Among all the carnage on the floor the bastards even had a break room. Also occupying the room were four more martyr/guards. They were smiling and pointing at Ankyer. One was shaking two fingers at Ankyer, the European equivalent of the Western middle finger, and another martyr/guard was waiving an AK-47 and pointing it at Ankyer.

The guard fired his AK-47, the bullet striking the acrylic window, creating a small hairline crack and fell to the floor. A second guard had opened his shirt revealing a suicide vest. Ankyer reached in his combat pack and pulled out his transponder. He backed down the hall away from the window and pushed the red button. Ankyer wasn't certain if the transponder's signal would penetrate the thick acrylic window, but nothing ventured, nothing gained. Ankyer gained. Multiple martyr vest explosions blew out the window and ejected a mass of red matter, vending machine parts and other flotsam across the hall and through another window opposite the first. "So much for blast proof rooms," Ankyer thought. "The AK-47 bullet must have weakened the window just enough."

A river of greyish green and red goo started spreading from under the door of the break room. Ankyer walked over to the former break room and looked in through the smoke and flames. The four martyr/guards had disappeared, heads and all. The room had actually contained and focused the blast through the window leaving the room a charred mass of rubble. The room's contents, including the martyr/guards, had disappeared. At the rate the martyr/guards were losing their lease on life, Paradise was going to run short of virgins, thought Ankyer.

Ankyer walked rapidly along the hall. He noticed more gas cylinders filling several rooms as he passed them by. Ankyer stopped at the steam generator room, reached under Tyson's arm and helped her up.

"It's time for us to go," he said. Ankyer and Tyson walked quickly down the hall through the anteroom door and out the security door. They trotted up the stairwell and out the door past the dead martyr/guard. Varna was there, still in a sitting position.

"Varna, 'relax', said Ankyer. The wolf walked up to Ankyer and sat at his feet.

"I didn't think a wolf could be trained," said Tyson.

"They can't," replied Ankyer. "But they can understand words and intent by the timber of the voice," continued Ankyer. "If he detected fear or concern in my voice he would instantly go back into guard mode. It's like having a high powered rifle with an exceedingly delicate hair trigger."

Ankyer, Tyson and Varna emerged from the basement stairs into the lobby of building 2.

"Where were you housed?" asked Ankyer.

"We were in a basement of building 3, but everyone except me is dead. There probably is no one in the building now,"Tyson replied.

"What about the guards? Where were they housed?"

"Building 4, I think. At least that's the building we would see most of them going in and out of sometimes,"Tyson said. As Ankyer started to reply, Varna lay down and started panting. Jake knelt down and checked the compression bandage on Varna's side. Frothy blood had started to seep out.

Ankyer reached into his combat pack and withdrew his secure tactical phone. He pressed a button on the side twice. There was a slight squelch and Neil's voice came through.

Neil said, "Go ahead Jake."

"Neil, Varna has been injured during the operation. It looks like he may have a punctured lung. We need to get him to a vet ASAP."

"We are on our way into your location now. We have an extra Black Hawk with us. You can load him in with you and head back to the hangar. We'll put a call into Father Bruno to have another helicopter pick Varna up at the hangar and medevac him back to his vet at the Monastery."

"Good idea," said Ankyer.

"Varna will take the hand off anyone else who tries to touch him. What's you're ETA?" "We're less than five minutes out," said Neil.

"There are five buildings, four in a semi-circle and one in the middle. Starting at the left of the semi-circle the buildings are numbered on the upper right hand corner. I am at building 2. I have a laboratory worker with me. Assume you are landing in a 'hot landing zone'."

"Roger that," said Neil. "We've been monitoring you in infrared via the satellite link. You've been busy."

"That's an understatement," replied Ankyer.

"We're here," said Neil. Three Black Hawk MH-60 stealth helicopters dropped down out of the night sky in front of building 5, followed by the MV-22 Osprey.

Neil walked up to Ankyer, who pulled his Draeger mask down.

"So what's the situation?" asked Neil.

"I've eliminated around fifteen guards both outside the buildings and inside building 2," said Ankyer. "Building 2 houses the labs where they converted the VX to nano VX. McGinty was involved in human experimentation. It's very nasty in the second sub- basement in there. They also executed all the scientific workers who, by the way, thought they were working on some kind of pesticide project." Ankyer motioned over to Tyson. "This is Emily Tyson. She's the sole survivor of the science staff. Emily has been very helpful and needs to be carefully debriefed. I'll take her back to the hangar with me and Varna."

Neil looked over at Tyson.

"We'll use the spare Black Hawk helicopter to get you, Emily and Varna back to the hangar," he said.

"There are also about 200 gas cylinders that may be filled with both VX and nano VX," continued Ankyer. "You're going to need a HAZMAT team to clear the cylinders. They are also going to be needed to remove the bodies of the people who were experimented on. They are probably all infected with VX."

"We've got FBI HAZMAT personnel and a CDC infection control team on standby as soon as you exfil out of here," said Neil.

"Three other things," said Ankyer. "The site is not completely secure. Emily thinks that the guards are housed in building 4. I've only eliminated guards I've encountered either outside or in building 2. Your team is going to have to secure the site before the CDC and the FBI HAZMAT people arrive. Most of these guys are wearing suicide vests so you need to go for head and neck shots."

"That shouldn't be a problem…" Neil started to say before he was interrupted by gunfire coming from a second story window in building 4. "Incoming!" yelled Neil and they all dropped down, Ankyer pulling Tyson down beside him.

"Do you want to try the transponder?" asked Neil. Ankyer pulled out the transponder and pressed the red button. There were two explosions, one on the second floor of building 4 and one on the first.

"It looks like the transponder works best in a 'line of sight' situation in a building or out in the open," said Ankyer.

"Some of them may have figured out someone is fucking with them," said Neil. Another burst of gunfire came from an outside wall of building 4. "Time to make things interesting. Stay down," said Neil.

He activated his throat mike and spoke a few muffled words. The Osprey MV-22 helicopter lifted off from its station one hundred yards from the buildings. It hovered fifty yards from building 4 and opened up with its General Dynamics, GAU-19/A, .50 caliber, six-barrel, Gatling gun firing at 8000 rounds per minute. The entire front of building 4 was obliterated within thirty seconds. There were several additional explosions in what remained of building 4. Probably suicide vests going off. The building was engulfed in flames, which were rapidly spreading to building 3.

"I'll bet that got their terrorist ass attention," said Neil.

An open backed pickup truck carrying at least six guards accelerated from behind building 4, headed toward an open field. The Osprey pivoted from its firing position toward building 4 and aimed at the rapidly receding truck. The Gatling gun fired again. The truck, which by now was almost a half-mile away, ignited with a massive explosion and fireball.

"Looks like the guards were all dressed to blow up," said Ankyer.

"Head or neck shots my ass," replied Neil.

Ankyer helped Tyson up from the ground.

"Neil, there are two more things." "I found what looks like a steam generator prototype for dispersing the nano VX," said Ankyer. "It's in building 2, the second subbasement about half way down the hall on the right. You need to get that to Doctor Finkel right away. It may help us determine how it's supposed to work and how effective it is."

"Roger that," said Neil. Two SEALS ran up carrying a litter.

"Where's Varna?" one asked.

"Over there," said Ankyer pointing about twenty feet away. They ran over, loaded Varna onto the litter, and jogged back to the Black Hawk. "We need to get out of here," said Ankyer. "The third thing is tell Doctor Finkel that McGinty left yesterday with Ibram el Farsi." Emily said they might be headed for Chicago but she's not sure."

"Ok," said Neil. "Once again you get to have all the fun, pick up frequent flyer miles and get the girl," he said reaching up and slapping Ankyer on the back.

"Clean living, Neil," said Ankyer. He took Tyson's hand and started running toward the Black Hawk. When they got to the helicopter, Ankyer helped Tyson in, and jumped in himself. The Black Hawk revved its engine and pulled up and out over the tree line and disappeared. The Osprey pilot landed several yards from Neil. The pilot opened the side window. "Who was that guy?" the pilot asked. "What guy?" Neil said.

DENVER INTERNATIONAL AIRPORT US ARMY RESTRICTED RUNWAY AND HANGAR FEBRUARY 20, 2012 8:47 AM MOUNTAIN TIME

The Black Hawk dropped down silently and came to rest just outside the hangar doors. A tow vehicle was connected to the helicopter and the Black Hawk was pulled into the hangar and parked in a maintenance bay. Ankyer jumped out of the side door and immediately saw the Holy Innocents Monastery's F/A-18F Super Hornet parked two bays over. Ankyer was approached by a short, round, bearded figure dressed in a surgical gown.

Brother Melbin, a veterinary-surgeon-turned-monk said: "Doctor Finkel didn't want to wait to get Varna back to us, so I'm making a house call. Ankyer smiled and gave Brother Melbin a one-armed hug.

"Careful," Brother Melbin said. I'm fragile.

"Sorry," said Ankyer, "but you don't get out of hugs."

"Where's my patient?" asked Brother Melbin.

Two of the Black Hawk's crewmembers had transferred Varna to a rolling cart and wheeled him over to Ankyer and Brother Melbin.

"Where do you want this guy?" one asked.

Brother Melbin pointed toward a brightly lit, draped area in the back of the hangar. "Over there," he said.

As Varna was being wheeled to the back, Ankyer noticed a man and a short Asian woman with long black hair, also dressed in scrubs, waiting by the entrance of the brightly lit area. "I called in a couple of my vet buddies from the area just in case," said Brother Melbin.

"In case of what?" Ankyer asked.

"Just in case," said Brother Melbin.

"I didn't know the extent of Varna's injuries so I've pulled in some experts in canine trauma. I promised them some Monastery fruitcakes for Christmas."

"You and Brother William are dangerous," said Ankyer.

"Part of our charm," said Brother Melbin.

Varna was wheeled into the enclosure, which took on the aspect of a field hospital operating room.

"So what happened?" asked Brother Melbin.

"Varna and I tangled with a large mountain lion. He killed it but got his side injured in the process. I put a combat bandage on but it looks like its leaking frothy blood."

"Ok. That's consistent with what Doctor Finkel told me. He said the mountain lion also bit you?" "On my left shoulder."

"Let me have the brain sample," said Brother Melbin. Ankyer reached into his body wrap and handed over the sample.

"I'll have it checked out for rabies when I get back."

The tiny Asian woman, who looked to Ankyer as if she weighed ninety pounds, walked over and said, "Bend down a little, you're too tall for me to see."

Ankyer did as she asked. She pulled at the body wrap material and slit it open with a scalpel she was holding.

"Nasty bite. Wait one."

She walked over to an instrument tray, picked up two syringes and walked back. She plunged one syringe and then the other into Ankyer's shoulder.

"Ouch," said Ankyer.

"Don't be such a big baby. They are antibiotic and tetanus shots," she said.

"Jake, this is Doctor Honey Pi and Doctor Murray."

Ankyer started to say something.

Doctor Pi said: "Before you say anything, it's my real name and its spelled 'Pi'."

"I would never have guessed otherwise," replied Ankyer.

"See your doctor whenever you get back from doing whatever you do. And stand by the door away from the operating table," Pi continued.

"You are filthy and smell terrible."

"It's been a long day so far," said Ankyer smiling.

"Doctor Pi is also an MD. She prefers treating animals to humans. So what do we have here?" asked Brother Melbin, as he walked over to the operating table.

Varna was not pleased and started to growl and bared his teeth.

"Oops," said Brother Melbin producing a syringe and injecting Varna's hind end with some purple fluid.

Varna's eyes immediately rolled up and his head went back down.

"Nighty night sweetie," said Brother Melbin

"That's by far the largest wolf I've ever seen," said Doctor Murray.

"He's a Mackenzie Valley Canadian Timber wolf," said Brother Melbin.

"He looks more like a Dire wolf, which doesn't exist any more," said Doctor Murray.

"He may share part of a Dire wolf's genome. We're looking at the possibility back at the Monastery," said Brother Melbin.

"Tell you what," said Doctor Pi.

"You keep your fruitcake and get me a fellowship at the Monastery. You guys are into some pretty cool stuff."

"Not a bad idea," said Brother Melbin.

"I'll check with my many bosses."

By that time Brother Melbin had removed the bloody combat bandage from Varna's side and was shaving the area around the wound. Doctor Pi was bathing the area with antiseptic and Doctor Murray had started a saline drip.

Brother Melbin asked Ankyer: "Got an idea as to what our friend's problem is?"

"I'd say he had a few fractured ribs, one of which punctured a lung," replied Ankyer. Doctor Pi was oblivious, busy spreading an incision she had just made.

"We have a bleeder here!" she said.

"Time to go to work, Jake. I'll let you know what happens. Don't worry," said Brother Melbin.

"Hey!" said Doctor Pi to Ankyer.

"If you hadn't put that compression bandage on the wolf when you did, he wouldn't have made it. The cat lacerated an artery. Your pal here would have been toast. Way to go big guy."

Just then one of the Black Hawk crew looked in and said: "Jake. Someone here to see you." Ankyer turned, opened the medical area's tent flap and walked right into Doctor Asher Finkel. "Jake, we need to talk."

Finkel and Ankyer walked across the hangar and into a small office.

"Jake, George Makin is dead."

"How did it happen?" Ankyer asked.

"He was picking up Hans Greffen and his family at their residence in Berne, so they could be transferred into our protective custody program. Evidently, a suicide bomber got access to the residence while they were there and blew everyone up, including George. We scraped some tissue from the wall and it's George's DNA all right. It looks like the Emir decided to punish Greffen for allowing his funds to be frozen. George was collateral damage." Ankyer sat down on a couch and Finkel pulled up a chair.

"There's more. Margie and Fred Bell have disappeared. They went to the Emir's estate as planned. We also had two CIA operatives there to provide backup if they needed it. Margie and Fred went into the estate with specific instructions not to stay any longer than an hour, no matter what. We haven't seen or heard anything from them for over three and one half hours. In addition to the CIA operatives, we have satellite visual and infrared input and no one has left those premises since Margie and Fred entered. This is my fault. I shouldn't have let George go to Greffen's and I underestimated the Emir when I designed the strategy to establish whether or not he's Saddam Hussein."

"Self recrimination is not going to resolve this problem," said Ankyer.

"This is a war."

"You're correct, of course," replied Finkel.

"What can I do?" asked Ankyer.

"I want you to go and get Margie and Fred," said Finkel.

"I don't know how much time we have. It may already be too late. I realize that retrieving people is not in your operational portfolio. I'm asking this as a favor."

"You never have to ask me for a favor," replied Ankyer.

"Thanks. The estate has at least four guards at the gate. I think given recent history we must assume they are wearing suicide vests. There are also a number of Doberman Pincers. We think five, that are given free reign throughout the grounds. As far as we can tell they don't bark, so it looks like military bark suppression treatment has been administered. Here are pictures of front, side and top elevations of the building itself taken from the satellite cams."

"What's that clear area on part of the roof?" asked Ankyer.

"We think it's a glass roof over a solarium or similar type room."

"I should be able to 'fast rope' down to the roof and possibly get in through that glass covering. I'll need a silenced helicopter."

"I have a Hughes OH-6A Cayuse Loach on standby."

"Is that the silenced 500P Penetrator version?" asked Ankyer.

"That's it. I also had two enclosed medevac stretchers attached just in case they are needed," replied Finkel.

"How do I get there fast?" Ankyer asked. "That's why I had Brother Melbin brought in on the Super Hornet," said Finkel. "I figured you could use it to quickly get to Long Island. And I didn't want to take a chance with Varna so I had the operating theater set up here. Your flight suit is in the ready room. Your combat pack has also been replenished and I included a new transponder in case the one you used on your last mission was damaged."

"Thanks. Did Neil tell you about the steam generator prototype?" "Yes. That could be a break for us. There are not many companies that manufacture that type of equipment. Hopefully we will be able to identify the manufacturer and trace locations where units have been delivered. The unit you found is on its way to the Monastery as we speak." "Neil told you about McGinty and el Farsi?" Ankyer asked.

"Yes," replied Finkel.

"They seem to be one step ahead of us," Finkel continued. "We are monitoring Chicago cell tower traffic. If el Farsi calls Malibi using his cell, we can track them down that way. We are a little concerned that if McGinty has concluded his nano VX conversion, they may kill him as a means to seal off that part of their plan."

"I would normally agree," said Ankyer, "except McGinty was engaged in human experimentation right up there with the Nazi's and Japanese. That may be enough to make him part of the team of these evil bastards."

"Could be," replied Finkel.

"By the way, I found a crumpled note in a room with McGinty's lab coat in it." Ankyer pulled out the note and gave it to Finkel. "1217 State. There's a State street in Chicago. I'll check into it," said Finkel.

"I'd better get going," said Ankyer.

"Thanks again Jake. I've cleared military air space for your trip. You should get there in about two hours. I've obtained a military traffic corridor at 52,000 feet. The Hornet has also been mounted with an auxiliary fuel pod so it's a direct supersonic flight. You'll be coming into Long Island Islip MacArthur Airport. There's a military hangar in the back. That's where the Loach is. Your other gear will be there as well."

"I'll get them back. Don't worry," said Ankyer as he left the office and walked toward the Ready Room.

As Ankyer approached the Ready Room, the Super Hornet pilot caught up with him.

"You're picking up a pile of miles on this trip," said the pilot.

"Hey Carl. Good to see you." They entered the ready room and Carl put two paper sacks on the table. "I figured you might be hungry. There's a burger joint just off the airport road, Jumpin' Jack's Burger Heaven. The home of the Wally Burger."

"Wally Burger?" said Ankyer.

"I asked the same question when I ordered and was told that Wally is dead, possibly from eating his own food, but his burger lives on. Anyway, I got you two double bacon cheddar Wally burgers with chili. There's Mountain Dew in the fridge over in the corner."

"Carl, are you trying to kill me along with everybody else?"

"Come on man. Are you some kind of wimp?" asked Carl.

"I'd show you what kind of wimp I was if I wasn't so damn tired." They both laughed. Carl brought over a flight suit.

"Looks like your camouflage wrap is shot to shit," said Carl.

"They have another one for you at the other end."

"Thanks," replied Ankyer.

"Be sure to have this one packed in with my other gear," he said.

"It might still come in handy."

"That's a Roger," said Carl.

While Carl was talking, Ankyer had stripped down to his shorts. Carl took his Wally burgers out of their wrappers.

"Whoa!" came an exclamation from the ready room doorway. Doctor Honey Pi was standing there looking at Ankyer.

"Wow, are you ever cut!" she exclaimed.

"You want a girlfriend? You didn't get that way from eating those for-shit Wally burgers. I could smell them thirty yards away!"

"Brother Melbin wanted me to let you know that we are finished with Varna. He'll be fine. We're loading him up on one of those black helicopters with all the guns and stuff for the trip back to the Monastery. Brother Melbin said Varna is the Alpha male in the wolf pack you guys have there. He also said that Varna would have to be kept from the pack until he regains his strength or they will eat him or something. What the hell do you guys do there, exactly? Don't answer that. By the way, your right triceps is slightly larger than your left. That doesn't mean bupkis unless you head into some kind of bodybuilding. If you decide to do that, let me know and I'll fix you up with a little more training. One thing's for sure, though. Nobody's going to kick sand in your face any time soon! I'm out of here."

And with that, Doctor Honey Pi turned and walked away.

"Was that my imagination or was there a really hot, short, Asian woman in here with a four lane wide attitude, a minute ago?" asked Carl.

"She's real, alright," said Ankyer.

"By the way, how's your Wally Burger?" asked Carl.

"Fabulous," replied Ankyer.

As they finished their meal Carl said: "We need to bail out of here. The Super Hornet's gassed up and ready to go. Do you want to drive or shall I?"

"You drive," said Ankyer. "I need to grab some sleep." Ankyer put on his flight suit. "Here's your helmet for the ride. We'll store your combat headgear and this moldy camo wrap with your other equipment on the Hornet," said Carl.

Ankyer got into his flight suit, picked up his flight helmet, and he and Carl headed out the door of the Ready Room walking toward the Super Hornet. Ankyer climbed up into the back seat of the Hornet and Carl into the front. The Hornet was pulled out of the hangar by a plane tug, and released. Carl closed the canopy and contacted the Tower.

"This is Super A Niner requesting clearance for takeoff. Over"

"Super A Niner this is the Tower. You are immediately cleared for takeoff. Proceed to military runway AA. All traffic into and out of the airport is holding pending your ascent directly to your assigned military corridor of 52,000 feet. Please ascend on a heading of 253 degrees, tactical squelch."

"Roger that," said Carl.

Brother Melbin and Doctor Honey Pi walked out the hangar door just in time to see the Super Hornet taxi to runway AA.

"Is the 'big guy' in the plane?" asked Honey Pi.

"He's in the back seat," replied Brother Melbin.

The Super Hornet turned on the runway and started rolling forward, the dual thunder rapidly rising in intensity. The plane increased its speed down the runway and lifted off. "That's a lot louder than a commercial aircraft," remarked Honey Pi.

"Wait," said Brother Melbin.

The Super Hornet executed a shallow bank to its assigned heading, tilting its nose up. Carl lit the engines' afterburners. The Super Hornet's engines screamed and the plane shot straight up and out of sight. Honey Pi stood there with her mouth open.

"Welcome to the world of Jake Ankyer," said Brother Melbin.

"Doctor Finkel asked if you would be willing to accompany him, Varna and me back to the Abbey. I think he wants to talk to you about a job."

"In a heart beat!" said Doctor Honey Pi.

"Excellent," said Brother Melbin.

"Why did you stop treating humans in favor of animals," Brother Melbin asked.

"The diversity of animals intrigued me," said Pi.

"But you've remained current in human medicine?" asked Brother Melbin.

"Absolutely. I'm Board Certified in internal medicine with a subspecialty in neurology." "You will find that useful," said Brother Melbin.

"Jake is not only a superb physical specimen, his mental acuity is off the charts as measured by his intelligence quotient results. He has a consistent IQ of 170 on a range of tests."

"You've got to be kidding," said Pi.

"Jake does have a little advantage. He has been neurologically enhanced." "At what research facility?" asked Honey Pi.

"At the Abbey. There is an advanced neurology lab there financed by the N.S.A."

"I can't wait!" exclaimed Pi.

"When is my interview?" Pi asked.

"You've just had it," replied Brother Melbin.

"There is an onerous, nondisclosure agreement you will have to sign. You won't want to sign it... but you will. Everyone does."

Doctor Finkel walked over. "Thanks for considering our little job offer. You will effectively have one patient, Jake Ankyer. He sometimes comes back from field assignments in worse condition than when he leaves. Although being bitten by a mountain lion is a first. We maintain a highly granular medical record on him, but several different physicians usually see him. We need one physician who can provide continuity of care as well as manage the specialty team. That would be you."

"Absolutely!" exclaimed Pi. "That definitely would be me."

EMIR'S MANSION
7 EARLY BIRD LANE
LONG BEACH
LONG ISLAND, NEW YORK
FEBRUARY 20, 2012
1:30 PM EASTERN TIME

Tallon started to wake. She felt as if she had been dreaming. Dark dreams. Questions. She fought them off. She couldn't move. She opened her eyes and vomited. She was still naked, but had been moved from the chair and immersed in the shallow end of the pool. Her ankles were shackled to the pool bottom and her wrists were spread and secured by short chains to metal loops imbedded in the edge of the lip of the pool wall.

"Ah, Doctor Tallon. You are back with us," said Malibi.

"We were having a conversation, you and I. I know about Holy Innocents Monastery. It sounds like a fascinating place. And Jake Ankyer! What an interesting man. I think you are in love with him. You wouldn't say what he does, but we'll find out. We'll be visiting the Holy Innocents Monastery and Mr. Ankyer in the near future."

"Fred," said Tallon weakly.

"Oh. You mean Mr. Bell. He's right here off to your right. Turn your head and you can see him." Tallon turned her head. Fred Bell was also naked and was lying face up on the floor with his arms and legs splayed out and his hands and feet nailed into the marble. Both his shoulders were black and blue with bullet holes and were seeping blood.

"Mr. Bell looks dead but he's not. Not yet anyway. Your job is to fill in some of the blanks from when you were questioned under sodium thiopental. Mr. Bell's job is to feel intense pain as an inducement for you to cooperate."

"I'll demonstrate."

"Mactar!" The huge man Tallon had seen before came into her field of vision. He walked over to Bell, placed a large foot on Bell's injured right shoulder and pressed down. Bell screamed until his voice changed into a weak whimper.

"See," said Malibi.

"He remains alive. How much longer depends on you."

"But before we begin, you had expressed a desire to have a conversation with the Emir. It would be unfair to cause you and Mr. Bell all the pain you are about to endure without at least achieving the objective of your visit."

"And now, Doctor Marjorie Tallon, pathologist and FBI agent, I have to leave for a few minutes, but before I do, I would like you to meet the Emir."

Tallon tried to turn her head and body but her range of motion, given her position in the pool, was limited.

"Hello Doctor Tallon," said a soft male voice behind her right ear. "How nice of you to come and visit us."

Tallon was slightly bent over due to the chains securing her wrists to the side of the pool. She could however, see that the man walking into her field of vision was about six feet two inches and guessed his weight to be around two hundred and twenty pounds. His hair was black with grey streaks, his eyes dark brown, and he had a mustache speckled with gray. She watched him.

"You are quite a beautiful woman and very desirable. I imagine you have your way with most men. Most men. But there are always exceptions to every rule. The exception to your rule is standing behind you. Abu!"

A hand grabbed the back of Tallon's neck, almost encircling it. The hand squeezed and Tallon immediately retched into the pool water.

The Emir continued, speaking softly. "Sheik Abu Mactar Kahn. He hates women. He hates the way they appear. He hates the air they breathe. There is absolutely nothing you could do or say to persuade him not to rip you apart, piece by piece. Nothing. If you tell us what we need to know, you will be spared that outcome. By the way, your friend Phillip Black is dead. Blown up along with Hans Greffen and his family. Was Mr. Black an FBI agent as well?"

Tallon noticed the Emir's eyes were expressionless when he spoke. His voice was monotonal as well. She studied the movement of his head as he spoke.

"See, Doctor Tallon, we know you are not an FBI agent at the moment. What we don't know is what you are. This charade you and Mr. Black played with Hans Greffen has not fooled us. No drug cartel, however large or influential, could have persuaded Heidi Riekert at the Swiss Financial Markets Authority to freeze our assets at INF. It had to be some other, much larger organization."

"My feeling is that we should kill you and Mr. Bell right now. Doctor Malibi is of the opinion, however, that you work for someone else; possibly someone who can damage our plans or at least interfere with us in some way. She has persuaded me that we should try to find out. Abu, leave the pool." Tallon felt the hand release her neck and heard some splashing. She saw Malibi re enter the pool area through double glass doors and hand what appeared to be a TV remote to the Emir. A shiver ran through her and her knees started to sag to the floor of the pool. The chains stopped her.

The Emir looked down at Tallon with vacant eyes.

"Do you know who Uday Hussein was, Doctor Tallon?"

"I'm sorry. I don't want to insult you. Of course you do. Uday was not very bright, but he could be creative when inflicting pain on others. As you may know, Uday was President of the Iraq Olympic Committee at the Salt Lake City Olympic games in 2002. Uday's soccer team did not do well, and when they returned Uday held a meeting in the basement of the Iraq Olympic Committee headquarters. Uday had the soccer team captain stripped naked and tied to the metal springs of a mattress. He then instructed a guard to connect a car battery. Uday decided right afterwards to piss on the soccer captain and completed the circuit as the battery was being connected. The soccer captain was electrocuted and Uday got quite a shock. But Uday also learned a lesson and applied his new appreciation of electricity to many others including the rest of the soccer team."

"Being close to Uday, he was happy to share his newfound knowledge with me. I don't have mattress springs of course, but let me show you what I do have."

A smile crossed the Emir's lips and he pushed a button on a remote control box he held. Tallon's spine arched, her eyes rolled up and she released a guttural scream that lasted for five seconds, until the Emir released the button. She sagged in the pool, her wrists bleeding from abrasions from the shackles.

"Quite a demonstration, wouldn't you agree?" said the Emir.

Tallon started to retch again and whimpered, trying to catch her breath.

"The circuit is completed by the pool's metal ankle and wrist restraints. The water you are in is salt water. It enhances the electrical conductivity and intensifies the pain of the shock many fold. You are young and evidently in excellent health, so you will not easily succumb to a heart seizure or stroke, or at least that is what Doctor Malibi assures me. Can you imagine the pain and torment you just experienced for five seconds going on for days? Weeks? I think not."

"You son of a bitch!" yelled Bell.

Abu Mactar walked over and mashed his heel into Bell's shoulder. Bell screamed and was then silent. "Is he dead?" asked the Emir. Malibi walked over and placed her fingers on Bell's neck. "No," she said. "Just passed out."

The Emir handed the remote control device to Malibi and spoke briefly in Arabic. He then turned and walked up to the glass doors, which opened automatically and closed after he passed through. Malibi walked up to Tallon.

"Unfortunately, the Emir has an appointment and has left the remainder of our conversation to me. Abu Mactar Kahn has remained to help out, so to speak. We have also been joined by one of our martyr/guards, Moobie. Now, you can save us all time, and yourself considerable discomfort, by telling us exactly who you work for."

Tallon whispered: "The FBI."

Malibi pressed the button on the remote. Tallon arched her back in a rictus of pain and yowled, blood flowing from her wrists into the pool. Malibi released the button after eight seconds, which left Tallon panting with tears streaming down her face.

"Break one of Mr. Bell's hands," Malibi said to Mactar Kahn. Khan walked over to the spread-eagled body of Bell and stomped on his nailed right hand with all his weight. Bell opened his mouth as if to scream but passed out.

"It would appear that Mr. Bell is using the device of passing out to evade his pain. A technique taught in army special forces Sere training I believe," said Malibi. "Unfortunately, that's not good news for you Margie," said Malibi.

"I'm going to leave for awhile. I think we all need a break. If I keep shocking you, you will swallow your tongue and choke to death and we can't have that...at least not yet. Abu Mactar Kahn and Moobie will stay here and keep you company. Don't try to talk to them. Abu Mactar Kahn will not talk to you and Moobie was born deaf and dumb. Think about this. You will eventually tell us whom you work for. No one we have ever encountered has been able to withstand the shocks. You may as well tell me what we need to know, when I get back, to save yourself pain. I might even let you and Mr. Bell live if I'm feeling generous. Who knows?"

Malibi turned to Abu Mactar Kahn. "You will be with Miss Tallon for awhile. I'll be back in several hours. Have dinner brought into the solarium."

Malibi then walked out the glass doors.

After Malibi left, Mactar Kahn instructed Moobie to go to the mansion's kitchen, have food prepared and to bring it back when it was ready. Mactar Kahn would think of ways to keep Tallon occupied in the meanwhile.

Tallon sank into the pool as far as the short chains would let her, the salt water stinging the wounds on her wrists and ankles.

LONG ISLAND ISLIP MACARTHUR AIRPORT LONG ISLAND, NEW YORK FEBRUARY 20, 2012 3:45 PM EASTERN TIME

Static in his flight helmet woke Ankyer up. "Super A Niner this is Islip MacArthur tower 'Over'."

"Islip MacArthur tower this is Super A Niner cruising at 52,000 feet in military air corridor 2577 Alpha, five miles out heading 78 degrees north east. 'Over'," replied Carl.

"Super A Niner you are cleared to land on tactical runway AC, heading sixty degrees northwest. Please taxi to the military hangar runway OO. Traffic at this facility is suspended until you land. Come on in boys, 'Over'."

"Thank you Islip MacArthur tower," said Carl. "We will be on the ground shortly. 'Over'". "Jake. You want to do the landing?" "Sure," he replied.

The Super Hornet executed a sharp right turn and dropped from 52,000 feet to 5,000 feet, banked left, lined up with runway AC, touched down at 250 miles per hour, reversed flaps, popped the drogue chute and came to a stop.

"Super A Niner this is Islip MacArthur tower ground control. Please taxi to ground taxi runway OO. We sure don't see that kind of landing here very often. It's definitely a story for the grandkids. Welcome to Long Island, New York. 'Over'."

"Roger that. Over," replied Carl.

"Nice landing Jake," said Carl. "You haven't lost your touch."

"I could use some more 'touch and go' time."

"I'll arrange it when I get back to the Abbey," said Carl.

Jake taxied the Super Hornet on runway OO, opened the Hornet's canopy, and shut down the engines when he rolled up to the hangar and the ground crewman crossed his batons. A crew chief ran a ladder platform up to the cockpit and Ankyer climbed down.

"You have an urgent call from Doctor Finkel on the secure satellite phone," the crew chief said, handing Ankyer the instrument.

Ankyer pressed the 'talk' button as he was walking toward a crewman waving Ankyer over to a small Ready Room. Ankyer noticed the Hughes OH-6A Cayuse Loach in a maintenance bay being loaded with 50-caliber ammunition for the dual canopy nose guns. "Doctor Finkel, Ankyer here. Any news about Tallon and Bell?"

"Nothing at this point," replied Finkel.

"We still have not heard anything and we are now convinced that the Emir identification plan has gone off the rails."

"What about the Black Forest laboratory?" asked Ankyer walking into the Ready Room.

"It was exactly as you described. Neil's SEAL team found two wounded martyr guards. They had nothing to add and the SEALS dispatched them on the spot. A CDC team is now on site. They said they haven't seen anything like it since the films of Auschwitz. This McGinty is a madman." "That's the same conclusion I came to. Now if only I could find the bastard," said Ankyer."

"On that score, one of the CDC techs is familiar with the steam machine prototype you found. It is only manufactured by two companies and is quite heavy. So heavy in fact that we suspect the machines are being delivered to the actual sites of the nano VX release. We are working to track that aspect down now. I expect that McGinty, being the narcissist he is, will want to be in the same neighborhood as one of the machines to see how well his brainchild works. I'll let you know as soon as we find out something," said Finkel.

"I have a couple other items for you, Jake."

"First, if you run into any more martyr/guards use the new transponder I've sent. Recall you had to obtain a guard's exploding vest cell phone to synchronize your transponder with the other exploding vest phones. The new transponder dynamically searches for signals and will automatically lock on, even if all the exploding vest phones are on different wave lengths."

"Excellent! What else?" Ankyer asked.

"You should have a new tactical camouflage wrap there by now to replace the one shredded by the mountain lion", replied Finkel.

"I think I'll wear the damaged one," replied Ankyer.

"But the rips in the wrap will interfere with the molecular camouflage conductivity across the entire garment," said Finkel.

"I considered that as well, but here's my thinking."

After Ankyer finished his explanation, Finkel said, "Brilliant! I never would have thought of that. If I didn't think Tallon and Bell's lives were in the balance, I'd suggest we try a couple experiments before you go."

"See. I told you my PhD you paid for at the London School of Economics would be useful some day," chuckled Ankyer.

"One other thing," said Ankyer. "I have no idea what condition I'll find Tallon and Bell in when I get there. What kind of medical support will I have?"

"We'll have medical personnel standing by at the Islip MacArthur military hangar. We have also enhanced the medical kit in your combat pack. In addition to the standard issue material and morphine, we have added two external monophasic defibrillators. You will also have two syringes of adrenaline and two syringes of magnesium sulfate in case Tallon and/or Bell present with any heart issues. When you find them, assuming they are still alive, call the Abbey on your tactical phone. Doctor Honey Pi will guide you through whatever you need."

"Honey Pi?" asked Ankyer.

"We are bringing her on board as a coordinating physician for you and other field operatives. You have a number of physicians working on you from time to time and we need a medical focal point. She has a strong neurology background and her veterinary credentials are helpful as well," said Finkel.

"Life just got a lot more interesting," replied Ankyer.

"She'll fit right in."

"We also have two CIA operatives, Oscar and Jason, on site about a mile from the road down to the Emir's mansion. They have a chain gun mounted inside the back of their SUV in the event you need additional tactical support. Their direct link is number 7 on your tactical phone. They are assigned to you, but are not cleared for Saddam Hussein information," said Finkel. "Ok," said Ankyer.

"I'll be ready to go in about thirty minutes. I'll contact the CIA guys before I leave. You know there's a pretty good chance Tallon and Bell are dead," said Ankyer.

"I agree," replied Finkel. "If they are dead, we have to make sure their deaths did not happen in vain."

Ankyer signed off from Finkel and inventoried the items in his combat pack, which had been delivered by that time to the Ready Room. He pulled out his tactical phone, pressed the channel button and scrolled down to '7'. He pressed the talk button. Two clicks later Oscar was on the line.

"This is Oscar."

"Oscar, this is Jake Ankyer. I've been briefed and you and Jason have been assigned to me for the moment."

"Roger that sir."

"What's your location?" asked Ankyer.

"We are a quarter mile from the mouth of Early Bird Lane. We have a satellite visual on the front gate area. It looks like there is a guard house with active players walking around."

"Those would be martyr/guards," said Ankyer.

"Martyr/guards?" questioned Oscar.

"They are all probably wearing suicide vests," said Ankyer

"Jesus!" exclaimed Oscar."

"No, Muhammad," replied Ankyer.

"Oscar, we have to get moving. My mission is to retrieve Tallon and Bell if they are still alive. I'll be coming in on a Cayuse Loach helicopter and will be landing about 200 yards from the mansion and going in from there. You and Jason need to stay put until you hear from me. I'll call on the tactical phone. You may have to tear ass down Early Bird Lane and do a 180 at the gate so you can get your chain gun into position. Depending on my situation, you may have to blow the gate open with it and take out the guardhouse and its occupants. If you hit the guards with the vests, you're looking at the equivalent of multiple IED explosions, so keep back from the gates if you have to open fire."

"They also have dogs up there," said Oscar.

"I think I can handle the dogs, but if you have to blow the gate and see the dogs, take them out along with the guards. I'm leaving here in 15 minutes and should be at the mansion in twenty. I will have the Loach fly over your position so you will know I'm on site." "Roger that," said Oscar. "Out," said Ankyer.

Ankyer replaced the tactical phone in his combat pack, retrieved his damaged tactical body wrap and put it on. He also put on the combat harness along with the crossbow and the H&K UMP 45 in the swivel leg harness. Ankyer walked over to a small refrigerator, opened the door and retrieved a quart of orange Gatorade. As he swigged it down, the Loach pilot entered the Ready Room.

"You about ready Jake?" the pilot asked.

Ankyer finished the Gatorade and said: "I'm ready when you are."

"Ok. We're out of here," said the Loach pilot."

They left the Ready Room and walked over to the Loach. Ankyer eyed the attached medevac stretchers. Ankyer turned to the pilot and said: "One of the people we're possibly medevac'ing is about six three and two hundred and forty pounds."

"Not a problem," said the pilot. We'll cram him in somehow."

Ankyer and the pilot got into the helicopter. A ground crewman detached the battery tender, and made a circling motion with his right arm. The pilot fired up the Loach and it lifted a foot off the ground and headed out of the hangar.

The pilot spoke into his helmet mike: "Islip MacArthur tower ...military aircraft ASD1 requesting clearance for emergency takeoff."

"Military aircraft ASD1 this is Islip MacArthur tower. You are cleared for immediate takeoff. Please vector out at 205 degrees North East. Over."

"Roger that, Tower. Over," replied the pilot and the Loach lifted off, reached its cruising ceiling of 16,000 feet at a climb rate of 2,016 feet per minute and a cruise speed of 155 miles per hour. Fifteen minutes later it was hovering at 12,000 feet one mile south west of the mansion at 7 Early Bird Lane.

"How do you want to play this out?" the Loach pilot asked Ankyer.

"Drop me on the roof of the mansion as close to the South East corner as you can. There are several chimneys blocking the view of some kind of solarium windows on the other side of the roof. After I'm out you can set down about 50 yards out from the building's North West corner, which visually places the mansion between you and the guardhouse at the front entrance. There may be two prisoners in the mansion I will need to evacuate and there are doors on the side where you will be waiting. I'll try to raise you when I'm on the way. You may have to come in and give me a hand if they are both incapacitated, so you will have to move the Loach closer to the doors. Don't get out of your seat unless I tell you. They have what appear to be military trained guard dogs that will tear you apart. I think I can handle them, but you have to be careful. What else do you have on the Loach besides the 50's?"

"I've got four Hellfire missiles that will reduce that building into a pile of ash."

"Great. If I get taken out doing this, use them," said Ankyer.

"Will do. They can say it was a gas explosion. A big one," replied the pilot.

"Ok. Hold onto your nuts. I'm going to do a silent descent with the blades auto rotating to about 100 feet. We'll get going again and I'll drop you on the roof."

"Let's do it," said Ankyer.

Oscar and Jason heard a faint whooshing sound and stuck their heads out of their respective windows of the SUV just in time to see the Loach dropping straight down at what looked like about 50 miles per hour. The helicopter then disappeared behind the trees.

"Were those Hellfire missile pods I saw on that helicopter?" asked Oscar.

"That's what it looked like to me," replied Jason.

"Holy shit," whispered Oscar.

ROOF
EMIR'S MANSION
7 EARLY BIRD LANE
LONG BEACH
LONG ISLAND, NEW YORK
FEBRUARY 20, 2012
6:18 PM EASTERN TIME

The Loach pilot dropped down to the southeast corner of the mansion and hovered about three feet above the roof. Ankyer jumped out and the helicopter peeled off to its assigned spot diagonally out 50 yards out from the northwest corner and set down. The Loach pilot armed his 50 caliber guns and set his radio to Ankyer's tactical channel, and waited.

Ankyer ran over to the edge of the glass portion of the roof. The glass was made of geometric shapes, which dispersed the sunlight, illuminating the room below but at the same time dissipating the heat. The occupants of the pool area could see the glow from the outside but not clear images. Ankyer, on the other hand, could see into the room below with clarity, and what he saw evoked cold, crystalline fury. The pool itself was almost Olympic size, a diving board at one end and what appeared to be a shallow area at the other. A naked figure lay outstretched by the side of the pool in a crucifixion position secured somehow at the wrists and feet. There was a great pool of congealed blood across the shoulders, some of which had dribbled into the pool.

"Fred Bell," thought Ankyer.

What infuriated Ankyer, however, was who was in the pool. The naked body of Margie Tallon was secured by short metal shackles just below the pool edge and shackled by her ankles at the bottom of the pool. Standing about three feet away from the pool's edge was a huge male mesomorph with the largest muscle mass Ankyer had ever seen…the human body equivalent of a Mack truck.

He was holding some kind of remote control device and continually pushing a button. Each time he pushed the button Tallon would arch her back and let out a scream, which trailed off into a whimper. The mesomorph looked like he was somehow making Tallon dance in the water, which was turning red with her blood. There was more blood each time she jerked in response to a push of the remote button.

Ankyer noticed a hatch cover a few feet from the glass roof. He ran over and carefully cracked the door open and peered down. There was a narrow flight of stairs, probably a maintenance stairwell to about the level of the pool. Ankyer adjusted his combat pack to accommodate the narrow enclosure and started down the stairs. He reached the landing. There was a door with a small rectangular window, which looked out on a foyer outside the pool area. He opened the door and stepped out into the empty foyer. In front of him were large, closed, double glass doors. Standing off to the side with his back to Ankyer was the mesomorph pressing the remote control button.

"Time for 'shock and awe'," thought Ankyer as he rotated the Heckler & Koch UMP 45 up from his hip and opened fire into the glass doors. Fifteen 45 ACP rounds from the thirty round magazine entered the double glass door at a rate of 600 rounds per minute. The glass doors exploded inward and glass blew into the front end of the pool area with a deafening roar. Ankyer saw the mesomorph drop the remote device and, without looking around, jump into the pool next to Tallon. Standing in three feet of water, he turned and grabbed Tallon's head with one hand holding her hair and the other hand her chin.

"Throw down your weapon or I will twist her head off," shouted Sheik Abu Mactar Kahn.

Ankyer immediately dropped the UMP 45 and stepped into the pool area. Abu Mactar Kahn assessed his adversary. The man standing at the side of the pool looked to be about 6 feet, 4 inches tall and about 240 pounds. He had different colored eyes, which made Kahn uncomfortable. He wore a strange garment, ripped in various places, of a type Abu Mactar Kahn had never seen. The front of the garment was crisscrossed by a harness, which held a knife handle hanging down on the left front shoulder. A small bow-like device was also secured to the front. Two small canisters, each of which hung from the right side of the harness, completed the man's image. At 7 feet, 380 pounds Mactar Kahn was confident he could overcome and destroy this man if he could get close to him.

"You come into the pool, soldier, and we will fight man-to-man for this woman. If you best me, she is yours. If I defeat you, she is mine to do with as I please."

Ankyer immediately inferred that the mesomorph's confidence was a function of the difference in their sizes, and his self-assurance in his own overwhelming strength. Ankyer looked at Tallon. There was fresh blood emanating from her wrists and circling up from her ankles under water. Her complexion was stark white and he could see her breathing was labored. Ankyer knew he had to get to Tallon quickly if she was going to live.

Ankyer walked over to the side of the pool, about twenty feet from Mactar Kahn. He removed his combat pack and jumped in.

"Ok, asshole, let's see what you've got," said Ankyer.

Abu Mactar Kahn grinned, released Tallon, and walked over to Ankyer. When he was within six feet of Ankyer, he lunged with incredible speed, belying his massive size. He closed with Ankyer, and lifted him, chest to chest with a bear hug. Ankyer had assumed the mesomorph would try and grab him around the arms to immobilize him, so he took a deep breath as the mesomorph started toward him.

As Abu Mactar Kahn encircled Ankyer with his massive arms, he said: "I am going to break your back and then rip you apart."

Instead of replying, Ankyer opened his mouth, clamped down on the mesomorph's bulbous nose with his teeth, and twisted his head, biting off the nose and partially exposing the mesomorph's sinus cavities. Blood and sinus fluids shot past Ankyer's head and the mesomorph screamed.

"I woo kwil yoo!" the mesomorph yelled, his diction affected by the alteration of his nasal passages.

Abu Mactar Kahn released his grip on Ankyer. In doing so, Kahn managed to pull the combat knife from Ankyer's battle harness. Kahn raised his massive left arm, hand holding the knife handle, and brought the knife blade down toward the top of Ankyer's head. Ankyer stepped his right leg between Kahn's spread legs, and blocked Kahn's descending arm with his own outward turned left arm. Ankyer then reached around with his right arm, grasped his left wrist and, with all his strength, pulled Abu Mactar Kahn's arm down sharply. Abu Mactar Kahn's left arm rotated counterclockwise, the opposite of its design, twisted off its shoulder, and was held in place only by now flaccid skin. Ankyer pivoted, pulling the arm from the skin holding it in place and dropped it in the pool. Blood started gushing into the water in great spurts. Kahn thrashed in the water, screaming. He reached over to the socket, which formerly held his left arm. His blood-drenched hand came away with bloody tendons and a partial rotator cuff.

Kahn's dismembered arm floated over to the pool wall. Ankyer walked over to the arm and retrieved his combat knife, still clutched by the arm's hand. Ankyer turned in time to avoid a half-hearted swing from Kahn's remaining arm. Ankyer stepped to the side, dug each of his thumbs and forefingers into Kahn's opposing carotid arteries, pinched and twisted violently. When he twisted Kahn's carotids, the blood flow to his brain ceased, causing him to pass out. Ankyer rolled the mesomorph over on his back to prevent him from drowning and pushed him along side Tallon.

Malibi exited the elevator and walked down the hall, returning to continue Tallon's interrogation, when she saw Ankyer rip Abu Mactar Kahn's arm off in the pool. Without another thought or hesitation, Malibi turned and ran for her life down the hall and back to the elevator.

Ankyer quickly levered himself out of the pool, returned the combat knife to its scabbard, looked around and saw a handcuff key on a cabana table. He retrieved the key and released the wrist shackles holding Tallon. He jumped back into the pool, reached down to her ankle shackles and released those. Having freed Tallon, Ankyer wrapped a wrist chain once around Kahn's remaining arm and snapped the clasp shut. He did the same to Kahn's ankles with the pool's ankle chains. With Kahn securely locked by the pool chains, Ankyer lifted Tallon out of the water to the side of the pool. Her breathing was labored.

She whispered: "Jake, Jake…" and then her eyes rolled up.

Her breathing became erratic and her lips turned blue. Ankyer ran over to his combat pack and carried it back to Tallon. He pulled his tactical radio out and pressed the number 8 button for the Abbey.

"Jake, this is Honey Pi. What's up?"

"I'm with Margie Tallon. She has been repeatedly tortured with electric shocks. She just passed out and her lips are turning blue."

"Put your hand on her chest," said Pi.

"Her heart is racing a mile a minute," replied Ankyer.

"She's got ventricular fibrillation," said Pi.

"Get the defibrillators. Hurry!" said Pi.

Ankyer reached into the combat pack and pulled the two defibrillator paddles out connected to a battery unit, placed them on Tallon's chest, and hit the red button. Tallon's body arched.

"She didn't respond," said Ankyer.

"Move the Joule dial up two notches and try it again," said Pi.

Ankyer did as Pi instructed. Tallon's body arched.

"Nothing."

"Her heart rate is dropping, fast. Shit. I think her heart stopped," said Ankyer.

"Do exactly as I say, big guy. Get the syringe labeled "adrenaline" and inject it into a carotid artery. Fast!"

Ankyer opened the combat pack again and removed the adrenaline syringe. He tapped the side of Tallon's neck a few times to elevate the carotid artery and injected the drug.

"What's she doing?" asked Pi.

"Her heart's going again," said Ankyer.

"What color are her lips?" asked Pi.

"Still blue," said Ankyer.

"Shit. You have oxygen there?" asked Pi.

"No," said Ankyer.

"Put your hand behind her neck, tilt her head back, breathe into her mouth four or five times, and then push hard on her diaphragm. Hurry!" said Pi.

Ankyer took five large breaths and expelled them into Tallon's open mouth. Nothing. Then Tallon threw up water and started breathing. Ankyer picked up the secure phone.

"She's breathing on her own. Looks like she had water in her lungs."

"Ok. You need to get her to a medical facility ASAP. Do not give her any morphine. I don't want her system depressed any more than it is."

"Will do although I'm still in a combat situation. I'll move as fast as I can."

"OK. Anything else?" asked Pi.

"Fred Bell. He's here out cold and crucified to the floor. It also looks like they shot him in both shoulders."

"Is he nailed?" asked Pi.

"Yes," said Ankyer.

"Through his wrists or his hands?" asked Pi.

"Hands and ankles," said Ankyer.

"Good. They didn't hit any tendons. You got pliers?" asked Pi.

"Yes," replied Ankyer.

"Good again. Pull the nails out. Be sure and pull straight up so you don't screw up the internal structures. How about blood loss?"

"There's quite a bit but it doesn't look like he bled out. Let me get the nails out so I can see his back."

Ankyer quickly pulled the nails out of Bell and rolled him on his side to examine the back of his shoulders.

"Looks like the bullets in both shoulders were through and through."

"Good," said Pi.

"You have a blood substitute in your kit?" Pi asked.

Ankyer looked in his bag.

"I've got a bag of BloodStat," he said.

"Good. Attach the bag to his arm with the strap and insert the needle into a vein."

A moment later, "Done," said Ankyer.

"Good. Put pressure bandages on him, front and back, and see if you can wake him up. I want to see if he has any mental damage."

Ankyer placed pressure bandages on Bell, reached in the combat bag, found an ammonia capsule and broke it under Bell's nose. Bell's eyes fluttered open, focused on Ankyer, and he said in a loud voice: "That big mother fucker nailed me to the mother fucking floor!"

Ankyer picked up the phone: "Bell's back with us," said Ankyer.

"Way to go big guy!" said Pi. "Give him a shot of morphine. Talk to you later," and the secure phone clicked off.

Ankyer reached into his combat pack and pulled out a morphine auto injector and hit Bell in the arm.

"That big bastard said he was going to castrate me," said Bell looking at his crotch. "It looks like you're timing was perfect. My nuts thank you."

"Fred, Margie had a heart attack. We need to get her and you out of here to medics. Your clothes are piled over there next to the champagne fountain." Ankyer helped Bell to his feet and asked, "Can you walk?"

"Damn right I'll walk."

"Good. Put on just your pants and shirt. Then grab my H&K over there."

"Roger that," said Bell.

Ankyer saw a stack of Turkish towels on a table. He ran over, pulled one off and carefully wrapped Tallon in it. Tallon's eyes fluttered and she focused on Ankyer.

"I've got you now, Margie. No one's going to hurt you any more," said Ankyer.

"Jake," said Tallon weakly. "I saw the Emir and I watched him talk to me. Jake, the Emir is not Saddam Hussein. He's a double."

"Are you sure?" asked Ankyer.

"Brother Arlot at the Abbey taught me how to recognize Hussein by the movements of his facial musculature over his skull. I'm sure. I may have also told them about the Abbey. I don't know. They had me drugged."

Tallon's voice tapered off and her eyes shut. At that moment, a door at the other end of the pool opened and Moobie, the martyr/guard, appeared pushing a cart loaded with sandwiches, bowls of salad and a bowl of fruit arranged as a bouquet of flowers. Ankyer reached into a pocket in his body wrap, pulled out the new transponder and hit the black button. Being deaf and dumb, Moobie could only mouth "Allahu Akbar" as he ran toward Ankyer.

"Fred, don't shoot him!" yelled Ankyer. "He's got an exploding vest on!"

Moobie ran halfway down the length of the pool pressing the button on the exploding vest's cell phone. Nothing happened. Ankyer ran down the side of the pool to meet Moobie half way. He placed his right foot behind Moobie's leg and hit Moobie sharply using his left palm in a sweeping uppercut with his fingers curled. The palm attack sent Moobie off the side into the pool, landing five feet out in the water. Moobie immediately sunk to the pool's bottom, dragged down by the weight of the exploding vest. Ankyer turned and ran back to the end of the pool yelling, "Fred, get down!"

Ankyer turned again and pressed the red button on the transponder. Two seconds elapsed. A large bubble formed in the bottom of the pool, shooting upward and terminating with a geyser showering pink water and bits of Moobie around the pool area. Moobie's head bobbed to the surface like a water polo ball.

"Boy," said Bell to Ankyer, "you are really something to work with."

Ankyer clicked his tactical phone twice. The Loach pilot came on.

"What's up? Sounds like you're busy in there."

"I've got my two captives, both alive," said Ankyer. "Pull the Loach up to the side doors. We'll be out in a few minutes. Watch out for the dogs. Oh, and give the hangar back at Islip a heads-up that we'll need two ambulances with medical teams when we get back there."

"Roger that," said the pilot. Ankyer heard a muffled voice coming out of the pool.

"I woo kwil yoo!" shouted Abu Mactar Kahn.

Bell walked up to Ankyer. "Anything I can do to help?" asked Bell. Ankyer tore off a piece of duct tape from a roll in the combat pack. He picked up the remote from the floor and handed it to Bell. Try the black button in the middle to see if it still works," he said. Bell put the H&K under one arm and pressed the remote's black button. Electricity coursed through Kahn's body causing him to arch his huge back and howl with pain.

"Looks like it still works," said Bell.

"I'll leave it up to you, Fred," said Ankyer. "Put a bullet in him, or duct tape the black button down. I don't think there's enough juice to kill him because he's so damn big. Your call."

"That's easy," said Fred and duct taped the black button down.

Abu Mactar Kahn thrashed around the water, his movements limited by the chains, which started to bite into his lone wrist and both ankles. Ankyer took a white phosphorus grenade from his combat harness, pulled the pin at the top and threw it into the pool. The grenade exploded, igniting the water in part of the pool. Ankyer threw a second grenade in, and the sheet of flame started to expand toward the mesomorph.

"Time to go," said Ankyer as he carefully picked up Margie Tallon.

She put an arm around his neck and buried her head in his shoulder. Ankyer, with Tallon in his arms and Fred Bell by his side, walked out of the destroyed glass doors and down the hall toward the elevator. Bell looked back to see Sheik Abu Mactar Kahn, shrieking from the constant electric shock as the white phosphorus flames in the water enveloped him.

Meanwhile, Zainab Malibi had exited the elevator and was running toward the front door, her objective being the grey, Porsche, 911 Carrera S Cabriolet parked five spaces down from the Black SUV that Tallon and Bell arrived in. As she was about to get into the Porsche, she thought about Tallon's Hermes Birkin bag.

"I wonder if she brought it with her?" Malibi mused.

She turned around, walked back to the SUV and looked in the front passenger window. Nothing. She then looked in the side back window and there it was! Malibi opened the door, dumped the contents of the bag on the ground and placed her purse in the bag. She then turned and started walking toward the Porsche. The Doberman hit her in the back, soft, inside upper part of her left leg, biting down and pulling away a large piece of her inner thigh. Malibi fell on her side and was immediately bitten on her face, a cheek and an eye was torn out and swallowed by a second Doberman. The scent of the blood caused the other three Dobermans that arrived on the scene to go into a feeding frenzy.

The Loach pilot landed the aircraft within fifteen feet of the northwest corner of the building. Four minutes later, Ankyer exited the building carrying Tallon in his arms and followed by Bell. Ankyer walked over to the Loach. The pilot opened the reinforced, Plexiglas, medevac stretcher cover. Ankyer placed Tallon inside, closing the cover over her. "You're on the other side, Fred. Sorry about the ride. It's all I could think of quickly." "Not a problem," said Fred. "I'm actually feeling a little woozy anyway," as he passed out and fell over.

Ankyer and the pilot picked Fred up and placed him in the medevac stretcher on the pilot's side.

"We ok for balance?" asked Ankyer.

"Yeah, we're good," replied the pilot.

"Fred's a big guy and I'm a lot smaller than you, so having him on my side and the woman on yours works out."

"Ok," said Ankyer." I need to make two calls and then we're out of here.

Ankyer thumbed his tactical phone.

"This is Ankyer. Over."

"Oscar here. Over."

"I'm just about finished at this end. Pull your vehicle into the front of the mansion gate and flip it around as we discussed. Take out the gate and the guardhouse. Shoot anyone you see. I'm concerned they may have a surface-to-air shoulder fired missile that could take the Loach down on our way out. They are all bad guys. I eliminated some up here but there have to be more. I'll call in backup for you guys. As soon as they show up you can take off so you're not identified. Over."

"Appreciate that," said Oscar. "Out."

As Ankyer was preparing to call Finkel, he noticed five Dobermans racing in his direction. One of the dogs appeared to have a toy in his mouth. As the Dobermans approached, Ankyer thought: "Ok. Here's where my idea for the damaged body wrap I used at the Black Forest factory works or not."

The Dobermans came within ten feet of Ankyer and stopped. They circled with their noses up and mouths open, except for the one holding the toy. Then they lay down with their ears back. The combination of Ankyer's body wrap pheromones from Varna, as well as the mountain lion, turned Ankyer into the most badass, Alpha male the Dobermans had ever encountered, instantly making Ankyer the Doberman-in-Chief.

The dog with the toy got up, padded over in front of Ankyer and dropped the toy at his feet. The toy turned out to be a wrist and hand clutching what appeared to be an expensive, although blood stained bag. Ankyer looked in the bag and found a wallet which, when he opened it, contained a driver's license, visible through a plastic window. "Zainab Malibi," read the license. Ankyer picked it up and tossed the wrist, hand and bag into his seat in the Loach.

Ankyer then called Finkel on the secure phone.

"I'm leaving the Emir's grounds. Both Tallon and Bell are alive. Tallon was tortured with electricity repeatedly. She had a heart attack and her heart stopped, but Doctor Pi got me through the resuscitation process successfully. Margie needs medical attention as soon as we get back to the military hangar at Islip field. She did manage to tell me that she was able to evaluate the Emir's skull configuration according to Brother Arlot's protocol and concluded that the Emir is not Saddam. It looks like the Emir has left here, I'm not sure where to. Also, I have reason to believe that Malibi is probably dead."

"How do you know?" asked Finkel.

"One of the Doberman guard dogs dropped a wrist with a hand clutching an expensive handbag with Malibi's license in it."

"The Doberman dropped it in front of you?" said Finkel.

"My pheromone strategy worked. I'm now their Alpha male."

"Excellent!" exclaimed Finkel.

"Another thing. I've asked the CIA people out front to pull in and eliminate the front gate, guardhouse and any guards in the area with the SUV's chain gun. I don't want us to get shot down on the way out with any surface-to-air missiles they may have. The Loach has four Hellfire missiles on board. We can obliterate the mansion on the way out if you think it would be useful."

"Leave it intact," said Finkel. "I will send in an N.S.A. response team to survey the mansion and see if there is any additional, useful intelligence we can collect."

"Ok," said Ankyer. "Have them treat the grounds as a hot LZ. There may be some martyr /guards and Dobermans wandering around."

"Thanks, Jake. The survey teams are on their way. We've alerted the county sheriff and police departments to a Federal action and instructed them to keep civilians outside a five-mile radius. I'll also contact the military hangar at the airport to make sure they have the appropriate medical personnel on hand when you arrive. I'll talk to you again after you return to the Islip hangar."

"Thank you sir." said Ankyer, and terminated the call.

He walked around to the medevac stretchers, checked on Tallon and Bell and climbed into the Loach. The pilot powered up the Loach and took off. As they rose they heard rapid, heavy gunfire coming from the entrance to the mansion grounds. In the distance they saw the CIA SUV pouring fire from the chain gun into the guardhouse through the smoldering remains of the gate. There were several large explosions. Two guards were running down the road, one holding what appeared to be a surface-to-air missile tube. "Stop them," said Ankyer.

The pilot banked the Loach and fired the twin fifty-caliber machine guns. Both guards exploded, also igniting the SAM and causing a large additional explosion. The pilot pulled back hard on the Loach's collective, and headed up and out toward the Islip airfield. In the distance they saw four Black Hawk helicopters headed toward the mansion. Doctor Finkel had wasted no time. Oscar and Jason stopped firing the chain gun, having destroyed the entire mansion entrance, together with its occupants. Oscar put the SUV in Drive and headed toward the entrance to Early Bird Lane. Jason turned to Oscar and asked: "You ever been on an operation like this one?"

"Not even remotely," replied Oscar.

"One thing is for sure," Oscar continued.

"I wouldn't want that Ankyer guy pissed off at me. He's a goddamn one man army."

LONG ISLAND ISLIP MACARTHUR AIRPORT MILITARY HANGAR LONG ISLAND, NEW YORK FEBRUARY 20, 2012 8:00 PM EASTERN TIME

After the Loach flew out of the immediate area of the Emir's estate, Ankyer called into the military hangar at Islip airfield and spoke briefly with the crew chief. He then shifted the wrist/hand and Birkin bag to minimize blood dripping in the cockpit, although most of the blood had started to congeal by the time they were airborne. Ankyer continued to look through Malibi's purse in the Birkin bag. He discovered a folded piece of paper, that upon closer inspection, he thought would be of interest to Doctor Finkel. He replaced the piece of paper in the purse just as the Islip airfield started to come into view.

The Loach pilot brought the helicopter into the military hangar at speed and then pulled up and settled the aircraft gently down in front of the hangar's main doors. As he cut the power the Loach was surrounded by medical personnel who quickly unlatched the medevac stretchers and moved Tallon and Bell to gurneys that had been positioned on each side of the Loach.

Two men in white coats, one for Bell and one for Tallon, bent over them for a few moments. Bell started calling out gibberish. He was given a shot by his "white coat", which had the instant effect of stopping Bell in his tracks and converting him to a smiling, snoring patient. Ankyer climbed out of the Loach and walked over to Tallon's "white coat".

"I'm Lieutenant Commander Parks and will be Doctor Tallon's physician for the moment. The other physician is Lieutenant Commander Walthour. I have spoken to Doctor Pi who will be coordinating their care while they are with us. Once they are stabilized, they will be transported by medical jet to a facility to be communicated to us by Doctor Pi. I've just checked Doctor Tallon's vitals. She is in good condition considering what she has had to endure. We will want to keep her with us for awhile to make certain her heart rhythms are stable. She's also lost a fair amount of blood and, while I can't be sure until I see x-rays, it looks like both her wrists and one of her ankles may have been fractured."

"Permanent damage?" Ankyer asked.

"Probably not physically. Emotionally things could be dicey. Prolonged torture can…no, will… induce PTSD in one form or another. I've discussed this with Doctor Pi and she indicated that the appropriate psychological support for Doctor Tallon would be available at her facility." As Ankyer and Parks were talking, Tallon and Bell were each loaded into one of the arriving ambulances. Medical staff climbed into the back of the ambulances, which pulled away at an increasing rate of speed.

"I understand you were with Doctor Tallon when she had the heart attack," said Parks. "Yes," replied Ankyer.

"Well, you should know that your intervention absolutely save her life," Parks continued. "Doctor Pi walked me through it," said Ankyer. As they were talking, Lieutenant Commander Walthour walked up.

"Doctor Walthour, this is the gentleman who rescued our patients," said Parks.

"I don't know where you learned your combat medicine but you definitely paid attention in class," said Walthour.

"The wounds to his shoulders caused the Chief to lose about half his blood. How did you ever get him to the helicopter? He's a very big man," said Walthauer.

"He walked out," replied Ankyer.

"Incredible," said Walthour.

Parks handed Ankyer a card with a phone number and an address.

"This is where we're taking them. Give me a call if you want an update on their conditions."

The crew chief walked up to them with a plastic box.

"Hold on a second," said Ankyer as he walked around to his seat on the Loach. He reached in and withdrew the wrist/hand clutching the bloody Hermes Birkin bag and placed it in the plastic box.

He handed the box back to the crew chief and said: "Take this back to the Ready Room for me and place a guard on it. I'll be back there in a few minutes."

The crew chief turned and started walking diagonally toward a far corner of the hangar. "You certainly lead an interesting life," said Doctor Parks.

Doctor Walthour said: "Nothing personal, but whatever you're wrapped in really smells bad."

Ankyer looked down at his body wrap. "It's been through a lot lately," chuckled Ankyer. "Thank you for taking care of my friends."

They shook hands. Ankyer turned and followed the crew chief. Doctors Parks and Walthour entered a waiting grey staff car, which pulled out gaining speed with its red light flashing.

GOLD COAST TOWNHOUSE
1217 STATE STREET
CHICAGO, ILLINOIS
FEBRUARY 21, 2012
8:00 PM CENTRAL STANDARD TIME

The street was quiet outside the townhouse. The snow had accumulated to slightly over two inches and was now limited to modest flurries. Ali el Abbas Abdul Fattah stood in the foyer immediately inside the front door looking through the small security window. He thought idly about his home back in Iraq. He much preferred the sand and heat of his homeland to the bitter Chicago cold and snow.

"Why would anyone want to live here," he thought to himself. His name, "Servant of the Opener of the Gates of Sustenance", was an important name and one, which he was certain, would occupy an exalted place in Paradise when his time came. The Emir had given him the nickname "Babba". Why he was not certain. No matter. The Emir had assured him that the many virgins who awaited him in Paradise would be selected from the very best, and already longed for him to arrive. He didn't know how exactly the Emir knew all this, but the Emir assured him that this was so.

The phone on the antique table next to the elevator chimed and an attached red light blinked. Babba adjusted the shoulder straps on his suicide vest as he walked over and picked up the phone. "Yes sir. I will do as you ask immediately sir," he said and replaced the receiver on the handset.

He had been busy preparing the townhouse for several days at the direction of the Emir, who was quite particular in his instructions. The townhouse library was now occupied by the Emir, Ibram el Farsi, and Doctor McGinty. Doctor Malibi was expected several hours ago but was probably delayed by the snow at O'Hare Airport. He would escort her to the library as soon as she arrived. He liked Doctor Malibi. She always called him by his full name.

The elevator door opened silently at the third floor and Babba emerged into the library. The fire, which he started in the fireplace an hour before, crackled and emanated a glow along with an aroma of oak, the Emir's preferred wood. The Emir, Doctor McGinty and el Farsi were seated at a highly polished mahogany table set with the tea service Babba had placed there earlier. The walls of the library were filled with books. Next to a ten-foot high stained glass window was a library table, which held a closed lap top computer. Sconces at various locations in the room shed a soft light on the occupants. Babba silently walked over to a small alcove and sat down in a leather chair next to a desk.

The Emir considered McGinty from across the table and spoke.

"Doctor McGinty, you are an unpleasant man. Ever since we rescued you from Mr. Rodrigues-Zappa, you have beleaguered us with your demands for money. Some would say that saving your life would be payment enough."

"We have a deal!" interjected McGinty.

"Yes, we do and we will honor our arrangement not withstanding our distaste for you. Since you have been involved with us, we have had some of our funds in one of our main financial institutions frozen; an expensive laboratory we own was destroyed; and now we have discovered that we are under suspicion by the American FBI or some other kind of police organization."

"I cannot be held accountable for your problems," said McGinty."

"I performed the tasks you set me to. I was promised $ 7,000,000 and I want to be paid."

"You will be paid, with interest," said the Emir.

"We decided to convert your payment to cut diamonds which have appreciated substantially over the past few months. They are worth probably $ 7,800,000 by now according to our gem experts. Babba, show Doctor McGinty his payment."

Babba removed a sack from the center draw of the desk he was seated, walked over to the table and gave the sack to the Emir. The Emir opened the top of the sack and poured some of the contents on the table. Even in the dim light, the diamonds sparkled.

"That's more like it," said McGinty.

The Emir continued, "We understand that the authorities who attacked the Black Forest laboratory found the bodies of a number of your test subjects."

"When el Farsi and I left, I instructed the guards to cremate all the remaining test subjects."

"I understand over fifty bodies were found in various stages of decomposition. It doesn't look like your instructions were followed," replied the Emir.

"That's not my fault," said McGinty.

"After all, they were just test subjects, irrelevant human waste. The important thing is that the nano VX steam generators worked!"

"I won't argue that with you," replied the Emir.

"Casualties are expected in any important enterprise. The problem is, that leaving evidence behind increases the risk of discovery, by the American FBI, for example." "That's not my problem," said McGinty.

"You were sloppy," said the Emir.

"Results count," said McGinty, not the miniscule problems you are talking about.

The nano VX steam generators will be set in operation over the next several days and will kill several million people if not tens of millions if the wind conditions are favorable. You'll have achieved your purpose. By the way, I had six steam generator devices ordered in addition to the test machine at the laboratory, but I am aware of only five operational locations. What happened to the sixth machine?" asked McGinty.

"It's not something you need concern yourself with," said the Emir.

"As you said, you performed the tasks we set you to and you deserve your reward."

The Emir scooped up the diamonds on the table and placed them in the sack with the others. He returned the sack to Babba. "Now, Doctor McGinty, it is time for you to reap your reward."

Babba pocketed the sack, pulled out two plastic handcuffs, and quickly applied them to each of McGinty's wrists, securing them to the arms of the chair. The Emir and Ibram el Farsi stood up from their chairs and walked over to McGinty. McGinty sat red faced and sputtering, saliva dribbling on his white beard.

"You promised!" he shouted.

"I promised you would be rewarded and so you shall be."

"Remove him to the basement and prepare him," said the Emir.

Babba placed a moving cart under the seat of the chair and wheeled McGinty and the chair into the elevator, and pressed 'B' for basement.

The elevator door closed silently leaving the Emir and Ibram el Farsi standing in the middle of the room.

"More tea?" el Farsi asked.

"Yes, thank you," replied the Emir as they returned to the mahogany table.

"Zainab Malibi should be here by now," said el Farsi, pouring the tea.

"I'll see if she is getting closer," as he took his phone from his pocket and pressed a speed dial number.

The phone rang five times and Malibi' s voice mail message came on.

"It is unlike Zainab not to call if she is running late," el Farsi said.

"No matter," said the Emir.

"McGinty can wait. We wouldn't want Zainab to miss McGinty's reward. She has worked hard to bring everything to this point. Tomorrow will be a great day for us and a day of sorrow for the Americans."

The two men sipped their tea as the snow began to swirl and fall faster.

LONG ISLAND ISLIP MACARTHUR AIRPORT MILITARY HANGAR LONG ISLAND, NEW YORK FEBRUARY 20, 2012 8:45 PM EASTERN TIME

Ankyer walked into the Ready Room. He opened the plastic box containing the wrist/hand, Hermes Birkin bag and Malibi's purse and cell phone. He pulled out his secure smart phone, took a picture of the sheet of paper with the list of locations and emailed it to Finkel. He also emailed a photo of Malibi's driver's license. The crew chief dismissed the guard in the Ready Room. A cart with sandwiches, two pizzas and coffee was wheeled in and the crew chief waived Ankyer over.

"We figured you would be hungry after your little adventure."

"Thanks," replied Ankyer.

"I'm starving," as he picked up two pieces of pizza, made a sandwich out of the slices, and ate them in three bites. Carl walked in with a flight suit and helmet.

"Do everyone a favor and get out of that camo wrap," he said.

"You're ruining everyone's appetite."

Ankyer walked over to Carl and gave him a fist bump.

"I gather we're going somewhere," Ankyer said.

"Your next batch of frequent flyer miles is taking you to Chicago in the Hornet. Call Doctor Finkel."

Ankyer changed into the flight suit and placed the camo wrap in another plastic bag and set it next to the bag with Malibi's arm.

"Carl, we need to get these bags to Doctor Finkel ASAP."

"Will do", said Carl. "After I get you to Chicago I'll continue on to the Abbey."

Ankyer poured a cup of coffee and walked over to a small table and chair, sat down and called Finkel.

When Finkel came on the line he said, "I heard that Margie Tallon and Fred Bell are en route to our intermediate medical facility there. Doctor Parks gave me an update on their condition. Margie is responding well to questions and her physiological readings are in the normal range, which is remarkable considering what they did to her. Fred is still groggy from the sedative he got which could put down an elephant. They are pretty sure Fred hasn't suffered any internal structural damage from the crucifixion, but we'll want to do full body MRIs on both of them when we get them back here. They are shipping them out tomorrow via military medevac and we'll have them back here with us by late tomorrow afternoon. Doctor Pi will be coordinating all their care at this end."

"Doctor Pi takes some getting used to but I'm glad she's on the team," replied Ankyer. "We've identified the manufacturer of the steam unit you found at the Black Forest, Colorado laboratory," said Finkel.

"They ship very few units of the make and model McGinty was using. We developed a list of shipping addresses and compared it to the addresses on the list Malibi had that you emailed earlier. Here's what we found."

A document appeared in the window of Ankyer's smart phone.

Selkirk's Steam Tech	Units	Malibi Addresses
ALBANY NEW YORK		
–530 MICKELBERRY LANE	1	X
DAVIS CALIFORNIA		
–77 INDUSTRIAL PARK WEST	1	X
CASPER WYOMING		
–2016 FAIRVIEW	1	X
SYLVAN CORNERS KANSAS		

–1217 STATE STREET	1	
CHICAGO ILLINOIS		
–10 SHOE FACTORY DRIVE	1	X
DESTIN FLORIDA		
–188B NEW FACTORY RD	1	X
BRICK NEW JERSEY		

"By finding the list in Malibi's purse, it appears you have given us independent verification of the locations of the steam generators and the nano VX distribution locations," continued Finkel.

"Except for Chicago," said Ankyer.

"We wondered about that," replied Finkel. "We don't think it's on her list because it's the one location she didn't have to remember since they are all familiar with it. We have concluded it may be the command and control location for the nano VX attack."

"Which is why I'm flying with Carl to Chicago," said Ankyer.

"Exactly," replied Finkel. "We are also deploying SEAL Teams, CDC HAZMAT units and FBI Evidence Recovery Teams to the other locations in addition to Chicago. If there is a chance, and we believe there is, that the Emir is in Chicago along with McGinty, and the Emir is Saddam, then the Priority Red Protocol is in effect. You need to go there to take active control of the situation prior to any of the latter ancillary units, except of course our SEAL team, showing up. Neil and part of our SEAL team will meet you at the Chicago O'Hare airport military facility. They will provide any cover and support you require. We have to be very careful that we don't inadvertently cause suspicion regarding Saddam, so we will have civilian clothes for you. The SEAL Team will be in civilian clothes as well. The FBI has also alerted the Chicago and State police that a highly classified government operation is underway and that Mary Hendricks from CIA and Mary Lou Hastings from the FBI will be coordinating their involvement, if any. It will be up to you to involve Chicago and Illinois law enforcement through me, but I frankly don't see any reason to at this juncture."

"I understand," replied Ankyer.

"Oh, and two other items," said Finkel. "The lab results from the mountain lion brain tissue sample came back. There was no evidence of rabies so you're clear in that regard."

"How's Varna doing?" asked Ankyer.

"He is doing quite well and is being watched over by Doctor Pi and Brother William. They expect to reintroduce him to the wolf pack in the next day or so. I must say that Doctor Pi and Brother William get along exceptionally well. Their personalities are remarkably harmonious. They became fast friends almost instantly. I suspect it's possibly because of their shared interest in Varna."

"Finally, when you pick up your additional equipment in Chicago, you will find a DNA matching kit, with three injectors included. The injectors are preloaded with Saddam's DNA profile. You insert the injector into the subject. The injector automatically extracts a blood sample, which is chemically analyzed and compared against the Saddam profile. It's a field test device. Not terribly accurate but it will give you a reasonable result. It should help you eliminate another Saddam double, if that situation happens to arise."

"Ok. I'll assemble my equipment and leave here shortly," said Ankyer. "Don't forget the transponder," said Finkel. "It seems these martyr people are always in the vicinity of the Emir."

Ankyer signed off, ate two more pieces of pizza, and walked back over to Carl.

"Ready to go?" asked Carl.

"Yes, said Ankyer." He handed Carl the plastic bags containing the damaged camo wrap and Malibi's wrist/hand with the Hermes Birkin bag.

"Ok," said Carl. "Doctor Finkel also asked me to let you know that you'll have a new combat pack waiting in Chicago."

"Thanks Carl. They walked out of the Ready Room and over to the Super Hornet.

"We have extra fuel on board again," said Carl. "Doctor Finkel wants you in Chicago ASAP so we'll have the after burners on all the way.

GOLD COAST TOWNHOUSE
1217 STATE STREET
CHICAGO, ILLINOIS
FEBRUARY 21, 2012
8:15 PM CENTRAL STANDARD TIME

Babba was seated at his appointed location in the foyer behind the front door. He had just returned from serving breakfast to the Emir and Ibram el Farsi in the townhouse dining room. They were in good spirits and praised Babba for his good work. So far Babba was having a good day. He had also checked on Doctor McGinty, who was not having such a good day.

Babba was now seated at a small table having his tea and a donut. The foyer was a pleasant place indeed. Beautiful tile floor. Beautiful pictures. Babba's only wish was that he could be with a Jihadist team to take the fight to the Americans. The Emir had told Babba that his day would come and to be patient. As a martyr/guard he was the Emir's to command and the Emir always said that patience is as much a weapon as an AK-47. As was his habit, Babba checked under his sweater to make sure his exploding vest was secure. He noticed that the green light on the cell phone was not on. That was most strange because he checked it often during the day and it was always on. Since the vest was padlocked to Babba and the Emir had the key, Babba would tell the Emir that the cell phone light was not working, at the first opportunity. At that moment Babba heard the door chime followed by the doorknocker. He looked through the security window in the thick oak door and saw what looked like the second button of an overcoat.

"Who is it?" Babba asked. He heard a muffled reply. He asked louder. "WHO IS IT?" He received another muffled reply and the doorknocker struck again. Babba walked back to a closet door, opened it and removed an AK-47.

Holding the AK in his right hand, he opened the front door a crack and said: "This is a private residence. No soliciting." He started to close the door but a large hand pushed the door open. Babba heard a whooshing noise…and then nothing. Ankyer stepped over Babba who now had a crossbow bolt in his forehead, followed by Neil, and picked up the AK-47. Ankyer bent over and pulled up Babba's sweater. There was the exploding vest with the cell phone light out.

"Not everyone's doorman carries an AK and wears an exploding vest. Looks like we're in the right place," said Ankyer.

"I'm sure glad you have that transponder with you," replied Neil.

"It's proven useful more than once over the past few days," Ankyer replied, leaning the AK-47 against a wall, taking off his coat and placing it over Babba's chair. Ankyer was dressed in a black, double breasted, pin-striped suit. The suit coat had slight bulges on each side, difficult to pick out due to Ankyer's large frame. The label on the inside read 'Gieves & Hawkes, □1 Savile Row, London'.

"Nice suit," said Neil.

"Doctor Finkel had it altered by the 511 military clothing division to incorporate concealed weapons pockets," replied Ankyer, as he stepped to one side to avoid getting Babba's blood on his Johnson & Murphy, Kiltie Tassel, wingtip dress shoes.

"Neil, if you wouldn't mind, I think I'm overdressed for the next step." Neil bent over and attended to Babba as Ankyer replaced the AK-47 in the closet and closed the entrance door. Neil finished with Babba and went over to Ankyer.

"The transponder should have deactivated any other suicide vests around here but I'll keep it ready just in case," Ankyer said. "Now let's see who else is inhabiting this rats nest." They opened the door next to the elevator and started climbing the stairs to the second floor.

The two men sipped their tea in the second floor dining room. The Emir had rung for Babba fifteen minutes earlier and Babba had not as yet appeared. The Emir was irked and pushed the call button several times. "Babba is useful for a number of things but refilling our tea does not seem to be one of them."

The dining room was twenty-feet by twenty-feet square and had light filtering in through floor to ceiling stained glass windows. The men were dressed casually and had just finished a hearty English breakfast of eggs, sausages, and toast. "Today is a great day," said the Emir. "Many Americans will feel the boots of the righteous crushing them into dust," as he lit a cigar. "We have done well," answered el Farsi. "Finding the McGinty infidel was good fortune. He was painful to be around but the result was worthwhile."

"I'm growing more concerned about Doctor Malibi," said the Emir. "She should be here helping to coordinate the release of the nano VX gas on the Americans."

Ibram el Farsi and the Emir heard a voice from the end of the room. "Malibi will be permanently delayed. She was eaten by your guard dogs." The Emir and Ibram el Farsi turned in their chairs and observed a tall, black haired and exceptionally well-built man standing in the doorway.

The Emir stood up and exclaimed: "How dare you interrupt us. Who the hell are you?"

"I'm your worst nightmare," the man replied, then pointed something at the Emir. The next thing the Emir heard was a whooshing sound and then a metal arrow-like barb entered his throat and plunged into the stained glass windowpane behind him. Blood shot out of the Emir's throat onto his shirt and he dropped, as he was a puppet with its strings cut, his spine having been severed. Ankyer covered the distance to el Farsi faster than el Farsi had ever seen anyone move. He backhanded el Farsi across the face, pulled his arms around the back of the chair and secured his wrists with plastic ties.

"You will die a thousand deaths in Allah's hell," said el Farsi. "Babba will be here shortly and you will receive a memorable death!"

"Babba's here right now," said Ankyer as Neil walked up behind el Farsi and dropped Babba's head in his lap. El Farsi bucked in the chair bouncing the bloody head off his lap onto the floor, where it lay with the whites of its eyes looking up at him. Ankyer reached into his suit coat pocket and withdrew what appeared to be a round cigar tube. He bent over and placed the end flush with the side of the Emir's neck and pressed a button. A needle shot out and then retracted back inside the tube. A small red light blinked on the side of the tube.

"Now it's your turn," Ankyer said. Ankyer retrieved another tube from his pocket and pressed it against el Farsi's neck. The needle shot deep into el Farsi's neck and retracted. A small green light blinked. Ankyer placed the tube back in his pocket.

"Neil," Ankyer said, "meet Saddam Hussein Abd al-Majid al-Tikriti." Saddam Hussein looked up at Ankyer with hate filled eyes. "Since this is supposedly 'command central' for the VX attacks, I figured he had to be one or the other of these two guys. Margie managed to tell me that the Emir was not Saddam based on the evaluation of his underlying skull structure. That left our friend here and I just confirmed it with the DNA matching kit injector courtesy, of Doctor Finkel. It's a rough test but I am told it is effective. The DNA reading has just been uploaded to the Abbey via secure satellite and is being confirmed as we speak," said Ankyer.

Just as Ankyer finished, the injector his pocket beeped three times. "Confirmation received," he said. "Welcome back to the planet Earth, Saddam."

"But I thought el Farsi was a gofer for the Emir," said Neil.

"That's what Saddam wanted everyone to think. With the Emir as the visible head, Saddam masquerading as el Farsi could move around wherever he wanted. His hatred for the US after they killed his sons made the VX project even more attractive, which is probably why he chose to stay close enough to McGinty to make sure the program was completed. It also gave Saddam the opportunity to observe the human tests, which he probably enjoyed." "How am I doing so far?" Ankyer asked, as Hussein returned a look of hatred and disgust.

"But what if the Emir tried to double cross him?" asked Neil.

"I think Saddam even thought of that," Ankyer replied. "I'll bet if his DNA and Malibi's were compared, there would be a familial DNA match. Now that I'm looking at him I can see certain family resemblances. I think Malibi was Saddam's daughter and was inserted as an aid to the Emir to keep an eye on him. Saddam had extensive facial surgery, but it's not perfect. There is also a vague resemblance between him and the Emir. I'm guessing the Emir is another body double Saddam had made up along the way. Once they got to the United States, he didn't want an exact match, so they both were surgically altered to reduce each other's similarities. He had billions of dollars he had pulled out of Iraq over the years, so money was no object."

"You think you are so smart American. Well it's too late. My martyrs are in place and prepared to initiate the destruction of more Americans than you can imagine. You can't stop it now," said Saddam.

"Oh. You must mean places like California, Kansas and Wyoming," replied Ankyer.

"How could you know that?" shouted Saddam.

"We know everything," replied Ankyer.

Saddam caught his breath and eyed Ankyer and Neil speculatively. "There are some things you don't know. But go ahead and arrest me. I have much money. More than you think. I will tie you up in courts for years. Jail me, but my brothers and sisters in Iraq will take me back and I will regain the country you Americans have stolen from me!"

"Where is McGinty?" asked Ankyer. Saddam laughed. "Garbage. We used him and let him go. He's gone."

Neil put his hand to his ear bud. He walked Ankyer away from Saddam and in a low voice said, "The team has finished its sweep of the building. There were three more guards, each with a suicide vest. The transponders worked perfectly. They are all dead. The team did find something in the basement you should see. We need to move on."

"Ok," said Ankyer and walked back to Saddam. "You should release me," Saddam said. "I can make you rich. You can have more money than you have ever dreamed of!"

"How can you do that when you are dead? You were hanged, remember?"

"I'm alive you fool!" Saddam exclaimed. Ankyer looked into Saddam's eyes for a moment and realization came to Saddam Hussein Abd al-Majid al-Tikriti. "No!" he yelled. "No!"

Ankyer walked around to the back of Saddam's chair, placed one hand under Saddam's jaw and the other hand on the back of his head and pulled and pushed at the same time. CRACK. Saddam Hussein's neck broke in exactly the position it would have been broken had he dropped through the gallows floor.

"Neil. Have four guys come up with two body bags ASAP and take them out to our unmarked ambulance. Now, what's in the basement?" Neil spoke briefly into his throat mike: "It's the guy in the chair that is Saddam. Make sure you get his body in the bag marked 'S'."

Ankyer and Neil walked to the elevator and pressed the lowest button on the panel to go to the basement. After Ankyer stepped out, Neil pressed the first floor button sending the car up to the four SEALs with the body bags. On one side of the basement was a Jaguar Ultimate sedan. Thirty feet further down was an open door with a SEAL waiving them over. Ankyer and Neil walked into the room and for the first time, Ankyer finally met Doctor Angus McGinty who had eluded him in Mexico and Colorado.

Angus McGinty PhD was seated on a high backed wooden chair. Next to him was a steam generator machine, the very steam generator machine that was missing from Malibi's list.

McGinty's throat had a vertical cut about three inches long that had been made at its base. A flexible tube had been run from the steam generator and inserted into McGinty's trachea and duct taped to his neck. Duct tape had also been used to secure McGinty's head to the back of the chair, and to secure his arms and legs. A self-retaining surgical retractor kept McGinty's mouth wide open. A water line from a spigot on the wall was connected to an inlet in the back of the steam generator…and then the steam generator had been turned on. The live steam was going up into McGinty's throat and coming out his mouth. The inside of his mouth and tongue were par boiled, and his eyes were melted. A tube coming from what looked like an oxygen cylinder was awaiting attachment to an inlet on the steam generator.

Another tube was coiled next to McGinty, evidently intended to be inserted into his mouth and from there connected to the building's chimney system a few feet away. They had, in effect, decided to incorporate Angus McGinty as an integral component of the nano VX steam machine designed to kill the people of Chicago. Undoubtedly, Saddam's idea of poetic justice.

The SEAL who waived Ankyer and Neil into the room said, "We found a partial roll of duct tape next to the guard you shot in the foyer on the first floor. It looks like he was the guard who was supposed to connect this guy up to the VX gadget. You got here just in time." Just then, McGinty started thrashing around in the chair. "The guy's still alive!" exclaimed Neil. "Shut that goddamn machine off," Ankyer said. He pulled out the Heckler & Koch Mark 23 from its holster and shot Doctor Angus McGinty once through the forehead.

Ankyer turned to Neil. "We need another body bag for him. We can take him along with Hussein and the Emir back to O'Hare. Doctor Finkel will have the bodies flown back to the Abbey. I'll get on the plane with them to save time. We also better get the HAZMAT team in to take care of the nano VX."

"We're calling them right now," said Neil. Another SEAL walked in with a body bag.

They removed McGinty's body from the chair and placed him in the body bag. "We'll take care of the HAZMAT team. See you back at the Abbey," said Neil. Ankyer slapped Neil on the back and headed toward the stairway up to the first floor.

When Ankyer walked into the foyer, he was met by one of the SEALs. "We've bagged and tagged Saddam and the Emir and the bodies are in the ambulance. There's a body bag on its way to the basement for the other guy. Well put him in the second ambulance. You can go in that one to O'Hare if you want."

"Works for me. Give me a few minutes. Thanks," said Ankyer as he walked over to a small alcove in the foyer and activated his secure smart phone link to Finkel.

"Bring me up to date," said Finkel.

"Saddam, the Emir and McGinty are all dead. We are loading them into ambulances for the trip back to the military hangar at O'Hare Airport."

"What happened to McGinty?" asked Finkel.

"They had him connected as an integral component to a steam generator and had live steam going up his throat and out his mouth. They were getting ready to connect him to a cylinder of nano VX and I think we got here just in time. Saddam and the Emir were probably getting ready to leave here and fly out of Chicago. I'm guessing that once they were airborne, the guards were going to turn the nano VX cylinder valve on and start poisoning the residents of Chicago. By the way, your CIA contact needs to give the police here a heads-up to secure a three mile perimeter around this building while the HAZMAT team dismantles this steam generator and gets the nano VX out of here."

"Done," said Finkel. "We are also beefing up the military escort for you to O'Hare and Chicago Police will be providing clear passage for you on the streets and expressways. As far as they are concerned, the military has just thwarted a potential terrorist attack but that's all that's been released."

"Ok," said Ankyer. "We'll lift off ASAP and bring the bodies back to the Abbey. By the way, one of the guards had what looks to be a large bag of diamonds in his pocket. If they're real they should be worth millions."

"Where are they now?" asked Finkel.

"In my pocket," said Ankyer.

"Bring them back with you and we'll figure out what to do with them later," said Finkel.

"Ok. See you soon."

Ankyer shut down the link and walked out the front door to the waiting ambulance. Neil intercepted him. "McGinty's in this ambulance. The other two are in the one up front. I've got SEALs in that one along with Saddam and the Emir. We don't want to lose Saddam again! I'm going to hang back here with part of the team until the HAZMAT types show up. Chicago cops have already blocked off street access to here and residents are being escorted out of the area. After we get the HAZMAT team squared away, I'm going back to Washington. Be sure to give Fred an arm punch for me when you see him back at the Abbey."

"Will do. Thanks, Neil." replied Ankyer. "See you later."

Ankyer climbed into the front seat of the ambulance containing McGinty. They followed the other ambulance with Saddam, the Emir and the SEAL team into the increasingly dense snow flurries.

ALBUQUERQUE INTERNATIONAL SUNPORT NEW MEXICO FEBRUARY 22, 2012 11:37 AM MOUNTAIN TIME

The team arrived within thirty minutes of each other at the Albuquerque International Sunport. They had booked four different flights to eliminate any suspicion from their appearance of a group. Muhammad Akim Abdul-Muhsi, Servant of the Reckoner, rented a nondescript grey sedan using the Paolo Verde driver's license and credit card he had been given. He then picked the others up at their respective baggage claim terminals. Each of them carried a medium sized duffel bag. Every thing else they required, including their instructions, would be provided at their next stop. Muhammad Akim Abdul-Muhsi drove the sedan past Sunport security and exited the airport on Route 40. He drove fifteen miles to a small, unincorporated town called Aztec Hills, where he pulled onto a side street and then into a large, dilapidated, garage.

They exited the car and were greeted by a short, older man with a scraggly beard. "Allahu Akbar," said the man. My name is Abu Altair, "the Flying Eagle"."

"Allahu Akbar". I am Muhammad Akim Abdul-Muhsi, Servant of the Reckoner. Do you have word from the Emir?"

"No, but no word is the same as word," said Abu Altair.

“Explain,” replied the Servant of the Reckoner.

“I was contacted by the Emir who told me if I did not hear from him I was to tell you to go ahead with the plan and that I was directed to supply you and the brothers with the materials you needed.”

“I understand. What do you have for us?”

The Flying Eagle led them over to a table on which was displayed an array of equipment. “I have been collecting materials at the direction of the Emir for over a month in case they were needed.”

“They are needed now,” said the Servant of the Reckoner.

“I have for you four AK-47s with four thirty round clips each; a box of twenty four fragmentation grenades; and four suicide vests with the usual cell phone attachment.”

“You have done well Flying Eagle,” said the Servant of the Reckoner.

“Thank you. I have also procured hunting clothes, including pants with deep pockets to hold your grenades and AK-47 clips. Finally, I also prepared bags of food and water for you.”

“Excellent,” said the Servant of the Reckoner.

One of the brothers opened the trunk of the sedan and they loaded all of the equipment from the table into the back of the car except for one of the AK-47’s. The Servant of the Reckoner inserted a magazine and jacked in a round.

The Flying Eagle said, “I envy you in a way.”

“Why would that be?” replied the Servant of the Reckoner.

“I am but a lowly suicide vest maker. I will never be called upon to make the supreme sacrifice so that I can avail myself of the seventy two virgins in Paradise.”

“Ah, I completely understand,” said the Servant of the Reckoner firing four rounds from the AK-47 at close range into the Flying Eagle. The noise was deafening and the smell of smoke permeated the garage.

“Why did you do that?” asked a brother.

“When the Emir gave me my instructions he told me to send the Flying Eagle to Paradise after we had collected our materials. Something about dead pharaohs taking their servants with them when they go to Paradise. I think what he meant was that we should be sure no one could interrogate the Flying Eagle to force him to tell about us. But I am not sure. I never liked Egyptians anyway."

"We need to leave because we have a long way to go. We can't take a chance on speeding and the American police stopping us."

"What about the Flying Eagle?" a brother asked.

"Leave him here where he is," replied the Servant of the Reckoner. "He is of no use to anyone now, least of all to us."

A brother opened the garage door. They got in the car and pulled out into the sunshine. It was starting to heat up outside, possibly reaching the low 60s today. Not the desert heat of the homeland, but it would have to do.

HOLY INNOCENTS TRAPPIST MONASTERY GILA NATIONAL FOREST NEW MEXICO FEBRUARY 22, 2012 12:00 PM MOUNTAIN TIME

It was quiet at the Abbey. There had been a light snowfall overnight, but the noontime temperature was an unseasonable sixty degrees and the snow had almost completely melted. The Abbey bell had just tolled twelve noon. The granite stone of the Abbey had shed the early morning moisture but there remained a few wisps of steam curling from the gables. Brother William, Honey Pi and Margie Tallon were walking back to the Abbey's main entrance, when they heard and then saw the Learjet C-20B circling for a landing at the Abbey's airstrip.

"I've got to go get Jake and bring him back for a meeting with Doctor Finkel," said Brother William.

"Can I go too?" said Tallon looking at Honey Pi.

"I don't see why not. It might not be a bad idea to be there to greet the knight in shining armor who rescued you from those assholes," said Honey Pi in her best professional vocabulary.

"Oops," she said looking at Brother William.

"Don't worry about it. Part of your considerable charm is calling things like you see them, and those people were definitely assholes!" he said chuckling. They split off,

Brother William and Tallon headed toward the Hummer, and Honey Pi for the front door of the Abbey.

Twenty minutes later, the Learjet had landed and taxied to the largest of three hangars at the edge of the Abbey's airfield. The pilot had shut down the engines and opened the hatch to the Lear's cargo bay. Brother Arlot, accompanied by two other Brothers, drove over to the cargo bay in a van. Brother Arlot got out, walked over to the Learjet, opened a small hatch cover and pulled a lever. A hydraulic lift platform pushed out from the fuselage and lowered itself. Lying on the platform were three body bags. Brother Arlot opened the top of each bag, examined the face of the corpse, and zipped the bags back up.

He nodded at the driver of the van who pulled up to the side of the jet. The two Brothers got out of the van and transferred the three body bags to the back of the vehicle.

While they were doing that, Ankyer opened the Learjet's cabin hatch and deplaned. He was still dressed in his Gieves & Hawkes suit. Brother Arlot walked over and shook hands.

"We need to get our guests here back to the Abbey labs as soon as we can," said Brother Arlot. "It is possible that some of the nano VX is lurking somewhere on them since they were around that nasty stuff. We also need to start preparing Saddam for his next trip."

As they were talking the Hummer pulled up. Tallon got out and walked over to Ankyer, wrapped her arms around him and gave him a big hug. She then grabbed his London School of Economics silk crested school tie by its Windsor knot, pulled his head down to hers and gave him a long, full sensuous kiss. When they came up for air, Tallon said, "Welcome home, sailor."

Ankyer replied, "With a greeting like that I'll have to save your life more often!"

"It turns out that my wrists and ankles were not fractured, so any time Jake, any time," as she gave him another hug. Brother William let out with an "ahem".

"Brother William!" said Jake. "How's your Internet business?"

"Thriving!" replied Brother William. "I've got all sorts of product ideas to talk to you about. We need to get back to the Abbey to see Doctor Finkel. That is if Doctor Tallon will uncouple herself from you."

Tallon released Ankyer who put his arm around her, and they followed Brother William to the Hummer and returned to the Abbey.

Doctor Finkel and Father Michael Bruno were standing in the middle of the Abbey library when Ankyer and Tallon arrived. Ankyer walked over, shook hands with Finkel and Bruno, and then went over to the library conference table and sat down. Tallon pulled the chair next to Ankyer, creating as little space as possible between them. Finkel sat at one end of the table, Bruno at the other end, and Honey Pi, who had just walked in, sat across from Ankyer and Tallon, keeping a measured gaze on Tallon.

Looking at Ankyer, Pi said, "How're you doing, big guy? Considering that you're probably classified as operational equipment, I'm glad to see you're still in one piece."

"Boy, you're really something," Ankyer replied. "I'm glad to see you, too," he said smiling.

Finkel said, "First, let me say on behalf of everyone here in this room, and all those associated with the N.S.A. Priority Red Protocol program, the deep regret we have for the loss of our friend and colleague George Makin. He was the consummate professional and died in the service of his Country without regard to his personal safety or security. While no one other than ourselves will know of his contribution to the safeguarding of this country, we will hold the memory of George in our hearts. His remains have been collected and returned from Switzerland. He will be buried here at the Abbey during a special, private memorial service conducted by the Brothers. George had no living relatives we are aware of, but we shall all attend the service in a few days time."

Finkel paused for a minute and then continued. "Based on the list Jake recovered from Zainab Malibi's remains, we were able to identify the suppliers of the steam generators and the locations for the nano VX attacks. We dispatched SEAL, CDC and FBI teams to each location, including Chicago. We were successful in preventing two-man terrorist teams in Davis California, Sylvan Corners Kansas, Destin Florida and Casper Wyoming from arming and starting the steam generator weapons. It seems that they were awaiting a call from the Emir, which never occurred because he had been dispatched by Jake."

"The SEAL teams at each location met resistance from the Emir's martyrs, who we are now referring to as terrorists, and killed all of them. I should add that each one of the martyrs was wearing a suicide vest, which would have exploded killing our teams and possibly spreading the nano VX debris over the area. Fortunately each SEAL team was issued a transponder, which was effective in neutralizing the arming mechanism in the vests. Based on that experience, we are providing the technology to the Department of Defense for use in disarming IEDs and exploding vests of suicide jihadists."

"Our teams also deployed 'Flybots', very small autonomous flying vehicles the size of a dragon fly, developed by the Defense Advanced Research Projects Agency. They were calibrated to detect air molecules containing VX. The Flybots did not detect any nascent VX within two miles of each of the Emir's sites, except one. One Flybot detected a positive hit for a barn, one and one half miles from the Sylvan Corners' steam generator site and radioed the GPS location back to the Sylvan Corners team. It turns out that the barn was some kind of a staging site, which contained one hundred large nano VX cylinders attached to a detonator, timer, and fifty pounds of C4 plastic explosive. The timer had twenty minutes left when it was discovered. Had the explosive detonated in that barn, given the wind in the area gusting at thirty miles per hour at the time, the magnitude of the explosion would have dispersed the nano VX throughout a very large segment of the Midwest, causing an incalculable death toll."

"Unfortunately, Brick, New Jersey was another matter. The terrorists at that location decided not to wait for the Emir's call. They turned on the steam generator, which started spewing nano VX-infused steam out through the building's chimney. Fortunately, it had started raining and the steam converted to liquid around the immediate area. This limited the damage, but not before six people and several animals had been infected and killed."

"The SEAL team, all wearing protective gear, entered the building to find the terrorists dead from VX exposure, and turned off the generator. The area has been evacuated for a diameter of four miles and a decontamination team from the CDC has been deployed. The CDC public relations division issued a public service announcement indicating that a laboratory in the area had an accident causing the release of toxic fumes."

Finkel paused and then continued. "N.S.A. has scientists evaluating McGinty's steam dispersal strategy to ascertain the extent of its efficacy, which is not clear yet. However, what is clear is that altering a toxic substance to a 'nano' form dramatically increases its potential for a destructive result, whatever dispersion technology is used."

At that moment, there was a knock on the door and Brother Melbin walked in.

"Jake. There's someone here who wants to see you." Varna came bounding into the room almost knocking Brother Melbin over and headed straight for Ankyer who stood up. Varna reared up in front of Ankyer, placed a paw on each shoulder and started licking his face.

"Varna!" said Ankyer. Ankyer put his arms around the massive wolf and gently brought him down to the floor. Varna had a dressing on his side and a saline bag attached between his shoulders.

"Be careful with that saline bag," said Brother Melbin. "I thought I was going to have to sedate him to get it on in the first place."

In the mean time, Tallon had moved from the chair and was kneeling on the floor. Varna padded over to her and started licking her face. "Get that wolf away from my patient!" exclaimed Honey Pi. Varna turned to Honey Pi, walked over to her and started licking her hand. "Good god. You people have turned a ferocious wolf into some kind of beagle." Everyone in the room laughed, including Finkel who was not much given to laughter.

Finkel asked if there was anything else to be discussed. Brother Melbin said: "The healing process in wolves is quite rapid. We will be releasing Varna back into the pack later today. It's a little early, but we need to get him into the pack dynamic to prevent another Alpha male from asserting dominance."

Finkel also asked Ankyer, Pi and Tallon to accompany him to the laboratory wing to discuss the Saddam corpse with Brother Arlot.

As they left the room, Honey Pi touched Ankyer's arm and hung back until they were alone. Honey Pi said, "Jake, a brief word. Our psychologist, Brother Carter, saw Margie when she came back. He indicated that she has a mild form of post-traumatic stress disorder resulting from the trauma she suffered at the Emir's. The usual form of PTSD requires a lengthy period of rehabilitation and clinical intervention. Brother Carter said that in Margie's case the PTSD should be quite short due to her very strong psychological core. I wanted to mention this to you since I've observed her getting as close to you as possible since you arrived. This is symptomatic of her PTSD. In such cases, the individual establishes an exceptionally strong need to bond to another person they see as critical to their wellbeing. In Margie's case your rescuing her from the mesomorph, coupled with the shocks she endured, has caused this clinical behavior. Her need to have close personal space with you should dissipate over a week or so. In the meantime, try not to show any discomfort with her edging into your personal space as that could extend her PTSD recovery."

"Thanks Doctor Pi. I appreciate the heads-up," said Ankyer. "The personal space won't become an issue since I like Margie a great deal and I don't mind being around her." "Hey you guys," said Tallon through the open doorway. "We need to get going to see Brother Arlot." Pi and Ankyer emerged from the library and Tallon immediately held Ankyer's hand as they walked down the corridor.

Finkel, Tallon, Pi and Ankyer walked into a large room with an extensive array of laboratory equipment. In the back of the room were two mortuary tables. One of the tables was empty and on the other lay a naked body. Brother Arlot waived them over. "I wanted to talk to you about our guest," he said. "First off, you're analysis was right on Margie - the EMIR was not Saddam. It was an amazing evaluation, considering the stress you were under."

Tallon shuffled her feet, not letting go of Ankyer's hand. Brother Arlot continued, "We did a digital comparison of a head MRI taken of Saddam when he was a guest of the US military in Iraq and a head MRI we did on our friend Ibram el Farsi here. The digital comparison was a perfect match along with the DNA comparison. This is without qualification, Saddam Hussein."

"How did you know?" asked Tallon, looking at Ankyer.

"Two things," Ankyer replied. First you told me that the Emir did not match the Saddam skull configuration when we were at the mansion. Second, Doctor Finkel gave me a field DNA matching kit with Saddam's DNA profile in it. When I finally caught up with the Emir I collected a blood sample from him and got a non-match. When I saw el Farsi, I noticed some underlying skull geometry that was similar to Brother Arlot's Saddam skull profile. I tried the test on him and got a match."

"That was really smart!" exclaimed Honey Pi.

"He's got a PhD," said Finkel.

"PhDs are not real doctors," said Honey Pi.

"I'm a PhD," said Brother Arlot.

"I'm also a PhD," said Finkel.

"Oops," said Honey Pi. "Just kidding!"

"Which brings us to the next part of our project," said Finkel. "We need to return Saddam here to his grave in Tikrit where he belonged in the first place. Any thoughts Brother Arlot?"

Brother Arlot replied, "First we need to replicate the gash in his neck displayed on the YouTube video." Brother Arlot picked up a color photo of Saddam's head, post hanging. "Do you have a scalpel handy?" asked Tallon, releasing Ankyer's hand. Brother Arlot handed Tallon a scalpel and she studied the picture. She then made an incision on Saddam's neck. She reached down and pulled under his jaw, pushing down on his collarbone, and separating the gash. "Perfect!" exclaimed Brother Arlot. "You obviously studied the Iraqi morgue video." "Thank you," replied Tallon reattaching herself to Ankyer's hand.

"The next thing we need to do," said Brother Arlot "is to try and approximate the current state of putrefaction of the body in the grave. The core sample the SEAL team extracted from the grave the first time around will be very helpful. We can match that to corruption levels of bodies in a similar climate environment to

Iraq's at a body farm we sometimes collaborate with. It's then a simple matter of immersing the Saddam cadaver into a desiccant to dry it out at the correct level and let larva work on it a little while in a bug tank. It won't be perfect but should be close enough."

"When will you be finished with it?" asked Finkel. "Give us three or four days," replied Brother Arlot.

"Perfect," said Finkel. "We'll leave you to it then."

"Oh, and one other thing. What are you going to do with the McGinty and Emir bodies?"

"We have them in cold storage at the moment," replied Brother Arlot. "We'll do autopsies of course. I'm particularly interested in McGinty. It's unusual for someone with a background such as his to demonstrate the florid, psychotic behavior we observed in his experiments at the Emir's Black Forest, Colorado laboratory. There may be some brain pathology there. There was never an opportunity to study the brain of the German monster Joseph Mengele or those Japanese scientists behind the human experiments in World War II. I've always suspected there was some kind of organic pathology involved in these extreme, educated psychotics. Dissecting McGinty may reveal organic anomalies even though the brain function itself cannot of course be evaluated. We'll keep all their brains. The rest of their remains will be cremated and thrown out with the garbage where they belong."

Ankyer said he wanted to pay a visit to Fred Bell. Tallon said she would go with him.

Pi said she had an appointment with Brother William. Finkel suggested they rejoin each other for dinner at the refectory around 7:00 PM.

GILA NATIONAL FOREST
NEW MEXICO
FEBRUARY 22, 2012
4:00 PM MOUNTAIN TIME

The grey sedan rolled to a stop on the dirt access road. The car had left the paved road in the Gila National Forest an hour prior to reaching its current location. The men peered out at the decrepit wooden sign in front of them. The sign read: Private. No Trespassing.

Government property. Biosecurity System.

"What's this 'biosecurity' mean?" a brother asked.

Muhammad Akim Abdul-Muhsi, Servant of the Reckoner, wondered about that himself. He was not told of any bio- security system. "I don't know," he said. "I do know that we have reached our destination. We should prepare ourselves."

The men exited the grey sedan and opened the trunk. They changed into the hunting clothes they were provided. They then helped each other don their suicide vests. They would activate the vests when they got closer to their targets.

"Our instructions from the Emir are clear," said the Servant of the Reckoner. "Kill as many of the American infidels as we can, then explode our vests in the survivors' midst and enter into Paradise."

"Allahu Akbar!" they all shouted.

A mile away, ears pricked up and heads swiveled toward the noise.

The four martyrs opened the case of fragmentation grenades and distributed them among themselves. They inserted a thirty round clip into each of their AK-47s and placed the remaining clips they were given in their hunting pants pockets. "This will be a great day for us. We will remain fearless and exterminate the foes of the Emir and Allah," said the Servant of the Reckoner.

They got back in the car and drove slowly around the sign to another overgrown access road. The Emir had told the Servant of the Reckoner that the Google map showed the road continuing for about four miles to a lake, behind which was a large stone building. That would be their destination, the lair of the infidels. The sedan continued on for two miles. They stopped and exited the car.

The Servant of the Reckoner spoke. "Now, activate your vests. We will divide up to increase our chances of victory over the infidels. If you encounter an infidel, shoot him. If you encounter a group, use one of your grenades. Save your vest for an explosion of glory inside the stone building. Go now and do the will of Allah. Allahu Akbar!"

The martyrs fanned out through the pine forest. Abdul-Alim, Servant of the Omniscient, was about two hundred and fifty yards into the forest when he thought he saw a shadow over his right shoulder. He swung his AK-47 around. Nothing.

He turned to continue his advance but a one hundred and sixty pound Mackenzie Valley Canadian Timber Wolf launched itself and fastened its fangs around his throat, knocking him over. A second wolf was ripping at his genitals. The ferocity of the attack caused the Servant of the Omniscient to lose his grip on the AK-47. He tried to curl into a ball but the weight of the wolves on his body prevented that. He did manage to push the button on his cell phone exploding his vest and the six grenades in his pockets. The Servant of the Omniscient and the two wolves merged into one protoplasmic mass, body parts flying in a one hundred yard circle through the pines.

Ankyer and Tallon were sitting on a log at the north end of the lake. Thirty minutes earlier they had visited with Fred Bell in the Abbey infirmary. Bell was not happy about his feet being wrapped in plaster and was particularly incensed at the bland diet he was being forced to endure. Tallon had told Bell not to be a big baby. Ankyer said he'd try and sneak in a large sausage and pepperoni pizza from the refectory later on. The prospect of the pizza calmed Bell down and he dozed off. After the visit, Ankyer had changed into 511 Covert Cargo pants and a Hawaiian luau shirt. A side pocket of the pants had a built in scabbard for his titanium/ceramic combat knife, which Ankyer carried out of habit. Ankyer, with Tallon in tow, decided to take a walk around the lake before dinner.

As they were sitting by the lake with Tallon holding Ankyer's hand, Tallon said, "You're not really going to sneak a pizza into Fred are you? That would be against my professional medical advice."

"Yeah, but your not his doctor and Honey Pi will never know, will she?" replied Ankyer.

"Never know what?" came a feminine voice forty feet behind them.

All ninety pounds of Honey Pi, sporting a long black ponytail, stepped out from some bushes holding a 12 gauge, Benelli M4 Super 90 Combat Shotgun accompanied by a broadly smiling Brother William who said, "I would never have guessed Doctor Pi was a..." Brother William never finished his sentence. Akim Abdul-Muhsi, Servant of the Reckoner, burst through the trees and shot Brother William in the back.

"Noooooo!" Tallon screamed. She pushed Ankyer off the log and covered him with her body. Ankyer rolled Tallon off and jumped to his feet.

In the meantime, Honey Pi swung her body 180 degrees, firing the Benelli M4 from her hip, blowing off the lower left leg of the Servant of the Reckoner. She followed with another shot blowing off the right leg above the knee as he toppled over. As his trunk hit the ground, the Servant of the Reckoner reached into his shirt.

"IED!" exclaimed Ankyer. Honey Pi fired a third shot and blew the top of the martyr's head off.

Honey Pi pulled a shotgun shell from a jacket pocket and pushed it into the hole in Brother Williams's chest. She then tore off a strip of her shirt, rolled Brother William on his side, and stuffed the material into the entrance wound.

"Am I going to die?" wheezed Brother William.

"No way, Bill," replied Honey Pi, as she stood up. "Nobody fucks with my patients or my friends. Nobody."

"Tallon ran over to Brother William, took off her blouse and wrapped it around Brother William's chest. "I think it's through and through but we need to get him back to the infirmary right now."

Pi said, "The Hummer is parked behind us. Let's load him in it and I'll take him back."

"I'll go with you," said Tallon.

Just then, they heard an explosion deep in the woods about a mile away.

"It looks like we're dealing with a team," said Ankyer as he picked Brother William up in his arms and ran to the Hummer. After Ankyer placed Brother William in the back seat, he said to Honey Pi, "How many shotgun shells do you have left?"

"Five or six in my jacket pocket," she replied, as she removed her jacket and gave it to Ankyer along with the Benelli.

"See you back at the Abbey," said Ankyer as he trotted back to the lake.

Ankyer reloaded the Benelli M4 and checked the remains of the Servant of the Reckoner. After examining the exploding vest's design, it was instructive to Ankyer that the explosive and shrapnel was affixed to the front of the vest and not the back, similar to the design he had encountered with other martyr/guards. It suggested that the Emir had sent a hunter/killer team to the Abbey, which was also consistent with Margie's earlier worry that she may have referred to the Abbey, somehow, during her drug induced interrogation. As he was considering how many martyrs might be involved, he saw a man running full tilt half way around the lake and headed in his direction.

Abdul-Warith, Servant of the Supreme Inheritor, was pleased that he was almost out of the woods when he heard the gunfire at the lake. He assumed that one of his fellow martyrs had destroyed some infidels and he felt a warm glow of pleasure at his back. He heard a low growl, turned to look back and discovered that the warm glow was in fact the hot breath of three immense wolves with their teeth bared. The Servant of the Supreme Inheritor pointed his AK-47 at the three beasts and pulled the trigger. He heard a metallic click. Jam! He tried to clear his weapon but one of the wolves leapt forward and grabbed his ankle in its teeth. He slammed the AK down on the wolf's back, causing it to release its grip. He turned and ran for his life, and unknowingly, toward Ankyer a quarter mile away. The Servant of the Supreme Inheritor didn't mind blowing himself up, but drew the line at being eaten alive by ferocious wolves.

As the figure approached, Ankyer stepped behind a large tree. The wolves sensed Ankyer ahead and in accordance with the wolf social structure, veered off to allow one of the two Alpha males in the pack, Ankyer, to initiate the kill. The Servant of the Supreme Inheritor looked over his shoulder and saw the wolves holding back. He knew his inner strength had cowed the wolf pack into submission. "Allah be praised!" he thought. He ran down the shoreline past a large tree and toward the remains of... Akim Abdul-Muhsi, Servant of the Reckoner!

When the martyr had advanced fifteen feet past the tree, Ankyer stepped out, trotted behind, closing the distance to ten feet. He fired four loads of the 12 gauge, Benelli M4 into the Servant of the Supreme Inheritor's back, causing the exploding vest to ignite and separating the martyr's head from the rest of his dissolving body.

Ankyer considered the situation. A martyr team, probably at the direction of the Emir and Saddam, had penetrated the Abbey's defenses with the intent of what? Probably trying to kill as many people as possible. How many martyrs were there, was the question. When Ankyer had encountered the martyrs at the Colorado facility, it seemed, that they were deployed in groups of four. There were also four guards at the gatehouse of the Emir's mansion. Probably reflected some strange design for Iraqi small unit tactics, which meant there was probably one more. But where? The first explosion he heard was about a mile away. The martyr Honey Pi killed showed up about twenty minutes later. Now this guy fifteen minutes after that. Where's the fourth martyr? On the leading edge or the trailing edge of the assault? The wolves came back to where Ankyer was standing and sniffed the now smoldering corpse. Leaving the wolves here would block the fourth martyr if he were on the trailing edge. The likely threat was therefore the leading edge. Ankyer concluded the fourth martyr was the leading edge and was probably already at the Abbey. He rubbed each of the wolves on their heads and said, "Guard." He then ran around the lake toward the Abbey, carrying the Benelli M4 at port arms.

Asher Finkel had been visiting Fred Bell in the Abbey's intensive care infirmary on the third floor. It was a light airy room with a large picture window and a view of the lake, positioned to capture the morning light. Finkel had been discussing Bell's recollection of the events at the Emir's mansion. Bell was curious about the transponder and Finkel had just shown one to him. They both had been startled by the explosions coming from the direction of the lake and looked out the window.

Abdul-Basir, Servant of the All-Seeing, was the leading edge of the assault. He had been able to gain entrance to a side door of the Abbey, while the explosions distracted those inside. He had noted that the part of the building he was in was four stories high and concluded that exploding himself on the third floor would cause the most damage. As he opened the door to the third floor landing, he noticed medical equipment and several beds. "A hospital! Even better!" he thought. He propped his AK-47 against the door, grasped his cell phone and entered the room.

He saw a very large man dressed in a hospital gown, probably a patient, talking to an older bearded man in a suit, probably a doctor. He rushed toward Finkel, wrapping his left arm around Finkel's throat and holding his now activated cell phone in his right hand. "You will now feel the vengeance of the Emir!" he screamed. Bell reached down to his bedside table and pushed the black button on the transponder he and Finkel had been discussing moments earlier. "Die infidels!" the Servant of the All-Seeing exclaimed and pushed the 'talk' button on the cell phone…nothing.

He pushed the button again. And again. Nothing. Bell walked over to the Servant of the All-Seeing, grasped the hand of the arm around Finkel's throat and twisted the hand counter clockwise breaking the wrist. Bell then ripped the cell phone, wires and all, off the exploding vest, grabbed the Servant of the All-Seeing by the throat, lifted him off the floor, walked clumsily on his casted feet toward the window, and hurled Abdul-Basir, Servant of the All-Seeing, out the plate glass window.

The Hummer driven by Honey Pi pulled up to the front of the Abbey and made a screeching stop, just in time for the body of Abdul-Basir, Servant of the All-Seeing, to land on its roof and bounce off onto the gravel drive. Honey Pi got out of the Hummer, looked at the body on the ground, and then up at Fred Bell who was wiggling his fingers at her and smiling.

"How many of these bastards are there around here?" she exclaimed as she opened the side door of the Hummer. She looked at Father Bruno who had just come running out of the front door. "We need to get Brother William to Brother McCabe's surgery, stat," she said. "Brother William's been shot. I managed to plug him up with a shotgun shell but he's leaking and I'm not sure how much internal damage there is."

Two Brothers ran out with a gurney, loaded Brother William on, lifted it up the front steps, and pushed it rapidly down the hall. Tallon exited the Hummer from the other rear door. "We should go and brief Brother McCabe on Brother William right away," she said to Honey Pi. By then Ankyer ran up. "I talked to two SEALs on the way in. They found a grey sedan about a mile in from the forest perimeter. There were civilian clothes on the ground and they said it looked like there was enough room in the car for four people, so we probably got them all."

Ankyer then looked at Honey Pi. "Where did you get the shotgun and learn to fire it so accurately?" Ankyer asked.

"I was my College's women's skeet shooting champion and I was teaching Brother William to skeet shoot," she replied. "That 12 gauge just about knocked me on my ass, but what the hell, it works, right?"

She then turned and ran up the stairs and into the Abbey after Tallon. "Boy, she's something," said Ankyer.

CEMETERY OUTSIDE TIKRIT IRAQ FEBRUARY 25, 2012 3:00 AM ARABIA STANDARD TIME

The SEAL teams had launched from a carrier deck and landed in two silenced Black Hawks, about two kilometers from the cemetery. The teams had covered the distance to the cemetery in about forty minutes. One of the SEAL teams had established a security perimeter around the cemetery, and the second team was busy digging up a grave.

A digger hit the lid of a box with his entrenching tool and they cleared away the sand and clay from the top of the box as quickly as possible. Two SEALs opened the lid and pulled out the body. They shined a low intensity red light on the body and checked it for signs of the drill holes another team had made when they extracted a core sample months ago. They found the drill holes and flashed the red light once out into the darkness.

Neil clicked his secure satellite smart phone twice. Both SEAL teams hunkered down and waited.

Upon hearing the clicks from the audio in his helmet, Ankyer jumped out of the cargo plane at 50,000 feet, followed by what appeared to be a rectangular shape with a bulb on the end. Ankyer's parasail flight suit was insulated against the cold but he was still uncomfortable as he and the other object hurtled through the dark. Ankyer's night vision, heads-up display showed a telescopic view of the SEAL teams far below. During his descent his altimeter registered "feet to target" and indicated he was then

5,000 feet above his mark. He depressed a button on his flight suit and the bulbous end on the other object spread open and a parasail chute deployed. The GPS-guided MMIST Sherpa Ranger, High Altitude Low Opening delivery vehicle slowed markedly as the GPS guidance system took over and the box attached to it swung gently on its short tether.

The SEALs on the ground monitored the Sherpa with their night vision goggles until it landed about thirty feet from them. A moment later Jake Ankyer silently swooped in and landed ten feet away.

Neil walked over and shook hands with Ankyer. They returned to the Sherpa and opened the payload container. In it was a bag containing the body of Saddam Hussein, aka Ibram el Farsi. The plastic surgery alterations had been methodically reversed by Brother Arlot to once again reflected Saddam's original appearance, except in an advanced state of decrepitude. They carried the bag to the open grave. They opened the bag and rolled the body into the open coffin, which was closed immediately and filled over with excavated dirt/sand by other SEALS. A bag of specially prepared soil was spread over the grave to mask any indication of disturbance.

While they were reburying Saddam Hussein, Neil double clicked his secure smart phone on the Black Hawk's frequency. Five minutes later, the two helicopters landed. The SEAL teams stowed the Sherpa Ranger in one Black Hawk and the body of the disinterred Saddam double in the other. The SEALS and Jake climbed into the Black Hawk and they lifted off.

The sand swirled around the cemetery and all was quiet as a trio of Camel spiders crawled over the grave.

EPILOGUE

CONSTABLE CLUB EMBASSY ROW WASHINGTON, DC APRIL 8, 2012 4:00 AM EASTERN STANDARD TIME

Asher Finkel sat in a leather, backed chair gazing out the Constable Club library window. A glow was just starting to manifest itself in the East and, within a few hours, would be washing over the cherry blossoms, which had been particularly abundant this year. The quietude of the morning, coupled with the advent of spring gave the appearance of hope and renewal that Americans looked forward to at this time of year. And yet, Asher Finkel knew that it was an illusion.

In spite of the terrorist attacks of September 11, 2001, and given the passage of time, Americans had relaxed their guard and let the Homeland Security bureaucracy replace their fear with the expectation that the government would protect them. Asher Finkel knew better. The withholding of communications from each other by the FBI and the CIA, while instrumental in permitting the 9/11 terrorist attacks to occur, gave rise to the Homeland Security Administration, designed to force government agencies to interact with each other.

As it became apparent that the imposed coordination of the US security agencies was ineffective, the previous insularity reemerged in a variety of forms. The then

President realized that a new solution was required to deal with specific threats to the Homeland. The National Security Agency was chosen. A massive data collection operation so secret that it was immune from normal Congressional oversight and other agency interference. Even with the selective involvement of various other agencies, including the military, the primary weapon utilized by the N.S.A. was kept a close secret by a very few. For all practical purposes, Jake Ankyer did not exist. "And it worked!" Asher Finkel thought to himself.

Finkel took a sip of his tea as the final embers in the fireplace started to die out. A confluence of circumstances had produced data in the N.S.A. that had energized the Priority Red Protocol and loosed Jake Ankyer on Saddam Hussein causing disruption of a plan, which could have had cataclysmic consequences to the people of America. A plan so venomous that its mere contemplation would send chills through a normal person. And Ankyer had stopped it. Not a fictitious 'James Bond' character, but a weapon, so intelligent and lethal, that it didn't...couldn't fail.

The Saddam Priority Red Protocol execution had not been perfect. They had lost George Makin, Margie Tallon had been subjected to excruciating torture, and Brother William had been shot. Finkel knew that they had to do better the next time. Casualties were always expected, but there was an equal expectation that the knowledge gained would minimize future operational mishaps. Brother William had recovered, due in large measure to Doctor Honey Pi's quick thinking, inserting the shotgun shell into his wound. Doctor Honey Pi. Finkel had grown to appreciate her sharp intellect and instant reaction to unanticipated events. Finkel thought about her as a possible replacement for him some day.

But not today.

Finkel had sent Jake Ankyer and Margie Tallon on the Lear jet to London for a month of R&R. There was a play Ankyer was keen to see, and he and Margie discovered they admired the same playwright. Tallon had recovered from her PTSD-related need for physical proximity to Ankyer. She continued to hold his hand now, because she wanted to, not because she needed to. Finkel knew that high intensity missions required low intensity denouement. Finkel wasn't concerned about the budget for their trip. The N.S.A. had moved the funds from Saddam's INF Banque Nationale, twelve billion euros, to the N.S.A. accounts and ultimately, Finkel's control. Another

Saddam bank in the Grand Cayman Islands yielded two billion euros more. McGinty's diamonds produced eight million euros, which Finkel thought would be useful for petty cash.

All in all, the Priority Red Protocol initiative would be amply funded for the foreseeable future, assuring the N.S.A. program's continued autonomy.

Asher Finkel reflected on all these things as his smart phone, which he had laid on the small table next to his chair, chimed. He picked it up and in the window saw the word 'President'. Jake Ankyer's vacation would likely be cut short.

The End

ACKNOWLEDGMENTS

During the creation of this book, numerous friends and colleagues have offered their insights and suggestions, all of which have combined to make the book hopefully, more interesting and informative. In particular, I would like to thank Marjorie Eskay-Auerbach, MD JD, for her editorial advice and medical counsel. I would like to acknowledge Mr. John Louis Larsen, a nationally prominent FBI agent, now retired, who reviewed the text for its law enforcement content and accuracy. Others who have made their mark on this book, either directly or indirectly, through their continued support, include Phillip Oczkowski, Jim Walthour and Nick Adami. I would also like to acknowledge Dan C. Harris who encouraged me to write this book and whose opinion I greatly value.

Every attempt has been made to make this book accurate in its portrayal of medical and biomedical science, military science, and other technologies. Nevertheless, any errors or inaccuracies in the text are the complete responsibility of the author.

Finally, I would like to acknowledge the contributions of my wife, Karen, whose encouragement and editing skills have made the book far better than it would have been otherwise.

Thank you.

D K Harris

D K Harris has been the editor of a number of biomedical and computer medicine journals, and a contributing editor to the Journal of the American Medical Association. He has been a consultant to the US Department of Defense, the US National Institutes of Health, US National Cancer Institute, and the US National Library of Medicine. Harris is a founding member of the American Medical Informatics Association and a Fellow of the American College of Medical Informatics. Harris lives in Glen Ellyn, Illinois with his wife Karen. They have one son.

33979938R00144

Made in the USA
Charleston, SC
27 September 2014